The Cassandra Prophecy

Also by Charles Wilson

Nightwatcher
Silent Witness

The Cassandra Prophecy

Charles Wilson

Carroll & Graf Publishers, Inc.
New York

Copyright © 1993 by Charles Wilson

First Carroll & Graf edition 1993

Carroll & Graf Publishers, Inc.
260 Fifth Avenue
New York, NY 10001

Library of Congress Cataloging-in-Publication Data

Wilson, Charles, 1939–
    The Cassandra prophecy / Charles Wilson.
      p.   cm.
    ISBN 0-88184-951-0 : $18.95
    I. Title.
  PS3573.I45684C37   1993
  813'.54—dc20   92-38238
                                               CIP

Manufactured in the United States of America

In memory of my father, Dr. Loys Charles Wilson, M.D., and my mother, Alberta P. Wilson; no son was ever more blessed.

Also, with special thanks for the material and advice they contributed to this work, R. Clay Mateer, former member of the United States Secret Service; Senior Chief Petty Officer Tom Hurst and Petty Officer 1st Class, Skip Turner, members of the United States Coast Guard, Gulfport, Mississippi, Station; J.B. Torrence, Sheriff, Rankin County, Mississippi; John Edwards, former polygraph expert with the Mississippi Highway Patrol; Sergeant Fred Dunlap of the Mississippi Highway Patrol; and Dr. Steve Hayne, Chief of Pathology, Rankin Medical Center. And finally, as always, to my chief critic, attorney and friend, Tommy Furby. Thank you all.

CHAPTER

1

Karen lay in the queen-size bed and looked at one of the stateroom's portholes, its thick glass revealing the blue-white quiver of lightning flashing in the darkness outside the yacht. Robert moved his hand down across her T-shirt to the buttons of her khaki shorts. She clasped his wrist and stopped him.

"Come on, Robert, I'm just not in the mood. All I can think about is how mad Daddy's gonna be if he calls and I'm not home."

"Will you chill out about that? You sound like you're seven instead of seventeen—daddy knows all, sees all. Tell him you got nervous about being alone—so you stayed with somebody. Say you called his room and didn't get an answer; hotel operator screwed up—you fell asleep. You can call him as soon as we get in—tell him you just woke up." He shifted his body so that he lay partly across her. His jeans and T-shirt were still damp from being on deck in the rain.

"God, Robert, if I *were* in the mood that'd turn me off."

"What?"

"Wet, dummy—your clothes are wet. It feels terrible."

"I'll take them off. How about that?" He smiled down at her. His dark hair, damp too, was plastered against his forehead. There was a drop of moisture on his cheek.

She kept looking at his face. She had never seen one that appealed more to her—or one more persuasive when he used his deep, dark eyes just so. *That's how he talked me into this,* she thought. She was a fool.

"You know," he said. "Maybe what I need to do is just set your old man down and lay it all out straight. Then you wouldn't have to be so uptight all the time."

"That's not funny, Robert. If Daddy knew about this . . ." She shook her head. "You don't know him like you think you do; he'd hurt you. I mean it; he would. God, if he even knew I was still seeing you—"

"Hey, lighten up. I was just picking. I'm not really crazy—not that crazy, anyway."

"I hope not." She nodded toward the empty beer can sitting on the dresser. "Go get me another one, okay?"

"That's not what you really need," he said, his smile coming back. "Trust Doctor Rodgers . . . He knows what's best for little Karen." He rolled away from her to switch off the table lamp, plunging the stateroom into darkness, then moved back against her, slipping his hand under the bottom of her T-shirt.

She grabbed his wrist. "Quit, Robert."

"Can't; gotta find that mood switch." He moved his face down to the side of hers and bit gently at her earlobe.

She couldn't keep from giggling.

"Ah, ha," he said, and nuzzled her neck. "I think I've found it."

"You didn't find anything. That tickled."

He caught the bottom of her T-shirt and raised it toward her head. She clasped her elbows against her sides, but the front of the loose garment easily lifted high enough to expose her unbound breasts, and she gave up, relaxing her arms. He finished removing the T-shirt then slipped off his own before leaning back to her and pressing his lips to hers.

At first she lay still, letting him do as he wished, but not responding; she was determined to show him. She tried to think of something else—the hum of the stateroom's air conditioner, the sound of the rain pelting the yacht's superstructure; she heard the steering station's radio crackling. But in only a few seconds she felt the familiar swirling slowly beginning to rise inside her.

Damn, she thought, irritated at allowing herself to become aroused, and she moved her arms around his back. His hands worked at her short's buttons and she lifted her hips to let him slip the garment from under them and down her strong, tanned legs. Her eyelids fluttered at his caress, and she gasped and raised her head to press her lips against his shoulder.

As she did, lightning flashed close outside the yacht, the vivid streak of energy bright against the portholes, bathing the cabin in a blue glow—and she saw the dark shape coming down the steps into the stateroom.

"Robert!"

At Karen's scream and her hands suddenly pushing frantically against his chest, Robert froze. Her eyes were wide.

"Behind you!"

Robert jerked his head around to see the shadowy form stepping toward the bed. For an instant he was stunned with shock, and then he came to his knees and twisted toward the figure.

The roar of a pistol shattered the quiet. Robert's head jerked violently from the force of the slug slamming into his forehead, and he toppled backward off the bed to the floor.

Karen screamed, came up off the bed and lunged toward the figure.

He caught her in midair and drove her back onto the bed where he came down on top of her, his hands already grabbing at her naked body.

She screamed again, leaned her head forward and caught a rubber glove-covered hand in her teeth, and bit as hard as she could.

The figure yelled in pain and tugged to pull its hand free. A fist slammed hard into the side of her face, stunning her. Dazed, she felt the hand pulling loose from her mouth. A piece of rubber remained between her teeth. A hand went around her throat, two hands, squeezing. Her arms were heavy; she couldn't lift her hands to try and pry away the fingers digging into her neck.

Pressing the full weight of its body behind its hands, the figure leaned closer. Another flash of lightning close outside illuminated the cabin, and through her blurring vision she saw the face clearly for the first time. She wanted to scream again, but couldn't. Her eyelids fluttered. Her hands, starting to lift, fell limply . . .

CHAPTER

2

The shiny U.S. Air Force jet banked above the bright lights of Biloxi and Gulfport and began its descent toward a runway at Keesler Air Force Base.

"Home sweet home," the pilot said into her mike. She didn't know why her passenger was on his way to Biloxi or what he did, only that Biloxi was his home and that he was a VIP, the hurried arrangements for his flight having been made by direct order of the Vice-President.

After receiving her instructions to make ready for the flight, she had awaited her passenger expecting an old, potbellied politician—an old one, anyway. She had been completely taken aback when, dressed casually in slacks and a dress shirt unbuttoned at the neck, an athletic-looking young man with thick, dark hair had walked up to her and introduced himself as Clay Rodgers. *To be young and handsome and powerful,* she thought wistfully, and then shook her head.

Clay Rodgers, sitting in the seat to the rear of the pilot, continued to stare out through the airplane's Plexiglas canopy. He was looking south, beyond the coast, across the waters of the Mississippi Sound to the shapes of the Barrier Islands.

To the islands' leeward sides he glimpsed an occasional dot of light—the mast lights of anchored shrimp boats. Several miles beyond the Barrier Islands lay the long chain of the Chandeleur Islands, then the dark vastness of the Gulf.

He finally forced his gaze back to the coast and up the beach past the brightly lit gambling boats, past Gulfport to the shallow water off the small town of Long Beach.

The *Cassandra* had been found there, four hundred yards offshore and aground on the mud flats. His brother's body, a bullet in his forehead, had been discovered on the floor in the *Cassandra*'s master stateroom. Clay turned his eyes away from the area and stared straight ahead.

He had been out of the country for a week—one of five Secret Service agents assigned to the detail accompanying the Vice-President to London. During his flight back to the United States, he had been called to the pilot's cabin for an emergency call patched through Washington.

He had said "Hello," and his stepmother had said "Robert is dead." Just like that. There ought to have been another way Donna could have said it, something to soften the blow, some easier way to tell a person his only brother had been murdered. Clay felt his stomach tightening again, and his eyes began to mist.

Donna was standing on the porch waiting when the cab deposited Clay in front of the house he had been born and raised in but had only been back to a couple times in the last few years. He lifted his worn suitcase and started up the sidewalk.

Donna had neglected to turn on the porch lights, and stood framed in the glow from the open doorway. All he could make out about her, except that she wore some kind of dark slacks and a lighter blouse, was the silhouette of her full, thick hair and the outline of her strong frame—her wide shoulders and wide hips making her solid waist small only by comparison.

His father was attracted to big, voluptuous women. Robert had been, too. Clay had always preferred a woman with a slender build, even a slight build if everything was in proportion. That was one of the few things in which they differed. In most ways they were more like triplets than brothers and a father.

All of them loved the water. His father, though turned forty-nine the week before, was still a great water skier. All of them liked gangster movies, hunting and fishing, working out and eating seafood. Robert had almost never dressed in anything except jeans and a T-shirt unless it was absolutely necessary to do otherwise, while their father had never liked wearing a suit; hated a tie. Clay himself had probably not worn a coat and tie more than a few dozen times prior to joining the Secret Service.

A lot of people said they even looked alike, though that was stretching things a bit. They all did have thick, dark hair. But Clay was only a little over six feet and possessed a lean athletic frame, while his brother and father were both a couple of inches taller and more heavily built.

As Clay stepped up on the porch, Donna shook her head sadly. "I can't believe it's happened," she said. Her eyes were red. She stepped forward and hugged him gently, the gesture bringing his own grief back to the fore. He had to stand quietly a moment before he could speak.

"Where's Dad?"

"He's in the bedroom."

Donna moved aside to let him enter, then stepped inside the house and shut the door behind them. She glanced across the small living room toward the hallway leading to the bedrooms. "The doctor gave him a sedative a couple of hours ago, but I was starting to worry it wasn't going to work. He just has drifted off."

"I won't wake him." He set his suitcase on the carpet and walked toward his father's bedroom door.

Opening it, he stepped quietly inside the darkened room and walked to the side of the bed.

His father, at first glance appearing comfortably asleep on his back with the covers pulled up to his waist, on closer study looked in anguish.

The thick, dark hair on his bare chest rose and fell noticeably with his rapid breathing. His face was tight, lines on it that Clay had never seen before. A man who had always looked much younger than his actual age now looked even older than he really was. Then his father groaned, his arm twitched, and he rolled restlessly to his side.

His turning revealed a rumpled red sport coat that had been lying under him. Clay carefully lifted the garment and laid it on the top of the dresser at the side of the room. He stood a moment longer, then turned and walked back toward the door.

In the small living room he sat in a chair across from the couch where Donna took her seat. He glanced back toward the bedroom, and shook his head. "He doesn't look good."

Donna nodded. "It's killing him."

"Do the police know any more yet?"

"They found a fingerprint they said had to be his—the killer's. It's really a print of part of his palm and a little bit of a finger. They said he was wearing surgical gloves and one of them must have somehow become torn. They said the print was on the headboard of the bed."

One thought had kept passing through his mind all the way from Washington. "Donna, why would Robert have been going out alone on the boat in the first place?"

"What?"

"Last night was Saturday night. We're talking about a twenty-year-old college kid on a weekend night. Do you think he didn't have anything better to do than be taking the *Cassandra* out— alone? If there had been a girl along, or one of his buddies; I could understand that. But going out by himself, that just doesn't make sense. I've been thinking about that ever since you called."

"I don't know. I hadn't even thought about it." She shook her head sadly. "I haven't been able to think of anything but his being dead."

Clay noticed her cheek tic, and he rose and walked over to the couch. Sitting down close beside her he put his arm around her shoulders.

Her lip trembled as she turned her face toward his, and he didn't know what to do. What he was now mentally experiencing was at the same time both the strength and the curse of his personality—in the company of others he was largely unable to show emotion of any kind and was usually awkward when he tried. It was a terrible mind-wrenching curse that often left him feeling guilty.

But that legacy he had unwillingly accepted from his mother was also a strength, when the need was to appear to remain cool and collected in circumstances under which most men would crack. That he was more than a little famous and counted among his fervent admirers the Vice-President of the United States, was due to his apparent ability to never become perturbed.

Before he could think of anything comforting to say to Donna, he heard the muffled moan from inside his father's bedroom.

He entered the bedroom ahead of Donna. His father, still asleep, lay on his side. He had been out of his bed. He now clasped in his arms the red coat Clay had placed on the dresser.

Donna leaned close to Clay. "Robert gave the coat to him for his birthday last week," she whispered. "I don't know how Robert saved up enough money to buy the coat—it's an expensive one. It made your father feel terribly guilty because he had cut off nearly all of Robert's spending money after he'd made such bad grades last fall. As soon as we came back from the funeral home this afternoon, your father went to his closet and got it out. He's kept it with him ever since."

CHAPTER

3

The cab left Clay at the darkened entrance to the boatyard, then made a U-turn up onto the highway leading back toward the tourist strip. The cab driver pressed so hard on the cab's accelerator that there was a brief squeal of rubber.

Clay shook his head in amusement. When on the way to the boatyard he had asked the driver to slow down, the man had surprised him by adamantly shaking his head.

"No chance, buddy," the man had replied. "I ain't got time to slow down. Prices goin' up ever day. I ran in and got some smokes while ago, and the damn things done gone to a flat two dollars. That's discounted ones. Hell, were only a dollar ninety-five a few months back; goin' for less than that 'round Christmas. Hell, man, no way I'm gonna slow down; gotta keep up."

Clay started across the firm mixture of crushed oyster shell and sand covering the boatyard grounds. He passed a small brick office building and a dry-docked thirty-eight-foot Hatteras

Sports Fisherman as he made his way toward the back of the small repair and fiberglassing complex.

Donna had informed him that the *Cassandra* had been returned to its berth by the Coast Guard, and he had decided he wanted to go and see it before he went to bed. He had felt like he *had* to go to the boat first.

At the back of the boatyard, he stopped at the entrance to a narrow, rickety wooden walkway jutting out a hundred and fifty feet over the dark waters of the Mississippi Sound.

At the far end of the pier and a dull white in the faint moonlight, was the *Cassandra,* an old, wide-bodied forty-three-foot yacht with a trawler configuration.

Known officially as a Gulf Star Mark II Motor Yacht when its series was constructed in 1970, it was one of the last boats whose owners received the best of both worlds, the vessel retaining the elegant—and more seaworthy—sweeping lines of the old sailing ships, but constructed of modern, minimum-maintenance fiberglass and powered by a pair of powerful 160 hp Perkins diesels. His father had bought it for $60,000 and reconditioned it, then spent much of his free time aboard it. It had always been his pride and joy. How would he view the boat now—the place where his younger son had been murdered?

Whatever lifting of his spirit had occurred at the antics of the cab driver, Clay was now suddenly solemn again. He wasn't sure whether he wanted to go onto the boat or turn around and go back to his house. He finally walked forward onto the pier.

A hundred and fifty feet farther and he ducked under a yellow CRIME SCENE—NO TRESPASSING ribbon strung across the end of the pier, then crossed a short metal gangway onto the boat. After sliding back the tracked door on that side of the main cabin, he stepped into the dimly lit interior of the boat.

He immediately noticed that intermingled with the smell of the salt air was the faint scent of fresh-cut roses, his stepmother's touch.

Nautically termed the salon, the main cabin was the *Cassandra*'s version of a living room—albeit a living room which had at one end a full set of steering controls sitting before a wide expanse of glass looking out over the boat's bow. Donna was just as finicky about how the salon was kept as she was the living room in her own home.

The small couch against the port bulkhead and the two easy chairs on the opposite side of the cabin were as nice as any pieces of furniture in their home. Even in the faint illumination cast by a small wall-socket light, the heavy wood end tables to the sides of the couch fairly glistened with polish. The brass lamps bolted to the tables' tops shined like new. The roses were in a large yellow vase sitting atop the built-in cabinets at the back of the cabin.

He stepped to the nearest end table and turned on a lamp. With the added light the black fingerprint powder jumped out at him. It was on the steering wheel, the gear control handles and the throttles.

There were other traces of black up and down the interior of both sliding doors leading into the salon, on the handrail of the steps leading forward down into the lower galley and on the door leading to the aft master stateroom—the place his brother's body had been found sprawled on the floor between the stateroom's queen-size bed and the dressing table.

Clay stared at the master stateroom door for several seconds, then walked to it. He steeled himself by taking a deep breath and releasing it slowly, then turned the door knob, opened the door and moved down the two steps into the cabin.

The police had stripped the bed of its covering. There weren't any bloodstains on the mattress. On the light blue wallpaper above the bed's headboard there was a curved line of small dark dots, their pattern making it look as if they had been applied with the flick of a paint brush. Between the bed and the dressing table, there was a large dried circle on the carpet, the place where his brother's head had lain after he had fallen. Clay stared for a long moment at the circle. Then he raised his gaze back to the head of the bed.

He saw the black smudge on the top of the box-shaped headboard where the police had lifted the killer's palm print. A rubber glove. Torn. How? What was there to look for that might give a hint to what had gone on?

He ran his eyes around the rest of the stateroom.

Other than the stains and the missing linens, everything in the cabin seemed in perfect order.

His Secret Service training regimen had included numerous criminal investigation courses, but he had only vague recollections of what the instructors had said. Since being assigned to the Vice-Presidential Protective Division, his training had focused almost entirely on how to spot *somebody* unusual—a nut in the area when a dignitary was on his way. Such a person usually stuck out like a sore thumb. But looking for *something* unusual, some kind of clue, was different.

He remembered back to what the crack detective on the Indianapolis police force had told him. It was during a joint federal/state investigation of a group forging government checks, and the detective had been working with him.

"What I do when I'm at a crime scene where there's no obvious clues, is just look around," the detective had said. "Not for anything in particular, but just look. If something makes me take a second look, gives me pause for thought, then I take a third look, a fourth; however many I have to take until I figure out what it was that caused me to take that second look. I don't ever let myself shrug something off after it's once made me take that second look."

Clay glanced around the stateroom again. Was he missing something? If the detective was here would he have seen something that made him take a second look; something that . . . He shook his head in exasperation with himself. *What in the hell did he think he was doing, anyway?* The police had a fingerprint. What was he going to discover that would improve on that—an autographed photograph the killer had left behind?

On his way back up the steps leading from the stateroom into the salon, he stopped and opened the hanging locker next to the steps.

The compact space was hung with various casual outfits of Donna's, and a couple pairs of pants belonging to his father.

In the salon he opened the doors to the cabinets that lined the back of that cabin. They were mostly filled with books—Donna was a big reader. One of the cabinets had been made into a small bar and contained a bottle of vodka and one of Benchmark Premium Bourbon. In the biggest cabinet there were a pair of scuba tanks complete with regulators attached, a pair of weight belts, flippers and masks. Then he saw the tiny piece of dried leaf.

He knelt and slid a stack of hard rock tapes aside and saw more signs of the drug.

His father had once asked him to speak to Robert about the evils of drugs, and Clay had, though he hadn't really thought there would ever be a problem like that. Not that Robert wasn't adventurous, to the contrary. He had been a kamikaze-type linebacker on the Biloxi High School team, his play always in complete disregard for his body, and he had totalled two cars and a motorcycle before he was eighteen. But he was also a health fanatic. He never drank or smoked and didn't like to be around those who did. But then Clay had known others who didn't consider "doing a little pot" as smoking. But how minor something like smoking pot seemed now, anyway.

He swept the remainder of the telltale fragments of leaf into his hand and slipped them into a pocket of his slacks.

The telephone on the end table nearest him rang. He moved to it and lifted the receiver.

It was Donna.

"When are you coming back to the house? I put fresh sheets on your bed."

The bed next to Robert's empty bed. He had forgotten he would have to sleep in that bedroom, the only other one in the house besides his dad and Donna's. There had previously been a third bedroom, his bedroom. When he had left for his career in the Secret Service his father had converted the room into an office and moved its bed into Robert's room. He thought again of the empty bed he would have to sleep beside. He didn't know whether he could stand that.

"Clay—?"

"Yeah, I'm sorry; I was thinking about something. I guess I'm about ready to come on back, now. How's Dad?"

"He's still asleep. I'm looking in on him every little while. Do you want me to fix you something to eat?"

"I'm not very hungry."

"What about a couple of sandwiches? I'll bet you haven't had a bite all day."

Not since he had received her emergency telephone call when he was on the plane returning to the States. But he really wasn't hungry.

"You need something," she insisted.

"Okay. A sandwich will be fine."

"Clay, if you don't mind, grab a six-pack out of the galley and bring it with you. There's plenty there. I restocked the boat Friday, but with us planning on taking the boat out yesterday I didn't think to bring any back to the house—we're completely out. I'm sure your father's eventually going to be asking for one."

After ending his conversation with Donna, he telephoned for a cab, then moved forward across the salon toward the steps leading down into the galley.

Just before reaching the steps, he stopped to look at the wires dangling from the steering station, where the thief had disconnected the equipment he stole. The compass, depth sounder and the single side band were gone. The Loran-C was still bolted to its bracket next to the steering wheel. The station's VHF radio was still there, too.

The thief had taken one piece of valuable equipment, the single side band, but then left sitting the expensive Loran and the radio in favor of two relatively inexpensive items, the compass and depth sounder.

Clay stared a moment longer. Maybe that's all the thief had time to get to before Robert arrived. Chief Langston had said it was his theory that the killer had hidden from sight when he saw Robert coming down the pier. After the *Cassandra* was away from shore, either the killer came out of hiding or Robert stumbled across him. After the murder, Langston felt that whoever committed it was afraid to return the boat to the boatyard and purposely beached it off Long Beach, then took the dinghy to shore.

It would make sense that after having committed a murder the killer would not be thinking about stealing anything else, just be trying to get away at that point.

That's what had more than likely happened. Given time, the thief would have probably taken all the equipment. Clay moved on past the steering station and down the two steps into the galley where he removed a six-pack of Coors from the refrigerator sitting next to the small sink.

Before leaving that area of the boat, he moved the few steps forward to the V-shaped bow cabin and glanced inside the compact space.

The two narrow bunks, one to each side of the cabin, were undisturbed, and everything in the cabin was in its proper place. Carrying the six-pack, he moved back through the galley and up into the salon.

He had switched off the lights as he left each cabin. Now the only lamp still lit was the brass one he had turned on when he first came onto the boat. He turned it off, leaving the salon's dim night light as the boat's sole illumination. He moved toward the open salon door.

Stepping from the cabin onto the deck, he glimpsed a car coming across the boatyard. It had its headlights turned off and was moving slowly. He watched in curiosity as it parked at the entrance to the pier.

It was a dark-colored Lincoln. Its interior light came on and the driver's door opened. A figure stepped out and started forward down the pier. In the dark, Clay could tell only that the person was a man—tall and heavily built.

Whoever it was, suddenly stopped and knelt on one knee in the middle of the walkway.

Clay continued to stare for several more seconds, then stepped back into the salon and walked to the steering station.

The binoculars he was looking for lay on the small chart table built into the bulkhead next to the steering station's compass mount. He set the six-pack on the table and picked up the binoculars then moved back to the open salon door and raised them to his eyes.

The man's head was bowed as he continued to pray, and Clay couldn't obtain a good look at the face. He could only make out that the man *was* big, had on a white sport coat, dark slacks and had thick, dark hair.

The man suddenly crossed himself and stood, looked directly toward the *Cassandra*.

Antonio Brouchard—the man everybody called "The Cajun."

Clay lowered the binoculars. *What would Brouchard—?* A sudden uneasiness settled over him. He stared a moment longer, thinking. Then he ran his hand into his pocket to finger the marijuana fragments he had swept from the salon cabinets.

Brouchard walked toward the *Cassandra*. Thirty feet from the end of the pier, he suddenly halted and raised his face to stare at the doorway of the dimly lit boat.

Clay pitched the binoculars to the couch, then stepped out through the salon door and onto the deck.

"Sorry," Brouchard said in a voice so soft it was difficult to hear him from where he stood. "I didn't know nobody be on board. Didn't see no car in the yard when I drove up. You're Clay Rodgers, aren't you, Robert's brother?"

Clay nodded.

The man moved up to stop in front of the yellow police ribbon. "I thought so. Just flew back from Florida, heard about your brother when I got off the plane. Thought a lot of that fellow. Didn't see how it would hurt nothin' to stop by here and say a few words for him." He nodded back to where he had knelt in prayer.

Clay couldn't help but be affected by the seemingly deep sincerity in the man's tone. "I appreciate your doing it, Mr. Brouchard. I just got into town myself, and wanted to come by here before I went to bed."

"How's your father and stepmother taking it?"

"Donna's doing better than Dad, right now."

"It was his flesh and blood, Clay—makes a difference."

"Yeah, I guess."

"You know, Clay, your brother was one of the few people ever came to me for advice—and then listened. Made me feel kinda proud of myself."

"My dad and Donna appreciated your talking to Robert for us, and I did, too."

The advice the man referred to had come the past winter. Robert, once again doing poorly in his grades, had suddenly decided he wasn't going back to L.S.U. for the spring semester and had taken a job at one of Brouchard's strip joints. Clay had received a frantic telephone call from his father and then telephoned Brouchard. Though it was the first time Clay had ever spoken with him, Brouchard couldn't have been any nicer. He had not only agreed to terminate Robert but offered to try to talk him into going back to school. And Robert had, not only returning to L.S.U. for the spring semester but later enrolling for the current summer school session.

"Well," Brouchard said. "I guess I better be getting on to the house—wife will be wondering what happened to me."

"I'm leaving in a minute, myself."

"Be proud to give you a lift."

"No, I appreciate it, but I've already called a cab. It's on its way." Besides, with Brouchard's surprising appearance, Clay now didn't plan on going to his house, at least not right away.

What had earlier passed through his mind when he had seen Brouchard walking toward the *Cassandra,* had given him pause for thought. And though the thought seemed unlikely, nearly impossible, he was going to do like the detective in Indianapolis had said—not shrug it off, but instead take a closer look. He knew just where to go to do that.

CHAPTER

4

The Beachfront Bar & Inn was more bar than inn. Only twenty-five double rooms out of the motel section's original one hundred and fifty had been salvageable enough to be rebuilt after Hurricane Camille had swept through the area, while the entire concrete block, hundred-seat bar had come through unscathed. Clay knew it to be the place where Brouchard sometimes ate, and frequently entertained. It was also where Linda Donetti worked. The cab let Clay out at the front of the place about ten minutes after Brouchard had driven away from the boatyard.

Inside the bar, the atmosphere was no different than Clay remembered it—dimly lit, with mounted fish of every description adorning the walls, tables covered with red-and-white-checked cloths spaced comfortably far apart, and, against one side of the building, small partitioned booths with doors you could shut and be in almost complete privacy.

It was nearly closing time and the only customer still in the place was a stocky, middle-age man sitting at the big round bar in the center of the room. He was talking across the counter to the bald-headed bartender. Linda, her back to Clay, was listening to the men's conversation.

She was as he remembered, too. She still wore her dark hair in a length gently resting on the top of her shoulders. Her tight cocktail waitress uniform displayed her small, almost boyish hips and her tiny waist. In her high heels, her calves were tight and slim, her ankles delicately shaped.

He couldn't see her face, but he had no doubt it was as beautiful as ever. He could still picture her captivating eyes, seemingly as big as half dollars, their light green color contrasting perfectly with her usual dark tan. He walked toward her.

The bartender noticed Clay first. A smile instantly appeared on the short little man's pale, round face. "Well I'll be damned," he said. "Look what the cat's drug in. What in the world brings you to—" Then his smile suddenly vanished, and he quickly added in a more subdued tone, "Hey, man, I wasn't thinking; I'm sorry about your brother." The middle-age man who had been talking to the bartender nodded his agreement.

Clay didn't know either one of them, but he nodded and smiled politely. "Thank you."

Linda had turned around to face him. "Hey," she said, a soft smile crossing her face.

She *was* still beautiful. It was hard not to stare at her eyes. He glanced at the two men and then back to her. "You have a minute?" he asked.

"Sure."

He gestured with his head toward the privacy of a booth. But as he walked beside her across the floor, old memories suddenly flooding back made him hesitant, and he stopped at the nearest table.

They sat down, Linda taking a seat directly across the table from him.

He leaned forward and rested his forearms on the table. "I wanted to ask you some questions about Robert."

Her brow wrinkled questioningly.

"Nothing about you two personally, Linda. I was wondering whether he might have mentioned anything to you lately about his being worried about something, or maybe somebody."

The wrinkles in her forehead deepened, and she stared directly into his eyes a moment before she spoke. "Clay, Robert and I haven't been out together in better than a year—I assumed you knew."

His brother had never told him. *Why should he have?* "No, I didn't know . . ."

She held her questioning look for a moment longer, then dropped her eyes from his and shrugged. "I haven't even laid eyes on him in, God, how long—? He hadn't been in here in months."

"Do you by any chance know who he was dating?"

"I don't have the slightest."

Maybe she could help him, anyway. "Linda, earlier I was out at the boat, and Antonio Brouchard showed up. Back in the winter, Robert worked for him for a few days. I know Brouchard comes in here all the time—or has that changed, too?"

"Antonio's in here almost every night." She nodded toward the nearest wall.

Mounted on the stucco finish was a large, framed color photograph of two smiling couples. One of the men was Antonio Brouchard. He had his arm around an attractive redhead. Clay didn't know the other couple.

"Antonio and my boss were cochairs of a big charity to-do last year," Linda explained.

Clay nodded and turned back from looking at the photograph. "Have you ever seen Robert in here with Brouchard?"

Linda shook her head. "No."

"Have you heard anything about Robert working for him, lately?"

"No, I haven't."

"Okay, Linda. Let me tell you what I'm worried about." She was going to think he was crazy. "Dad called upset during the

Christmas holidays. Robert had quit school and gone to work at
one of Brouchard's clubs. The way I looked at it was that Robert hadn't been doing anything but wasting his time at L.S.U.,
anyway. Maybe a couple of years in the real world was what he
needed, and then he'd go back to school and do better. The
job's being at a strip club didn't bother me like it did Dad,
either. What did bother me was the rumors I'd heard over my
years growing up here about Brouchard's possible involvement
in narcotic trafficking."

At his mentioning the trafficking, he noticed a brief smile
cross Linda's face, but she didn't say anything, only continued
to listen.

"When I called Brouchard, he was quite polite. End of a long
story—he advised Robert to go back to school and Robert did.
But tonight, when Brouchard came down to the boat, it got me
to wondering if Robert really did quit working for him.

"I know that sounds crazy, but with the light load he was
carrying in school—just a few hours a week—that left him with
all kinds of free time to do something else. And with him living
at school, there was no way Dad knew what he was doing, or
where he might be at any given time. After seeing Brouchard I
started wondering if . . ." Linda was shaking her head in dis-
agreement.

"Clay, I don't know what's got you thinking like this. Even if
Antonio was into drugs—and he's not, take my word for it—
Robert wouldn't have done something like that. I can't believe
you think he would've."

As guilty as he already felt about the thoughts he was harbor-
ing about a dead brother, he wished she hadn't said that. "I'm
not saying I think he did, Linda; but somebody killed him—for
some reason. There are kids down here, good kids, who have
gotten—"

"Clay, you're looking for something that's not there—let it
go. I knew Robert pretty well myself—some ways better than
you did. He wasn't the type—no way. I thought the police said
he came up on somebody robbing the boat?"

He nodded and leaned back in his chair. "That's what they

think—probably did." It was only that there were those things he felt didn't make sense about the murder. Mainly, Robert's taking the *Cassandra* out by himself on a weekend night. Then there was the equipment that wasn't stolen, while the less valuable pieces had been. Despite the logical explanation he had thought of for that, he still wondered about it. Finding the pot in the salon cabinets was no big deal until Brouchard, the man Clay had heard rumors about all the time he was growing up in Biloxi, had walked down the pier.

Clay shook his head. He knew that what was really bothering him was the possibility of Robert's killer never being caught, and he didn't want that to happen due to something being overlooked, however unlikely. But wild, emotional guessing wasn't going to help, either. He needed to leave police work to the police.

A soft smile lit Linda's face. "You're a big name down here, now. I guess you are everywhere—the guy that saved the Vice-President's life. I saw the whole thing on CNN. I can't believe you weren't scared."

"I was scared as hell."

"You'd have to be crazy not to have been. But you surely didn't look like it at the time." Her smile faded. "I couldn't help but feel sorry for that poor kid they shot."

"Yeah."

"Will you tell me about it?"

"If you saw the CNN tape that's all there was to it."

"I mean from the beginning—what you were thinking. I'd really like to hear it. Maybe if you're going to be in town for a few days . . ."

"Yeah. I'm going to stay over long enough to make sure Dad's doing all right. Maybe one night before I fly back to Washington we can have dinner together."

Though he meant the invitation only as an opportunity to ask her more about Robert, the guilt that he suddenly felt was overpowering. It came from the memory of that night in Washington.

"I'd like that," she said.

*   *   *

In the cab on the way back to his father's house Clay thought back to the time Linda had shown up in Washington when he was undergoing his Secret Service training.

His father had called a few days prior to her arrival and said that a Linda Donetti had phoned to obtain Clay's apartment number.

"She's the girl that Robert's dating," his father had reminded him, "and brothers don't do things like that to each other."

Clay had laughed. He had no interest in a high school senior and doubted seriously she had any interest in him. He had only seen her a couple times previously, and both of those times when she was in the company of Robert.

She had called the next day from Union Station, as soon as she got off the train. Nothing had been out of the way about her call. She had explained that she and two friends who had just graduated from high school with her had decided they wanted to see Washington before they started looking for jobs. Her mother had not liked her coming to Washington alone, or the same as alone, accompanied only by two other seventeen-year-old girls. But Linda had reminded her mother that Clay was in training there and said she would call him as soon as she arrived, and wouldn't do anything without first asking him if it was safe. Her mother had said, "Now, baby, maybe he don't want to be handed such a chore as a surprise." Linda had replied, "He'll be happy to see me, Mama."

She was right, and when he experienced that very feeling as she talked over the telephone to him, he had thought back to his father's call.

The first night the three girls went out together, and the second night he went with them. The third night the other two girls had decided they wanted to go to a play, something Linda didn't want to do, and she asked him if he'd mind taking her around to the clubs.

They had left the last club a little before three in the morning. In the back seat of the cab on the way back to her hotel, they had melted into each other's arms—just like that. He had then leaned forward and informed the cab driver they had a change of destination. Instead of her hotel, they had gone to a nearby motel.

He had awakened the next morning with Linda's tight body curled against him, and he had immediately felt a great guilt. He was almost certain his dad somehow knew, and he prayed that Robert would never find out. But that didn't stop him from making love to her one more time after she had stirred and pulled herself across his chest to look down into his face with those big green eyes. When they left the motel, he had told her it could never happen again. He made it clear to her he was never going to put himself in a position where it might.

Though obviously not feeling any of the guilt he was suffering, she agreed. But he could tell she didn't mean it, and didn't think he did. He had. But he had thought of her often. And now here he was thinking of her again, and, with his brother dead, it was making him feel guilty all over again.

CHAPTER

5

Clay drove his rented Ford Taurus along the road that followed the south bank of the big lake on the L.S.U. campus. His father had awakened upset that morning, complaining that all of Robert's belongings were still in his dorm room with nobody to pick them up—as if nobody cared. He wasn't going to allow that to continue, he said; he was going after them.

Clay had glanced at Donna, her face showing her worry at how his father was acting, and then he had turned back to his dad and told him that he would get one of the workmen at the boatyard to go after the things. But his father would have none of a stranger going after the belongings—not Robert's, not now.

Clay had again glanced at Donna, and then said he would go after the things. There was no way he would've allowed his dad on the road in the condition he was in. Besides, the trip would allow Clay to question Robert's roommate about who Robert had been dating, and to ask if Robert had mentioned anything about planning on taking the *Cassandra* out over the weekend.

Robert's roommate was waiting in his room. His name was Barry Chapman, the son of a well-to-do furniture manufacturer from Tupelo. Well-built, with a mop of thick, brown hair, and dressed in jeans and a ragged, purple sweatshirt lettered with the words GO TO HELL OLE MISS, the boy was sitting on his bed when Clay walked into the room.

"Mr. Rodgers?" the boy inquired as he came to his feet.

"Yes, and you're Barry Chapman. Glad to meet you."

"Yessir. Glad to meet you, sir."

Clay shook the offered hand, then glanced at the clothes and other belongings piled on one of the beds.

"I've got some of my friends to carry the stuff down the stairs to your car, Mr. Rodgers. It'll only take me a minute to round them up." The boy started toward the door.

"Wait a minute, Barry."

"Sir?"

"Did Robert happen to say anything to you about what he was planning on doing Saturday night?"

"No, sir. The police asked me that. I didn't even see Robert after I left the dorm for classes Friday. I went on to Tupelo for the weekend and didn't come back until last night."

"Was he dating anyone in particular—somebody steady—or was he dating around?"

"Last few months he's been sticking with one, pretty much— really all the time. He spent a lot of nights in Biloxi, not just weekends."

"Biloxi? What's her name?"

The boy shook his head. "I don't believe the police think I was telling them the truth, Mr. Rodgers, but I really don't know." He spread his hands in a plaintive gesture past his sides. "I don't know why, but Robert wouldn't tell me who she was. I know it sounds crazy, but that's the way it was. He just . . ." The boy suddenly looked surprised.

"Jesus," he added. "I didn't even think about it when the

police were here. Man, are they ever gonna think I was lying now." He pointed to a lockbox on the end of the bed. "He received a letter every once in a while. He always put them in there. I know it was from her—had to be." He shook his head in bewilderment. "I can't believe I let that skip my mind."

Clay walked to the bed.

"I'll go get the other guys, Mr. Rodgers." The boy turned and left the room.

The box, a small metal one, was locked. Other than the box, Robert's belongings consisted mostly of clothes—jeans and khakis, a variety of both short- and long-sleeve pullover and buttoned shirts, a pile of underwear and socks and two pairs of tennis shoes. There was also a jam box; a small, portable television set; a windup alarm clock and a black shaving kit. As he continued to stare at the things, Clay felt his eyes moisten. He took a deep breath, exhaling it audibly.

As the roommate and three of his friends came back into the room, Clay pointed to the lockbox. "Do you know where the key is?"

"No, sir. Robert always kept it on his key ring."

Clay glanced around the room. "I need a screwdriver, or something like that, something I can use to pry it open."

All of the boys shook their heads. Clay reached to turn the box on its back and pressed with his thumbs against the metal siding next to the lock. The box was constructed of extremely thin metal. He lifted it off the bed and laid it on the floor.

Pressing the toe of his shoe against the latch, he exerted sharp pressure twice, and then, harder, a third time. The latch sprung and the lid popped open. The four boys looked at each other as Clay picked up the box and laid it back on the bed.

The few envelopes, addressed to Robert in handwriting and bound with a rubber band, had no return addresses.

Clay slid a sheet of lined notebook paper from the first envelope.

Dearest Robert,
It seems silly to be sitting here in class writing you when I
talked to you only a couple of hours ago, and will be seeing
you when school is out. I wish you could go to the game
with me. I think we've got a good chance to be state
champs.

I love you, I love you, I love you, I love you, so much—I
really do.

Love and kisses.

The letter was signed, "Me, myself, and I."

"Me, myself and I," he repeated aloud. The boys all looked at
each other.

When school is out.

A college girl would have been more likely to have written,
"when class is out" or "when the period's over," not "when
school is out."

State champs.

The author of the letter had to be a high school girl.

Clay slid the sheet back into the envelope, and opened the
next letter.

Seven letters in all, and all signed, "Me, myself, and I." None
of them gave any better clue than the first one had as to the
writer's identity.

As Clay dropped the packet of envelopes back into the box,
he saw a key.

He lifted it from the box. It was a safe deposit box key. His
eyes narrowed with his thought. He turned to the roommate.
"You know what this is to?"

The boy leaned forward to look. "Maybe a safe deposit box
key?"

Clay nodded. "Yeah, but you don't know where the box is—
Robert never said anything about it?"

The boy shook his head. "First time I've ever seen it. Aren't
safe deposit boxes in banks?"

Clay nodded again. "Is there a bank on campus?"

"Gosh, Mr. Rodgers, I don't know."

"Do you have a phone book?"

The boy glanced around the room. "Some place."

They found it scooted under the bed.

There were nine banks in Baton Rouge. Counting the branches, over a hundred places in all to call.

When Clay began telephoning the banks and their branches, he started with the ones nearest the campus. The third one he called was the one with Robert's name listed among the holders of safe deposit boxes.

But being a brother had no bearing on the ownership of a box. Clay would have to obtain a legal order from the judge who was going to handle the estate, the branch manager had said, rather curtly, before anybody could gain access to the box.

It only took a single call to Washington, and within forty-five minutes the Vice-President's office had called a Louisiana Congressman who had called a judge who was hoping to be nominated to the federal bench one day, and Robert's safe deposit box was being opened.

The tall, skinny branch manager still didn't like it. A scowl across his face, in his hand a faxed copy of the judge's order to open the box, he stood outside the vault and glared through his thick spectacles at what was going on.

Clay stood next to the bank employee who now inserted the bank's key next to Robert's, turned the locks, and then opened the compartment's small door. As the employee moved out of the way, Clay slid the narrow, gray metal box partly from its slot, and raised its hinged top.

The box was literally stuffed full of money. Tens, twenties, even hundred dollar bills, were crammed inside the narrow, oblong space; thousands of dollars, maybe as much as forty or fifty thousand. Robert hadn't suffered any deprivation in coming up with enough money to buy the red sport coat. He hadn't been killed by a burglar, either.

CHAPTER

6

After arriving back in Biloxi, Clay drove to the police station and told the chief about the money in the safe deposit box, then went straight to the Bradford-O'Keefe Funeral Home. Inside the funeral home, he asked if he might be alone with his brother for a while, then quietly visited with him for better than an hour.

After leaving the funeral home, he drove to his house where he explained to Donna what he had found in the safe deposit box in Baton Rouge. His father was asleep, having grown so despondent the doctor had again sedated him.

After Donna assured him she could look after his dad and would call Clay if any problems arose, he picked up his suitcase and went straight to the boatyard. He had decided that he would stay on the boat for a couple of days, partly because of his aversion to sleeping across from Robert's empty bed, but also because he was hoping that in staying on the *Cassandra* he might eventually notice something that would give him a clue to what had happened that night.

Once to the boat, he stripped the yellow ribbon from between the pilings at the end of the pier and carried it aboard with him where he stuffed it into the waste basket under the galley sink. He engaged the burglar alarm system then went directly to the small cabin in the bow.

There, he found his service automatic in his suitcase, laid the weapon on the port bunk, then slid fully clothed onto the narrow, starboard bunk, folded his arms behind his head and lay back on the pillow to rest for a few minutes.

He stared up through the Plexiglas hatch above his bed. It was nearly seven-thirty. The setting sun's last rays gave the soft bank of white clouds passing above the hatch an orange hue. He could smell the roses, and everything was quiet: the boat was gently bobbing, and the bed soft. A pelican on its way to its roosting place glided silently over the boat. In another moment, Clay was asleep.

The quiet darkness aboard the *Cassandra* was shattered by the sound of an alarm, its shrill beeps pulsating high-low high-low, high-low.

Clay jerked upright in his bunk in the bow cabin and swung his feet to the floor. The moonlight coming in through the portholes afforded enough illumination for him to see that nobody was in the galley. He stepped from the cabin and hurried to the porthole over the dinette table in the galley where he looked out toward the pier.

Linda, in the same cocktail uniform she had worn the night before, her purse held in her hands clasped at her chest, was backing away from the *Cassandra*.

Clay hurried into the salon. There, he turned the alarm off, then slid the pier-side salon door back and stepped out onto the deck.

"Linda?"

She shook her head nervously. "I'm—I'm sorry. I heard from one of the deputies about the money you found in Robert's safe deposit box. I know how bad that's got to be bothering you. Donna said you were out here; hope you don't mind my coming by."

"Course not. Come on in."

"When I stepped to the deck off of that . . ." She nodded toward the gangway.

He smiled. "A pressure pad under the welcome mat. It's off now."

Inside the salon, he gestured to her to sit on the small couch. "Would you like a drink?"

"Yeah, please, I would."

He stepped to the cabinets and opened one of the doors. He glanced back across his shoulder. "Bourbon and vodka—that's it."

"Bourbon will be fine. A little ice."

He got a glass and ice from the galley, then walked to the cabinets and lifted out the bottle of Benchmark. Back at the couch he handed her the drink, then sat beside her.

"You're not going to have anything?" she asked.

"Not right now."

"God, I feel like a sot."

He smiled.

She drank almost a third of the strong liquid with her first swallow, then placed the glass on the end table beside the couch before turning back to speak to him.

"As soon as I heard about the money I wanted to come over and apologize for misleading you last night." She shook her head. "I still can't believe he would be involved in anything like that."

"In a way I can't, either. I keep hoping there's some reason other than drugs for the money. But at the same time I know there's not going to be." He noticed how Linda was staring directly into his eyes, then she bit her lip and closed her eyes for a moment. She suddenly stood.

"I'm sorry for busting in on you like this," she said. "I have to go now."

What in the hell? he thought. He rose to his feet and clasped her elbow, turned her around to where she faced him. "Hey, slow down. Is something wrong?"

Her eyes moistened as she stared into his. "That's what I want to know," she said. "What did I do wrong, Clay; that time in Washington? I know you liked me. More than liked me—I could tell. And then you wouldn't even talk to me again. What did I do wrong?"

He felt terribly awkward. "Nothing Linda. Robert was my brother."

Her brow wrinkled, and she shook her head. "He didn't care. We were just friends, that's all. We only went out together for fun. Great fun, but that's all it was. We even fixed each other up. God, the first time we had a date he was only a freshman in high school, two years younger than me. He just stopped me in the hall one day and asked me to the senior dance. Nobody had asked me yet, and I didn't know if they were going to. He was cute, and my being a senior I didn't want to miss my last school dance, so I went. We were just buddies after that. We went out together when we didn't have a date with somebody else. I mean it was a good deal for both of us, for years, but only as buddies; never anything else. He had to have told you."

What reason would he have had to tell me? Clay thought. He shook his head. "After that time with you in Washington, I never mentioned you to him. I certainly wasn't going to ask him if he would mind my taking you out."

"Why didn't you ask me?"

He didn't answer.

She stared directly into his eyes. "You silly, stupid man," she said. "You wanted to, didn't you?" And, suddenly, just like that first time in Washington, she moved into his arms.

When she finally pulled her lips back from his, there were tears running down her cheeks.

"Clay, the first time I saw you, when the three of us went out on the boat together during spring break, I fell for you, then. I couldn't get you out of my mind. Do you really think my idea of fun as a seventeen-year-old was to take a trip to Washington? It was because you were there. And everything worked out great.

But then when you left me that next morning you said, 'No more.' What was I supposed to do, start calling you? Beg?"

He pulled her back to him and they began to kiss again.

An hour later, Linda lay cuddled close to him, one leg lying across his thighs and an arm draped across his chest. Clay lay quietly, staring up at the cabin's overhead and the Plexiglas hatch.

Linda pulled herself up on one elbow so her face was above his. "What are you thinking about?" she asked softly.

Immediately following the overpowering pleasure he had experienced with her, his mind had moved to thoughts of his brother, and he had felt a deep sensation of guilt. Maybe the guilt was a reminder of what he had done in Washington—even if she wasn't his brother's girlfriend at the time, he had thought she was. Maybe the guilt came simply because of having just experienced such pleasure when he should be in mourning—he didn't know. But he hadn't allowed himself to continue thinking like that, and had quickly forced his thoughts on to what he could do to help uncover the killer. He had been thinking about that ever since, and he had come up with an idea.

He looked up into her eyes. "There's something you could help me on," he said. "I don't know anyway to do it without you. Yet, I don't know if I should ask you to."

"Try me."

"You could help me get some fingerprints."

Her brow wrinkled.

"Linda, the police found a print on the *Cassandra* that has to be the killer's, a part of his palm and a finger. He was wearing rubber gloves. Somehow, one got torn. When somebody picks up a glass his hand is like this." He held his hand in front of her eyes and cupped it, forming a C. "Part of the person's palm and part of their fingers will be pressed against the glass."

"Yeah, so . . ."

"When Brouchard and his friends are drinking, they're going to leave prints on the glasses. If you can get the glasses to me, I can see if any of their prints match the ones the police found on the *Cassandra*."

"Why do you think—"

"Linda, we both know that Robert was involved in some way with drugs. If the rumors about Brouchard are for real, and if Robert was working for him, and they had some kind of falling out, then maybe whoever killed him is walking in that bar every night—one of Brouchard's men. It's a long shot, but what's there to lose?"

"You're way off base, Clay. First of all, Robert wasn't working for Antonio. He couldn't have been without me knowing about it—I'm around Antonio too much. Second, I don't care what the rumors are, there's no way Antonio's involved in trafficking. Prostitution, maybe some other things; he's no angel. But I've heard him complain about drugs. Not the ethical argument; but how stupid it is to mess with them—the heat from the DEA and all. I know what I'm talking about."

"Linda, last night you were just as positive that Robert couldn't be involved in something like that."

"I know, but . . ." Her eyes suddenly brightened. "Clay, I don't even think Antonio was in town Saturday night. He came by the bar Friday; told my boss he was leaving later that night, going to Florida on a business trip. I remember he was bitching about having to go."

Clay nodded. "Yeah, when he came down to the boat he said he'd just got in from Florida. But that doesn't account for somebody who might work for him. That's why I need prints of as many of the people around him as you can get."

She was silent for a moment, then she shrugged. Slowly a soft smile replaced the serious expression she had worn as she disagreed with him. "Okay, sure, I'll get your prints for you, why not?"

"Good. You're going to have to keep your fingers off the outsides of the glasses, and store them where they're not touched by anybody. And you're going to have to remember which glass was used by which person."

"I can do that."

"One more thing, Linda. Even if Brouchard's innocent of anything to do with Robert's murder, he might be involved in something else. If they find out what you're doing, you could be in danger."

She smiled. "He's not going to be involved in anything that serious . . . But, okay, I won't have any problem doing it without anybody knowing. I'll be careful. I promise." She moved her lips down to his ear.

"I'll do it, and I'll be careful," she repeated. "And now I want you to love me. And I *don't* want you to be careful. I want you to love me as hard and as wild and as long as you can."

CHAPTER

7

The club was located a block off Bourbon Street and down an alleyway. The entrance to the place was a wide, single door constructed of weather-blackened two-by-ten planks held together by strips of cast iron. A hand-lettered sign nailed above the door simply stated:

"THE JOINT."

There were a score of such clubs in similar locations around downtown New Orleans. Some of them were surprisingly nice inside and attracted the tourist crowd, and some of them were dilapidated and filled with local riffraff, plus an occasional simple-minded college student who didn't know any better.

Inside the thick door, a set of warped wooden steps led downstairs where loud hard-rock music was blaring from a thirty-year-old jukebox.

On a stage in the middle of the club, a too skinny, middle-age stripper with stringy, blond hair and sagging breasts tried helplessly to coordinate her movements with the impossible rhythm of the music.

Sitting on metal folding chairs at tables surrounding the stage were a half dozen aging members of a motorcycle gang, a pair of stoned, transvestite prostitutes grown weary of plying their trade on the streets up above, a few winos, and, at separate tables and sitting by themselves, an out-of-place farmer from the Mississippi Delta and a slim, narrow-faced man of medium height. The slim man had short, lightly graying brown hair and sported horn-rim glasses. He was wearing gray slacks and a thin, V-neck sweater over a T-shirt. He was one of the few sitting around the stage who was paying any attention to the blonde.

Antonio Brouchard, his dark-skinned face appearing almost featureless in the dim light, sat on a stool at the bar. He was the only one at the bar, and was the best-dressed man in the place; wearing white slacks and a dark blue sport coat over a light blue silk shirt, with his feet encased in a pair of alligator shoes. A couple of the motorcycle gang members had stared when he walked into the place, but had quickly lost interest in him when he had quietly averted his eyes from theirs.

The song now finished on the jukebox, the blonde lifted a thin, cotton robe from where she had dropped it in the middle of the stage. She thrust her arms through the robe's wide sleeves and pulled the garment around her body.

At the corner of the stage, she slipped into her spike heels, then stepped off the raised wooden platform and slowly made her way through the tables toward the bar. When Brouchard glanced at her, she forced a tired smile to her face until he turned away and stared back toward the stage.

The slim man rose to his feet, remained at the side of his table a moment as he finished the last of his drink, then turned and made his way to the stairs. He began climbing them on his way out of the place.

Outside in the alleyway, it was starting to rain, a light summer drizzle. The slim man quickened his steps as he turned deeper into the alley on his way to his apartment in a run-down old building a few blocks from the club.

Antonio Brouchard appeared at the door of the club and looked down the alley after the man. After a few seconds, Brouchard stepped from the doorway of the club and followed in the direction the man had disappeared.

Reaching the entrance to his apartment building, the slim man paused at the canopy-covered doorway to fill and light his pipe. A light gray wisp of smoke remained behind him as he swung open the wrought iron gate to the building's open hall-way and started up the stairs leading to his second-floor apart-ment.

Inside his apartment he used his heel to kick shut the door behind him, flipped on the room's overhead light and moved to sit in an easy chair placed close to the front of an old television. After turning the set on, he leaned back in the chair and drew a long deep drag from the stem of his pipe.

At that moment the apartment door opened and Antonio Brouchard stood in the doorway. The man sprang to his feet, his pipe dropping to the floor in the process, but he didn't move any farther when he saw the automatic leveled at him.

"I'm Antonio Brouchard."

The man's eyes widened and he began slowly moving his head back and forth.

Brouchard shut the door behind him and turned the dead bolt. He motioned with his pistol for the man to move toward an old-fashioned iron radiator in the corner of the room.

A few minutes later, the slim man securely handcuffed to the radiator, Brouchard walked to the center of the room and picked up the man's still smoking pipe.

Brouchard went back to the radiator. He slid his automatic into the waistband of his slacks, then leaned over to pull a six-inch switchblade from his sock, and snapped the weapon open.

"Charlie Bailey used you as the go-between. Who did you take it to?"

The slim man, his eyes intent on the blade of the knife, shook his head.

Brouchard raised the pipe and, inverting it, placed the open bowl on the man's upper shoulder at the base of his neck. As smoke seeped from between the rim of the bowl and his skin, the man's eyes closed and he moaned softly.

Brouchard used his knife to tap the bottom of the bowl, dislodging the packed hot tobacco to lie against the man's skin.

"Arrrgg!"

Brouchard quickly slipped the tip of his blade between the man's lips and past his teeth, and the man quit moaning. Sweat popped out on his forehead and ran down his face. He began shaking.

"Jeffcoat," he gasped in pain. "Johnny Jeffcoat!"

"Where?" Brouchard asked as he removed the pipe bowl and slipped the knife blade from between the man's lips.

The man flicked his shoulder sending the smoldering tobacco falling to the floor. "In Gretna—he lives there." The man tried to see down to the painful blister at the base of his neck.

"Go on . . ." Brouchard said in a soft voice. "The address?"

Antonio Brouchard stepped from the run-down apartment building and swung the wrought iron gate shut behind him.

On the building's second floor, the slim man lay next to the radiator in the front room of his small apartment. His heart, now stopped, was no longer pumping great spurts of blood from the cruel, jagged gap in his throat.

Across the street from the apartment building, a couple of runaway children had just taken up residence for the night in a back corner of the alcove of an abandoned department store.

When Brouchard had emerged from the apartment building, clanging the wrought iron gate shut behind him, the children had raised their heads and stared. But when they saw he was staring back at them, they had quickly dropped their heads and huddled down in the corner again. Brouchard walked across the street to stop at the entrance to the alcove.

The boy might have been thirteen, the girl, maybe eleven. They were both dressed in ragged jeans, with the boy wearing an army surplus camouflage jacket over a thin, dingy cotton sweatshirt, and the girl wearing a worn, brown leather jacket over a T-shirt. They both had stringy, brown hair, and both wore it at shoulder length. The boy raised his head again. The girl refused to look. Both of them were scared.

Brouchard glanced back across his shoulder to a second-floor window in the old apartment building, then turned back to stare at the children who had seen him as he exited the building.

After a few seconds he shook his head in pity, then reached into his pocket and pulled out a wad of folded money. He peeled two twenties from the wad and, stepping forward, held out the bills.

"You'll have to sleep somewhere else tonight," he said. The boy, his eyes narrowing, carefully reached up for the money and took it from Brouchard's hand. Then the boy quickly scooted back tighter in the corner with his sister. She still wouldn't look.

"Somewhere else," Brouchard repeated, and stepped back to allow the children to move.

The boy tugged at his sister and the two came to their feet. They quickly edged around the back of the alcove out onto the sidewalk, and hurried up the street.

Brouchard watched until the two shapes had disappeared into the night, then he glanced up into the sky. It had quit drizzling, so as he started back to where he had parked his car he slipped his coat off and slung it over his shoulder.

CHAPTER

8

At Clay's urging, Linda had promised she would ignore him if they met in public over the next few days. Then he had walked her from the *Cassandra* to her car and sent her on her way before the sun rose.

After she left, he showered and shaved, dressed in a dark blue suit, then went to the funeral home.

Donna was there. His father had left a few minutes before to go home and get the red sport coat. He had decided he wanted Robert buried with the coat in the casket.

Clay hugged Donna, then walked with her into the room where his brother lay. It was all he could do to keep his tears from starting again, though he had thought he had cried himself out when he had visited with his brother the day before.

After a few minutes, he turned and walked from the room, then waited for Donna in the main lobby. When she joined him her eyes were red.

"You going to be okay?" he asked.

She nodded.

"If you're sure, I'm going to run down to the police station for a minute. Then I need to go by and speak with Jennifer."

Donna nodded again.

Biloxi Police Chief Robert Lee Langston, a powerfully built, thick-shouldered man with a gray flattop, was leaning forward in his chair thumbing through a stack of papers on his desk when Clay knocked on the office door.

"Yes."

"I'm Clay Rodgers. I telephoned earlier."

"Yes, I thought that's who you were. You certainly bear the family resemblance. Come on in." The chief came to his feet, rolling down his uniform sleeves and buttoning them as Clay came forward. The two shook hands across the top of the desk.

"Won't you have a seat?" the chief said, nodding at the wooden chair pulled up to the front of the desk. Then he sat back in his seat. "Would you like a cup of coffee?"

"No, thank you. I only have a minute. I have to go to an attorney's office when I leave here, and then I have to be back at the funeral home before eleven."

"Okay," the chief said as he leaned back in his chair and crossed his arms across his chest. "You wanted to know how I thought your brother's case was going. Well, I'll be frank. We don't have a suspect in mind yet, and that's not very encouraging. A large percentage of the murders that are ever going to be solved are solved in the first forty-eight hours. After that . . ." The chief shook his head.

"On the positive side, we do have the partial palm print. That's in our favor if we ever get a suspect. And we have the serial numbers off what was stolen—maybe he'll try to pawn the stuff rather than go through a fence. Other than that, all we can hope is that he's out running his mouth somewhere and talks to the wrong person."

Clay nodded. "Yeah, but a pro wouldn't be so likely to be running his mouth, would he?"

"You're thinking pro because of the money you found, and because you think that translates back into drugs and some kind of dispute arising out of that?"

"Where else could he have gotten that much money?"

"Let's hope we come up with a reasonable explanation. I wouldn't like to think Robert had been into something like that; it would tarnish my image of him."

Clay stared at the chief for a moment. "Yeah . . . Well, I appreciate you letting me have the stuff I asked for."

"My pleasure," Langston said. He reached to a side of his desktop and picked up a square, blue plastic container and a sheet of paper. "Here's a copy of the print we lifted off the headboard, and this is the fingerprint kit you asked for. But I don't think you're going to be able to find anything the lab people didn't. They spent a lot of time on that boat—doubt they missed anything." He leaned across his desk and handed the container and sheet of paper to Clay.

Clay gathered them into his hands and rose to his feet. "If anything new comes up I wish you'd let me know." He had written two telephone numbers on the back of a small card, and he handed it across the desk. "I'm going to be staying on the boat. You can ring the first number and get me when I'm on board. The second is to an answering machine if I'm not in. It's also the number I'm going to put in the paper for anybody that might have any information about the murder—I'm offering a reward."

The chief looked at the card a moment, then slipped it into a top drawer of his desk. "If I learn anything new, you'll know about it five minutes after I do."

"Thank you."

"Reward might help," Langston added as he came around the side of his desk. "Never can tell, somebody might have noticed something out of the ordinary that night, but not real sure it's any of their business—until they hear there might be some money in what they know."

The two exchanged handshakes again, then Langston accompanied Clay to the door.

"We'll do all we can, Mr. Rodgers. I can promise you that. Funeral's at one, isn't it?"

"One-thirty."

"I'll see you there."

Clay nodded and started down the hall. Walking toward him was Antonio Brouchard. He was dressed in an all-white suit with a black tie. At his side was the same attractive redhead who had appeared with him in the framed photograph hanging on a wall in the Beachfront Bar & Inn.

She appeared to be in her late thirties. Her well-developed body was vividly exhibited in a tight, yellow, dress stopping just above her knees.

Brouchard stopped in front of Clay. "Afternoon, Mr. Brouchard."

"This is my wife, Angela."

The woman nodded and smiled. Up close she was not as attractive as Clay had first thought. Her face was a little too hard, and her makeup a little too thick. She held out a hand and squeezed his firmly, holding the grip for just a moment too long before breaking it.

The police chief joined them. "Hi, Mr. Brouchard. Ms. Angela."

The man shook the chief's hand. "Langston."

"I have all the information lying on my desk, Mr. Brouchard. If you could help us on this fund drive, you don't know how much we'd appreciate it."

"Clay," Brouchard said, looking back at him. "I'm going to have to get along. I got a lot going today. I'll be at the funeral."

Clay nodded and smiled politely.

Brouchard lingered a moment longer, his eyes studying Clay's face. Then he shook his head and spoke with real sadness. "I been feeling real sorry for you, boy; real sorry."

"Thank you."

Brouchard nodded, turned and started down the hall. As Clay moved toward the station's exit, he glanced back over his shoulder as the two men disappeared into the chief's office. Angela smiled back at him before she stepped through the doorway.

CHAPTER

9

Jennifer Toney's one-woman law firm was in Gulfport, Biloxi's adjoining city. The firm was on the west side of Highway 49, in the next to last block before the highway dead-ended into 90 and Gulfport Beach's commercial area containing the Gulfport City Marina and Gulfport Yacht Club, the Marine Life Oceanarium and the Coast Guard station. Clay arrived at the firm twenty minutes after leaving the Biloxi Police Station.

Jennifer's secretary announced Clay over her intercom as he took a seat in a straight-back chair against the wall. In less than a minute the client Jennifer was in conference with, an old gray-haired black man in a dark business suit, walked from her office, and she appeared in the doorway.

With a beige summer dress clinging casually to her ample but well-formed figure, her blond hair flowing gently down to her shoulders, and makeup perfectly applied, she gave the impression of a woman years younger than her mid-forties, an attractive woman. But more important than her looks, his father had always reminded him, was that she acted like a woman.

"She has a private pilot's license, you know, with an instrument rating," his father had told him, "in addition to her degree in law. She can stand her ground against anybody. Yet you'll never meet anybody that acts more like a lady. I'd be for all that women's lib stuff if there were more that acted like her; probably the only feminist I ever met I could be happily married to."

But Clay had known better. With his father's background of sailing the world as a hand on a freighter from his mid-teens until he married, and the extended periods of loneliness he had endured on his long trips away from home, all he looked for in a woman was one who would devote all of her time to him when he was home.

And he hadn't changed much after he had married and stayed home from the sea. Clay had grown angry more than once when his mother had been browbeaten by his father into doing something she really didn't want to do.

Thinking about that, Clay's thoughts moved once again to the time she had climbed out of her bed at his father's insistence, dressed and left the house for beer, never to return.

Experiencing the same angry emotion that he always felt when he remembered back to that instance, but now with his father in such deep grief, Clay suddenly felt guilty.

Jennifer gave a last nod to the old black man as he walked from the office, and then she came toward Clay. He stood and the two clasped hands.

"You've had a rough time of it, haven't you," she said in a gentle voice. "Are you coping with it okay?" She then shook her head and smiled softly. "Of course you are, at least as well as anybody could be expected to. Your father always said you were a rock. Don't tell him I told you, but he's always telling me how you should have been the one of his two boys he should have named after him; said you would be the one to have carried the name forward with pride. Yes, he's extremely proud of you, Clay."

He smiled politely. "Thank you."

"How's he doing?"

"Not real good."

Jennifer nodded and sighed. "That's what Donna said. She told me that he was in Jackson on business and called in just after she'd heard, and she had to give him the news over the telephone. She said he just started groaning, couldn't say anything. My heart goes out to him." She shook her head. "Well, come on in." She took Clay by the arm and walked with him into her office and to a chair in front of her desk. As he took his seat she went around to her tall leather chair.

After she sat she shook her head again. "I wish you would keep me apprised how he gets along," she said.

"I will."

"Good, I appreciate that. Now, before we get into what you telephoned about, I want to speak with you for a minute about the reward you said you were going to post. Are you positive you want to put up the entire hundred thousand CD? I know it's none of my business, and I know your father has concurred, but that's a great deal of money. I'm concerned that you two are letting your emotions direct you into a premature decision. Something might break on Robert's case any day, someone come forward without the incentive of a reward. But if you've already posted it, you know they're going to claim it." She leaned back in her chair as she continued.

"Clay, I don't mean to sound presumptuous but your dad's business is not a gold mine; he's always having cash flow problems. He might need that money someday. Even if he doesn't, it might be the only thing coming to you when he's gone. The boatyard's not going to be worth much with no one to run it. Again, not meaning to butt into your personal business, but I'm aware your Secret Service Agent's pay isn't exactly making you rich—you could use that money someday."

"I've already thought it all out," he responded. "It is what I want to do. And, like you said, Dad feels the same way."

She nodded. "Okay. Explain to me again how you're going to divide the reward."

He nodded. "Fifty thousand dollars for information leading

to the conviction of Robert's killer, fifty thousand to anybody
that can bring in conclusive evidence of who's behind any drug
trafficking going on in this area."

"Why are you so certain that drug trafficking and Robert's
death are related?"

"The only way he could have come up with the kind of money
he had in his safe deposit box was through drugs."

Jennifer was silent for a moment. "Clay, how much has your
father ever told you about me?" ·

He knew from the look on her face that she didn't mean as a
lawyer. "Not much of anything, really."

"Your father was the first man I ever loved."

Clay thought he had controlled his reaction to her statement,
but he must not have, for Jennifer smiled and nodded.

"I thought that would surprise you," she said. "Your father
told me he had never confided anything to his family regarding
our past relationship." She smiled. "Guess he worried that your
mother, and then Donna, would have been on him to employ
another attorney.

"When I first met him he was crewing on a freighter running
short routes across the Gulf between New Orleans and the east
coast of Mexico. During that period he was home considerably
more often than was normal for him.

"I met him at a club one night, and that was it. You know how
good looking a man he is." She smiled and stared directly into
Clay's eyes. "Like all of you are—three peas in a pod, both of
you boys coming out looking like him. I look at you and I can
almost go back to then." She stared into his eyes a moment
longer, then shook her head wistfully.

"Anyway, he swept me off my feet. He thought a lot of me,
too. I believe he might even have eventually asked me to marry
him, except that I decided to break it off; really for two reasons.
First, to him, women were put on this earth specifically to serve
men. Me, maybe I'm too extreme to the liberated side. But he
was every bit as strong the other way—stronger.

"The second reason I broke it off was that he was a woman

chaser like you wouldn't believe. I wasn't able to abide that."
She raised her eyes directly to Clay's.

"Clay, I'm not telling you any of this to tarnish his image. I
know with you it's not going to anyway. I've said what I have so
that you would realize I'm on a personal level with your father,
that he confides in me things other than just legal and business
matters.

"He was experiencing a great deal of difficulty with Robert,
not only the grades. Robert chased everything that wore a skirt
—from girls so young that if the situation had gone the wrong
way he might have been in some real legal trouble, all the way
up to women of, well, any age. Are you familiar with the woman
who runs the Beach Buff Arcade in Biloxi?"

Clay shook his head.

"She's my age, Clay, and married. Because your brother
slipped out with her, your father had to face a gun-carrying
husband a couple of years back. And that's not the only time I
know about Robert being involved with a married woman.

"The point is, Robert's killer could as easily have been an
angry husband. For that matter, even the money could have
come differently than you've decided; through some other
means outside of drug trafficking. About a year ago Robert
came to me to get him out of a bookmaking charge he incurred
at L.S.U."

Clay closed his eyes briefly.

"He requested I not tell his father. I intended to, if it started
looking bad for Robert. But I was able to pull some strings with
a D.A. who's an old friend, and bailed him out of trouble. I can
still remember Robert telling me that money was no problem in
his defense. Any amount of money, he said. And that was before you said he had thought about going to work for
Brouchard."

Clay shook his head. "That was just Robert's big talk. He
probably didn't have a dime."

"Maybe, but when I said bookmaking I didn't mean he was
only placing bets for a couple fraternity friends. He had a big
operation going. He might have done better financially than we

thought. That money you found in his safe deposit box didn't necessarily have to be drug money—that's the point I'm making."

Clay nodded. "It might not be, but it might be, too. I once worked with a detective who told me that if something about a crime gave pause for thought, that you shouldn't shake it off. Too many things have started me thinking that Robert wasn't killed by a thief, but that his murder was in some way connected to drugs. I've got to try and find out whether it was or wasn't—I can't just shake the thought out of my mind and go on like it never occurred to me."

"Clay, you're inexperienced. Everywhere you look you're going to find something that, as you put it, gives you pause for thought. Even an experienced investigator would be hard pressed to stay logical if something happened to one of his loved ones. I knew a detective, too; he was a homicide whiz. One day his sister was found raped and beaten to death in her home. The first thing this detective did when he arrived at the home was to decide that one of the officers already there investigating the scene was a prime suspect. The detective's sister had been hit several times in the right side of her face. The officer was left-handed—that's all. The detective told me that in the state of mind he was in when he saw the officer use his left hand to fill out his report, that was all it took. He said if they hadn't eventually found out who had killed his sister, that he would probably still be wondering about the officer. Sure, his sister being hit in the right side of her face indicated a left-handed assailant, but don't you think the detective jumped to a hasty conclusion? He did because of his being personally involved with the victim; his sense of logic, of reasonable probability, was gone."

Clay leaned forward in his chair. "I understand what you're saying. But I'd still like to hear about Brouchard. You told me over the phone that you would tell me what you know about him."

She smiled. "You're hardheaded like your father, too." She leaned back in her chair. "Okay. Brouchard came into this area as an orphan in his late teens, somewhere out of south Louisiana Cajun country. Old John Dupree gave him a job as a ticket-taker at his strip joint. Couple of years later Brouchard had worked his way up to bouncer, and then to Dupree's bodyguard. When Dupree was charged with intent to distribute, he deeded the club to Brouchard in order to keep from having it shut down. Whatever the real understanding was between the two, it ended six months into Dupree's sentence when there was a racial fight up at the state penitentiary and Dupree got his throat slit. Since then, Brouchard's opened three more clubs.

"There have always been rumors about his being involved in drugs. Yet, rumors are all I know them to be. Somebody could have not liked Brouchard and started the rumors, maybe some prissy somebody that was offended by the way he made his living. We are still in the Bible Belt. Running strip joints is not exactly looked upon as the most Christian work in the world.

"But look at it from Brouchard's point of view. What do you do to start making a living when you come to town broke, uneducated and a teenage orphan. You don't open up a medical practice and start seeing patients.

"Actually, with his charity work he's taken a lot of the sting out of what he does; the fund-raising he's always into has gained him a fair degree of respect over the years.

"Other than for a few violations for some under-age kids getting in his clubs, he's only been in trouble with the law one time as far as I know, when he became involved in a fight and used a knife on a man for making a pass at Angela. For a while he faced an 'assault with intent to kill' charge, but it was later dropped. Angela, that's Brouchard's wife, was a featured stripper at one of his clubs before he married her; she's still quite an attractive woman."

"Yeah," Clay said. "I met her earlier, today."

"They have one child," Jennifer continued. "A daughter from Angela's previous marriage. I would imagine that the child's about a senior in high school by now. Brouchard adopted her shortly after he married Angela.

"So there you have it—charity work, good marriage, loving

father. One, two, three—outside of the stigma of the clubs, he gives every appearance of a man trying to be a good citizen. But there are some chinks in his armor.

"For one thing, admittedly insignificant—but to show that not everything's perfect in Brouchard's world—his marriage is not as solid as everybody thinks it is. His wife came to me a few weeks ago and told me she was considering a divorce. She wasn't sure she was going through with it, and said she'd be back in a few days to talk more about it, but for me not to telephone her. She never came back."

Clay was silent for a moment. "And I guess you can't tell me what he'd done to cause her to be thinking about a divorce? Right? Ethics?"

"Oh, come off of that, Clay," she said, smiling and flicking her hand at him. "Only don't be repeating it; I wouldn't want it to get back to her husband. It's really nothing that tells you anything about Brouchard other than that he's not quite as perfect as he appears. He has a mistress. Evidently he's had her for a long time—according to Angela. Angela said she had thought he'd broken off the relationship, but then shortly before she came to me she found a canceled thousand-dollar check for, as Angela put it, 'the whore's latest services rendered.' I know the girl. Works down at the Beachfront Bar & Inn. A very attractive little thing by the name of Linda Donetti."

CHAPTER

10

After the graveside service for his brother was over, Clay drove Donna and his father to their home, and visited with them until his dad decided to take a nap. Then Clay drove to the *Cassandra*.

Once aboard the boat, he walked around the deck to the far rail, leaned against it and stared out across the Sound.

His thoughts were mainly of his brother, but a particular image of Linda kept popping into his mind.

He had not seen her at the funeral home, but she had come to the cemetery and stood silently among the several dozen people in attendance. When the service was over, she had continued to do as he had asked, not speaking to him in public, and had walked slowly to her car. Not once had he noticed her look his way until after her car had started along the gravel road that ran through the cemetery.

At that time she had looked back across her shoulder and,

definitely staring at him, held the stare for a long moment before facing forward again. He kept visualizing her doing that.

He knew what Jennifer said about Linda's relationship with
Brouchard. But he also knew that in the cabin with him on the
boat Linda had not been faking her feelings or how she had
reacted to his lovemaking. He just knew that. He nervously
thumped his fingers on the polished wood of the rail. *He just
knew that,* he told himself again. Then he felt a sensation of
guilt at being given over to thoughts of Linda so quickly after he
had buried his brother. He raised his face to stare out over the
water.

It was a beautiful summer day, the Gulf breeze light and
warm, the sky a brilliant pale blue with only an occasional puffy
white cloud to be seen.

A couple hundred yards out into the Sound, a gleaming white
Hatteras Motor Yacht passed by. A flock of sea gulls flew over
the yacht, banked and came down close to make sure it wasn't a
fishing vessel. As the birds rose back into the sky, a large pelican glided through their midst, momentarily scattering them.

A ski boat pulling a pair of tanned teenage girls in white one-
piece bathing suits plied the calm waters to the leeward side of
nearby Deer Island.

The last time he had taken the *Cassandra* out on such a day,
Robert and his father had been trolling shiny flashing spinners
off the stern. They had caught a half dozen red fish before they
had reached the Ship Island pass into the Gulf. The good times
—but there had been the bad times, too. There had been the
worst time.

Clay thought about his father and how he looked lying in his
bedroom. Was the pain-twisted face and the anguished breathing all because of Robert's death, or was their father going back
to that time when he had nagged his wife, Clay and Robert's
real mother, into going after some beer?

Faye was her name. His father always drank a couple of beers
before he went to sleep. But there had been none left in the
house that night and, busy finishing up a proposal he had promised to deliver to a yacht owner the next morning, he didn't

want to waste the time it would take to go after a six-pack. Instead, he had nagged Faye into going to the store for him despite the fact that she was suffering from a headache and had already undressed for bed.

The next time they saw her, she was lying in intensive care, her car having been hit by a drunk driver as she had turned into the small strip center where the beer was sold. Horribly mangled, she only lasted for twelve hours. To Clay's knowledge, his father still couldn't drive by the accident site, detouring around it whenever he had business in that part of Biloxi.

Eventually everything returned to as normal as it could without a mother in the house, until, a little over two years later, their father had taken a woman out to dinner. His doing so had angered Robert deeply. Clay felt differently, glad that their father could once again enjoy being around someone of his own age, and Clay had shamed his brother into agreeing.

The woman their father had taken out had been Donna. A few months later they were dating steadily; to be married the following Christmas. Robert had never gotten over it. Was that when he changed? Clay looked at the rope the Coast Guard had left lying on the forward deck after they had towed the *Cassandra* back to the boatyard. Robert, as a little boy, had always carefully coiled the ropes; had to have them just exactly right. He had also made straight A's in grammar school, would become almost depressed when he made less than an A even on a single test. Clay looked at the rope again.

Maybe Robert hadn't changed.

The lines being coiled perfectly in place, and Robert dissatisfied, even depressed when he brought home anything less than an A—he was an *extreme* person.

So why shouldn't he, when he grew older and his preferences moved from cruising and schoolwork to the world of driving, dating and drinking, have gone overboard in that direction, too?

Remembering Robert's extremes, and their mother's always preaching about moderation, and then how it had been her

words to Clay which, however unintentionally, had taken away
his right to moderation, he shook his head at the irony of it all.

"Moderation is the key to a happy life," his mother had often
said. Then there had come that night. As she lay broken and
slowly dying on her hospital bed, she had asked for the others to
step outside a moment and then gestured with her hand for him
to come close.

He was going to have to be the family rock she had whispered
to him through her swollen lips. He was going to have to take
care of the others.

Robert was only a child, she had continued. His father was
more bluster than anything, not nearly as tough as he tried to
act—not when it came to real responsibilities.

As Clay held his mother's hand, she had asked him to swear
to her that he would always be strong for them—for her.

And when he had sworn as she asked, she had suddenly
smiled, and the pain had left her bruised face. Her eyes had
then slowly closed, and he had known she was gone, and that
she had taken his words with her, and that his words were all
she had been able to take with her. He knew there was no way
he would ever take them back from her.

Clay looked again at the rope lying on the forward deck, then
moved to it and curled it into a proper coil. He stepped up onto
the bowsprit and stared down into the murky water and drifted
back into reminiscing.

His mother's death had been in the late spring of his junior
year at Biloxi High School. He had been a decent athlete, more
fast than anything, and had started for the Indians as a football
wide receiver both his sophomore and junior years. But his senior year he didn't get to participate in sports.

That was the year his dad, still depressed and not able to
work as hard as he had before his wife's death, had allowed the
boatyard to get so far in debt he was about to lose the business.
Honoring his oath to his mother, Clay had quit all his school
activities and, allowed to leave school at twelve each day, had
begun putting in as many hours at the boatyard as any of the

regular hands. Robert couldn't help; he was only eleven at the time.

Slowly, the business began to do better, and Clay spent the next two years splitting his time between work at the boatyard and study at Gulf Coast Community College.

His junior and senior years were spent at Ole Miss where, convinced for the first time that the boatyard and his father were going to make it, he had finally relaxed and began to enjoy his college years—enjoyed them too much.

When he graduated the surprisingly high cumulative average he had maintained while working full time had dropped to a three point. Most students would have welcomed such an average, but it was not high enough to get into medical school, where he had originally thought he wanted to go. But then, becoming a doctor had really been more his mother's idea—and he had sworn no oath about that.

He flirted with law, even took the LSAT and made a twenty-eight—borderline with his average. He probably could have been accepted into law school somewhere, but never really tried outside of a pair of applications to the Ole Miss and Mississippi College Schools of Law, and both of them had turned him down.

He loved the water and contemplated for a time going to work full time at the boatyard. But he knew from the years he had worked there that his dad was demanding and headstrong. And Clay was no longer a child. He knew they'd be clashing.

Other than a couple of family trips to Disney World while he was still in grade school, he hadn't seen much of the world outside of what he viewed on television. But he had heard about the many places to see as his dad related his adventures in the ports he had visited around the world.

The Secret Service had suddenly popped into Clay's mind. He didn't know where the idea came from. He hadn't remembered seeing a commercial or any other kind of advertisement. He had finally decided on giving it a try. Such employment would obviously afford some travel, there was a decent income to be made, and an adequate government pension when he retired—if he should decide to make it his career.

After joining the Secret Service, he had spent his first eight weeks in a federal law enforcement training center at Glynco, Georgia.

His criminal investigation courses touched lightly on nearly everything to do with law enforcement: evidence, federal court procedure, search and seizure, organized crime, psychology for law enforcement, sources of information, undercover operations and on and on. An endless list, but, as he had discovered in the last days, not covered in enough detail for the way he needed the knowledge now.

His second eight weeks of training were spent in Washington, D.C., with firearm training, protection techniques and other outdoor exercises held at nearby Beltsville, Maryland. Then he had been assigned to the field office in Indianapolis.

He spent two years there, mostly working counterfeit and forgery cases. The third year he applied for an open position on Gerald Ford's protection detail. It was the plum protection detail, a laid-back job of protecting a polite and easygoing former President who lived in Palm Springs and spent most of his time on a golf course there. The assignment particularly appealed to Clay because acceptance would have meant he would have worn golf togs much more often than a suit and tie.

Of course he didn't have enough tenure to win the assignment. He did, however, shortly afterwards, receive notification over the teletype that he had been assigned to temporary duty as a member of an advance team that was to fly ahead of the Vice-President on one of his upcoming overseas tours.

First Clay's team had flown to Paris, where he had a relatively relaxed time standing a security post at the airport as the Vice-President arrived, spent a scant few hours, then departed for London.

Clay's advance team of special agents then became a "jump team" who leapfrogged the Vice-President's London stop where another team of advance agents was already in place, and flew on instead to Manila, the next scheduled stop on the Vice-President's itinerary after his two-day stay in England.

Manila *had not* been a relaxed time for Clay. It was there that the Secret Service's Intelligence Division had developed a frightening case. There was the possibility that a communist terrorist group might make an assassination attempt on the Vice-President.

The possibility of an attempt alone wasn't the frightening part. The Intelligence Division of the Secret Service always had rumors to investigate and be on guard against. What was frightening about this particular alert was that, if an attempt was made, it would be done by a fanatic wired with dynamite rushing forward to explode himself as close as possible to the Vice-President.

In such a scenario how could the fanatic be stopped? Even if the terrorist was apprehended while still far enough from the Vice-President to be no danger to him, there would still be the huge crowds all along the motorcade route. Dozens, even scores of bystanders would be killed if the man exploded the charges that were supposedly going to be wired to his body.

And what of the agent unlucky enough to perform his duty well enough to spot the fanatic before he rushed forward to make his attack?

It wasn't a case of having to shoot before being shot. A quick movement of the fanatic's hand and both he and any agent close enough to stop him would be gone.

But most of the rumors developed by the Intelligence Division were only that, rumors; and Clay hadn't been unusually tense as he stood his post on the sidewalk along the motorcade route. Then he saw the young man edging through the crowd.

It was really a child, thirteen, fourteen maybe. Dressed in a ragged pair of long cotton trousers and a billowing pullover shirt, the boy was nervously moving his eyes from side to side.

As Clay moved closer, he saw the beads of perspiration on the boy's face. The loose shirt was the perfect camouflage for a string of dynamite wired around the thin body.

It happened so fast after that moment that it was hard to remember everything in exact detail.

The boy's eyes locked on his. The expression that had immediately crossed the frightened, dark face told Clay there was no doubt he had discovered the assassin.

The Vice-President's motorcade was still a mile away. Clay had raised his wrist to his mouth and spoken into the little mike rubber-banded to his watch.

The motorcade immediately stopped, the Vice-President's limousine and the two chase cars making abrupt U-turns and speeding off to a predetermined "secure area."

The boy, unaware his quarry would not be passing by, had edged closer to the street. Clay had taken a deep breath, then suddenly shouted for everyone to clear the area.

For a minute nobody had moved, except to look at the white man who had uttered the loud shout. Then, the few in the crowd who understood English repeated in the local dialect what the tall American had said about explosives. Screams had rent the air, and the crowd had scattered in every direction.

Clay had waited for the boy to explode the charge, but the youngster, his face dripping sweat, had only stood there.

Within minutes only Clay and the boy were left on the deserted sidewalk; a couple of other Uzi brandishing special agents stood a few hundred feet away.

The command had come through Clay's earpiece to back away, to attempt to get some distance and a tree trunk or the body of a car between him and the boy before the Uzis opened up. The boy, noticeably trembling, his hand hidden under his shirt, had suddenly started crying.

Clay had spoken to him, trying to keep his voice calm and steady as he did. "The Vice-President's been warned. He won't be coming this way." Then Clay had cursed the language barrier.

But the boy turned and glanced down the empty street, and Clay realized the youngster did understand English.

"You will die," Clay had continued, "and I will die, and for nothing."

The boy was by then trembling so hard his body was literally shaking, and Clay had feared the dynamite charges might go off from an accidental movement of the hand thrust under the shirt.

The boy suddenly stopped crying, and his face had tightened. For a moment Clay thought the youngster had decided to explode the charge. Then, reacting to whatever thought had worked its way through his brain, the youngster started crying again and began shaking his head back and forth, back and forth.

Clay had forced a smile to his face, as big and as gentle a smile as he could make, then slowly reached to pull his nine-millimeter automatic from its holster.

The boy's eyes widened.

Clay pitched the pistol to the sidewalk, where it clattered and slid a couple of feet along the concrete.

The boy looked at the weapon, and back to Clay. Clay signaled by cupping both of his hands and wiggling his fingers toward himself, urging the boy to come forward. He had made sure to keep his smile big and friendly.

"Nobody's going to hurt you," Clay had said gently. "Your mother will hug you tonight rather than cry for you. Let's take the charges off."

Without a moment's hesitation, the boy had immediately slipped his shirt over his head to reveal a dozen sticks of dynamite wired around his body. He began unstrapping them, and in a few seconds had laid them on the sidewalk. He started backing away from the dynamite.

Clay, still forcing a smile, and with his hands held calmly at his sides despite the perspiration burning his eyes, took a step forward toward the dynamite.

A shot had rung out and the boy's head was knocked violently backwards, the blood erupting from his forehead spraying Clay.

Two more sharp reports followed the first, though they were not needed. Clay had shut his eyes and dropped his head.

When the Intelligence Division agent stopped beside him,

Clay had shaken his head. "I was as close to the dynamite as he was. He could have never got back to it before I tackled him. There was no reason for him to have been shot."

The agent pointed to the rooftop across the street. "It was one of the Filipino soldiers, not our people."

Clay had glanced to the rooftop and saw several soldiers patting the back of the one who had fired the shots, congratulating him.

Standing next to the soldiers was an American television crew who had filmed the entire confrontation, and Clay saw himself often on television over the next several days. Courtesy of CNN, on his way back to the United States there were people in two different airports in two separate nations who recognized him and wanted to shake his hand.

He had landed a permanent position on the Vice-President's protective detail, and received a ten thousand dollar bonus for risking his life in the protection of a member of the executive offices, the bonus a benefit seldom awarded and little known by the general public. The last special agent to receive such a bonus had been Tim McCarthy, who received a similar bonus after the John Hinckley assassination attempt on President Reagan, and was then made a member of the protective team surrounding Nancy Reagan. He was the special agent always seen closest to her in public appearances.

More important to Clay at the moment, was that after the Manila incident the Vice-President had personally told him, "If you ever need anything, anything at all, let me know."

Clay had already taken advantage of that pledge in getting the safe deposit box opened. There was a good chance he would be taking advantage of it again before he returned to Washington.

A shout pulled Clay from his thoughts. It had come from the ski boat, now dead in the water in the middle of the channel leading toward Biloxi Bay.

The boy who had been steering the boat was standing and waving his arms at another small ski boat filled with similar age youths.

The boy's next shout drifted across the wind to Clay. "Out of gas!"

Clay started to smile, and the thought suddenly struck him: *Fuel!—the* Cassandra*'s fuel tanks!*

Why in hell hadn't he thought of that before?

He stepped off the bowsprit and hurried down the deck to the salon. Inside the cabin, he moved to the interior steering station.

The calibrated fuel gauge showed the main tank nearly seventy gallons from being full.

His gaze fell on the six-pack of Coors sitting on the chart table; the beer Donna had asked him to bring back to the house. He hadn't thought of it since he had laid it on the chart and went with the binoculars to study Brouchard kneeling in prayer. Donna hadn't mentioned it again. He wondered if his dad had ever asked for one. He shook his head. His dad wasn't doing well at all. He stared at the six-pack for a moment longer, then moved to the telephone.

Donna's cousin, Lila Delaney, visiting at the house, answered the ring and handed the receiver to Donna.

"Yes."

"Donna, did Dad top off the *Cassandra*'s tanks after you all had her out?"

"Gosh, I'm sure he did, but I don't remember him doing so."

"Is he still asleep?"

"Yes."

He always topped off the tanks, both the fuel and fresh water tanks while Donna tidied up the inside of the boat. Then everything was ready to go the next time they went out.

"Clay, for the life of me, I can't remember—wait a minute. Yes, he did! On the way home in the car he told me to remind him to call the fuel truck the next day, that he had nearly drained the pier tank when he filled up the *Cassandra.* He said he didn't like the pier tank being that low on fuel; was afraid water might condense in it and end up in the *Cassandra*'s tanks. I never did remind him to call. Why?"

"There's around seventy gallons gone, now. That's enough

for the *Cassandra* to have gone thirty-five to forty miles one way before starting back here; maybe a little less in high seas or against a current. But in which direction—to where?"

"Clay . . ."

"Uh, huh."

"Clay, I don't want you to take this the wrong way, but you're letting this . . . Clay, you need to let the police do the investigating. I'm afraid if you keep thinking about it it's going to get to you. Why don't you call them and tell them about the fuel and then come on out here and let me fix you something to eat —you haven't eaten, have you?"

"Yeah, I ate breakfast." A half a sweet roll and a cup of coffee—all he had felt like eating. "I'm okay."

He replaced the receiver and walked to the steering station to stare at the gauge again.

Thirty-five to forty miles one way, and back to Long Beach. Robert hadn't been killed right after taking the *Cassandra* from its berth. He had gone somewhere first. At least the *Cassandra* had gone somewhere first, whoever was at the controls. But where?

Then it dawned on him. Robert's making big money in drugs, his having the *Cassandra* at his disposal: the Safety Fairway incoming freighters traveled as they made their way toward Gulfport Harbor was just south of Ship Island—Robert had gone out to meet one of the ships. *He was ferrying drugs to shore!*

Clay hurried to the telephone.

After he punched in a number and a secretary answered, it was only a few seconds until Jennifer was on the line.

"Clay."

"Jennifer, I need a favor. I want you to call the Port Authority and find out the names of any freighters that came into Gulfport Saturday night."

There was a moment of silence before she spoke again. "You think Robert took the *Cassandra* out to meet one of them."

"Yes, but I don't want to be the one making the call. If they realize who I am, they might guess why I'm calling. I want to get the names of the freighters, first, and then think about it a while before I go any further. I may want to go through Washington rather than local law enforcement. Besides, if a freighter did dump drugs over that night, then they'll do it again, with someone else to ferry the drugs to shore. I don't want the word to get out that anybody suspects what they're doing."

After replacing the receiver, Clay, absorbed in his thoughts, leaned back on the couch.

Barely three minutes passed before the telephone rang.

"Hello."

"Clay, there weren't any."

"What?"

"Nothing came in Saturday night. The last freighter to dock in Gulfport was a Russian ship in to pick up a load of frozen chickens—Thursday. It departed Friday night."

After replacing the receiver Clay sat in silence for a moment. Finally he stood and moved back to the steering station where he stared at the fuel gauge.

So where had the *Cassandra* gone that night? What was thirty-five to forty miles from the boatyard? And in what direction? West? East? Straight out into the Gulf? Or out past the Barrier Islands and then west or east. Or . . . He shook his head in exasperation. Knowing the amount of fuel used was absolutely useless information.

CHAPTER

11

The *Victory* was a wide-bodied ocean-going trawler, over twenty meters in length. Its hull was heavy steel painted dark blue, the color specifically chosen by its owner, Soung Ming, to make the vessel less visible when it was moving at night without running lights. It sat at the Gulfport City Marina, at the end of the pier nearest the open water, and took up two regular berths.

Soung Ming also leased the two next nearest berths, in order to distance the trawler from any other boats. A crewman, a guard actually, could be found standing on the *Victory*'s bowsprit, staring up the walkway that anybody wanting to reach the vessel would have to walk down.

Inside, the accommodations were as spacious as could be found on most any yacht under a hundred feet. You could enter the superstructure from either of two side doors, from a forward entrance under the bridge, or through an aft passageway.

All but one of the entrances were always kept locked and bolted, with a crewman constantly standing at the unlocked one.

The interior steering station was forward of the upper salon, not in it, and separated from the salon by a thick steel bulkhead.

The salon itself was a good twenty feet long and fifteen feet wide, resplendent with plush furnishings. Usually the only persons who could be found there were members of the crew, except for the times Soung Ming held business meetings there with some of his Central American partners.

There was also a lower salon, forward down the steps from the first. This salon was just as wide and ten feet longer than the upper. It was decorated with a variety of expensive furniture. The bulkheads were covered with imitation gold leaf painted with brightly colored Vietnamese figures. Soung Ming was sitting in a big overstuffed chair against an aft bulkhead and next to the passageway leading down into his ornate master cabin.

Soung Ming was both tall and fat, and anything but weak. His fat only covered but did not replace the wide strong muscles similar to those of a Japanese Sumo wrestler.

His long black hair was slicked back and held in a rubber band, producing a short ponytail. Three thick gold chains hung around his neck. He wore a flowered shirt unbuttoned to his navel, his stomach protruding through the wide gap between the sides of the material. This day he also wore an enormous pair of white Bermuda shorts and sandals. He held a thick Cuban cigar curled tightly in his left hand, and in his right held what was left of half a barbecued chicken. He was pointing with the chicken at the thin Vietnamese man who stood before him. His voice was loud.

"No one who works for me himself is allowed drugs." He raised the side of chicken back to his mouth.

The man nodded his head repetitively before he spoke. "No, sir, he shouldn't have. He won't again." The man being discussed was the thin Vietnamese's cousin.

The young, silk-pajama-clad Vietnamese woman who had been reclining on the couch to Ming's right rose slowly to her feet and walked around to his side. She reached down with her long fingernails and ran them gently across the side of his face, then began to massage the beefy folds around his neck.

Ming looked back at the man in front of him. "No, he *won't* again."

A coldness ran down the thin man's spine, but he was careful to show no expression.

Ming, satisfied with the man's lack of reaction, relaxed his stare. He tore the last of the white meat loose from the chicken breast and dropped the bone into the wastebasket sitting at the side of his chair. Then he plopped the meat into his mouth.

"The charter boat goes out tonight," he said around the bulge in his cheek. "This time I go along."

"Sir, do you think that's a good idea?"

Ming's face raised, his eyes reading again.

"I mean I know it is a *wise* idea," the thin man quickly added, "but I am thinking of you, sir. There is always risk."

Ming dropped his gaze and nodded. The woman leaned the softness of her breasts into the side of Ming's face, then moved her lips down to his ear and whispered.

Ming came to his feet. His thick legs spread wide enough so his massive thighs would not rub together, he walked in the shuffling fashion of a Sumo wrestler toward the passageway to his stateroom. Giggling, the woman hurried ahead of him.

"Sir."

Ming halted without looking back. "Sir, what about the Secret Service agent?"

"The same as since he arrived—keep watching him."

"You are aware he's said he will not be leaving until he solves the death of his brother."

"We shall see . . . It is easy for him to boast of what he is going to do. But I believe he shall grow weary and return to Washington. If not, we shall wait and see how much of an inconvenience he becomes to us." He shuffled forward again.

CHAPTER

12

The Beachfront Bar & Inn was closed, but all its interior lights were burning brightly and the bartender was on duty.

Antonio Brouchard was dealing the cards. He was still in his white suit, but now without a tie. Sitting to his right was a narrow-faced New Orleans politician with long, oily black hair, dressed in a shiny blue suit complete with a flower in the lapel. To Brouchard's left sat a broad-shouldered graying man, pale and sunburned, wearing coveralls—the owner of a farm and garden supply store thirty miles inland.

Directly across from Brouchard sat the last of the foursome, an unusually handsome, athletically built man in his middle thirties. He had thick blond hair, cut full and hanging nearly to his shoulders, and he wore a light blue dress shirt and dark blue pants. Linda had never seen him before tonight.

As she carried a fresh round of drinks toward the table,

Brouchard bet five hundred. Nobody folded, the men throwing their cash on top of his.

She used a napkin to keep her palm and her fingers off the glasses as she set the drinks before the men. When she picked up the empty glasses, she did so by inserting her forefinger inside them with only the tip of her thumb on the rims of the glasses.

At the bar she set the tray out of reach of the bald-headed bartender standing at the cash register. She looked at him and smiled.

"Freddie, I thought you were going on in?"

Recounting the cash in the register for the third time, the bartender shook his head irritatedly. "Can't get this damn thing to balance out." He glanced at the tray of glasses. "Hand those here."

She ignored the request. "How much are you out of balance?"

"Seventeen damn dollars."

She laughed. "Go on home. I'll get it to work out. If I don't, I'll put the seventeen dollars in out of my pocket. You've been on duty for over twelve hours now. You're going to have a heart attack one of these days. I lay in bed all day. I'm wide awake. You can do me a favor sometime."

"Okay, if you're volunteering. Try to get this damn thing balanced. I don't want to be paying all my overtime back into the son-of-a-bitch."

"I'll have it balanced before I leave—guaranteed."

He untied his apron, laid it over the bar and smiled at her.

She followed him to the door, kissed him on his fat cheek, then let him out and locked the door behind him.

Back at the bar, she carefully placed the glasses in a paper bag, and leaned over to place the bag in a cabinet at the bottom of the bar.

"Linda!"

The sudden shout startled her, and she felt part of the color drain from her face. She raised her head back above the counter and looked toward the men around the card table.

"Linda, be bringing us another round, honey."

She pulled her order slip out of her pocket and began preparing the drinks.

Clay relaxed at the realization of what the sharp, shrill noise was that had awakened him. The telephone rang a second time. He swung his legs out of bed and stood, reached to pick up his 9-mm service automatic from the other bunk, then unbolted the door from the crew's quarters and walked through the galley and up into the salon.

He lifted the receiver to his private number. "Hello."

"Clay, this is Jennifer. Hate to bother you so late. I'm down at my office and just received something in by fax that you're going to be interested in."

He looked at his watch. "Down at your office—this time of night?"

"Clay, you recall when we were discussing Brouchard and I told you about him arriving here as a teenage orphan? The story is supposed to be that his father and mother went out hunting one night and never came back. That's not exactly the straight of it, as my granddaddy used to say."

"What do you mean?"

"When you were questioning me about Brouchard, it started me wondering about what kind of background he came from, had his parents been in any kind of trouble. You know, things like that. It wasn't real important. But it stayed on my mind.

"Late this afternoon I remembered I knew a sheriff over there named Brouchard, too. Thought he might have been of kin, at least known of Antonio or his family. He didn't, but he said he'd see what he could find out.

"He contacted me about an hour ago and told me he'd found something he thought I would be interested in. After he read it to me, I asked him to fax it to my office right then."

"Jennifer, are you trying to build the suspense or something?"

Her soft laugh came over the phone. "Brouchard's mother did go hunting one night and never came back. At least that was the report Brouchard's father gave the police. By the way, she was Italian, that's where he got his first name.

"But back to the story. A few weeks after Brouchard's mother was mysteriously misplaced, Brouchard killed his step-father."

"What?"

"The fax my friend sent over was a copy of his confession—really his defense. Listen and I'll read it to you."

Clay laid his automatic on the end table nearest him, sat on the couch and leaned back against the backrest. He didn't turn on a table lamp, preferring instead to remain in the quiet, peaceful darkness as he listened:

Statement of Antonio Louis Joel Brouchard given to Detective R. E. Armistead investigating the death of Jon de Marcel Champhene, stepfather of Antonio Louis Joel Brouchard.

"My stepfather came in drunk after midnight. It was raining and storming bad and he was very wet. He stripped his clothes and dropped them on the floor as I came out of my bedroom. He told me to get him a towel. He was real drunk and fell down twice while drying himself. He laughed and looked down at his privates. Told me to look what was happening. Said he couldn't get his clothes off no more without that thing jumping up. He asked me if I was like that. I started back in the bedroom. He hollered at me and told me to come back, said what was wrong with me. I told him nothing. He told me to come over and dry his back for him. I didn't want to. I knew he was queer. He had a man in our house. Never knew the man's name, but he was a big black fellow. Scared me when he would look at me with them black eyes, staring. This was a few days after Mamma had disappeared. The man stayed there a week. They didn't get out of bed one day when I came in, and I saw them. That's why I was knowing what was going on. And that was why I didn't want to dry my stepfather with a towel. He told me to do it again; hollered again. I said no, that I was going over to my Aunt Louise's house. He said I was going no damn where and he stood up and come after me. I started toward the door. He knocked me on the floor. I was trying to get up, but he knocked me back down. He got on top of me, was beating me; hurting me bad. I told him to stop and I'd do what he said. He said okay get in bedroom, and I did. He made me take off my clothes and made me lie down on the bed, and he did things to me. I was crying and he slapped me. Told me to shut up. Told me at thirteen, it was time I learned about things. Told me if I'd shut up I'd like it. He hit me a lot more times. I quit crying, but I was still scared. Then he got up and went over to the stove and got a can of grease. He greased himself and me and then got—got up on top of me and hurt me sumpthin bad. He then took a bath. When he came back out of the bathroom he laid himself down on the bed. Told me to go get him some whiskey. I went to the kitchen, opened a cabinet door under the sink and made a noise thumping bottles together so he would think I was getting him some. I went then over to the fireplace and got the shotgun. There was a box of shells in a drawer and I knew where they were. I broke down the shotgun and loaded it. I stepped back into the bedroom. It was dark, but I could make out his outline lying on the bed with his back to me. The first time I pulled the trigger, the gun didn't fire. I ran back to the drawer and got another shell out of the box. I made sure the gun was cocked. I then returned to the bedroom. He was still on the bed with his back to me. I stepped in the doorway and shot him in the back of his head. I put my clothes on and went outside. It was raining and lightning. I don't remember what I done next. I remember I was scared and crying. When I was driving through town I ran through a stop sign and police stopped me. They took me back to my house and found my stepfather's body. The reason I hadn't done told them what happened had been because I was so scared. I don't know why they didn't find that shotgun. I pitched it out the window on the road because it scared me. I don't remember where on the road. I'm sure if they keep looking they'll find it."

Clay remained silent after Jennifer finished reading the statement.

"Well," she said. "What do you think about that?"

He wasn't sure. "He's lied to everyone here about what happened to his parents, but I can see why. Something like that is not what you want everybody to know."

"Yeah, Clay, and you want the other possibility? It's only Brouchard's word—certainly could be self-serving. How are we to know that he didn't murder his stepfather maybe because he'd had a fight with him—for whatever reason? What I read you could be the statement of a hell-of-a-smart kid manufacturing an excellent set of extenuating circumstances.

"Did you notice at the end of the statement that the police hadn't recovered the murder weapon? Of course you would think if Brouchard admitted killing his stepfather, he wouldn't be averse to guiding the police to the location where he disposed of the gun. That is unless he had carried it a considerable distance from the house and sunk it in the swamp, or disposed of it in some similar manner—an action which would indicate that he was thinking lucidly, rather than frightened like he was contending he was.

"Another thing, the part about the black homosexual with his father. This was rural Louisiana, nearly thirty years ago. If Brouchard wanted to make his stepfather look extra bad, what better way to do it back then than by saying he was a homosexual? And not only that, but had made love to a *nigger*? A lot of rural, Bible Belt whites—and that's what the jury would have been made up of back then—would have gotten a double shock out of that. In fact, what actually ended up happening was that Brouchard never even went to trial. Grand jury didn't bring an indictment; termed it justifiable homicide. Did Brouchard murder his stepfather and get away with it by playing on prejudices of that time, or did he avenge himself on somebody who had brutally raped him? Well, that's it, except my friend over there said Brouchard went to live in a foster home for a while, then disappeared from the area at about the same time as he showed up over here. What do you think?"

Clay saw the quick glint of light reflect against the wide windows in front of the steering station.

"Wait a minute, Jennifer."

He reached for his automatic, then went to the salon door. He slid it partly open and looked toward the boatyard. A car was stopped at the entrance to the pier.

He stepped back to the phone. "Jennifer, something's come up. Thanks for the info. I'll talk to you tomorrow."

"Just a minute, Clay, I wanted to ask you; have you had any bites on your reward notices, yet?"

"Only a kook—wanted to put me in contact with the spirits— and a couple newspaper reporters wanting to do an interview with me about the rewards, human interest stuff, they said. Might take them up on it—get the word about the reward better circulated."

"How's your father doing?"

"He's taking it hard, Jennifer. If he doesn't start coming out of it soon I'm going to be worried." He glanced across his shoulder through the salon window to the men coming down the pier. "Jennifer, I have to run."

"Okay, keep me informed. Be careful." He replaced the telephone receiver, and moved back to the door. He watched the two shadowy figures as they neared the *Cassandra*.

They stopped as he slid the door the rest of the way open. He kept his automatic hidden behind his thigh.

"Clay Rodgers?"

"Yes."

"DEA. We have a message for you from Washington."

Clay felt his adrenaline begin to work. The *Cassandra* was docked a long way from anyone being able to see or hear what might happen on it. He took a deep breath, tightened his grip on his pistol's handle. "Come on in."

He stepped to the nearest end table and turned its lamp on, then remained there until the two men walked through the door.

The man in the lead was a middle-age, well-built black of around six feet. He wore a blue sport coat over a white shirt and had on gray slacks. His partner, a slim Hispanic in his middle thirties, was around five-ten, wore a dark red sport coat, blue shirt and a pair of cream-colored slacks.

The black agent produced his identification, flipping it open. His name was Richard Becker.

Upon seeing the identification, Clay relaxed. He laid his pistol on the end table and turned back to shake hands with the agents.

"Angel Morales," the Hispanic said as he grasped Clay's hand. "Third generation New Yorker. Last time a member of my family was this far south we were riding with Santa Anna."

Clay smiled, and looked back at the lead agent. "A message?"

"We're it," Morales answered.

Becker spoke in a husky voice. "We've been assigned undercover work in this area for a few days. A friend of yours in Washington told us to come by and say hello."

I'll be damned, Clay thought. The first notice of his rewards had only that morning appeared in the newspaper, and the word had already reached the Vice-President.

Becker held out a small, white card. "The number I've scribbled on the back—if you have a problem, call it. There're two more agents flying in tonight, four of us all together, and one of us will be monitoring that number at all times."

"The rainbow coalition," Morales said, "at your beck and call."

Becker smiled. "The agents flying in are Vietnamese. By morning there will be a pair of Vietnamese, fresh from Miami, and this wise-cracking, dumb-ass Mexican from South Texas looking for work along the docks."

CHAPTER

13

Chung Lam Vu sat on the edge of his cot in his cell on the top floor of the three-story Gulf City jail. A slight man with tousled dark brown hair, and wearing a loose set of flowered cotton pajamas, he more resembled a teenage boy than the thirty-year-old man he was. He had across his lap a newspaper. He was carefully reading for the tenth time a reward notice he had first seen when he was eating his dinner.

He raised his face and stared blankly for several seconds past the bars at the front of his cell, then came to his feet. After slipping on a pair of open-toed sandals, he walked to the bars, peered down the hall and yelled for the jailer.

A few seconds later the door at the end of the cell block opened. A lanky, gray-haired man wearing cowboy boots and dressed in jeans and a long-sleeve khaki shirt stepped into the cell block and strolled slowly down the hall.

"Boy, what you be hollerin' at me for this time of night? You up and gone crazy?"

"I want to use the phone."

The jailer wasn't happy with Vu waking him up from the light sleep he had been enjoying at his desk in the processing area outside the cell block. He shook his head.

"Vu, old buddy, I'm afraid you're gonna have to wait 'til in the mornin'."

Vu stuck two one-dollar bills through the bars. The jailer glanced toward the only other occupied cell on the floor, quickly grasped the money and thrust it in his jeans pocket. He stuck a key in the lock to Vu's cell.

"Okay, Vu, now you stand back away from the door, boy." The small Vietnamese backed to the center of his cell. After opening the barred door, the jailer moved a few feet down the hall, reached to unsnap the restraining strap from the hammer of his pearl-handled revolver and nodded for Vu to step outside his cell.

With the jailer carefully staying several feet behind the Vietnamese, the two walked down the hallway and out a door into the cell block's outer processing area.

Vu, still followed by the jailer, walked to a pay telephone on the wall. He looked across his shoulder. "Private, okay?"

The jailer gave no indication he had heard Vu's request, only moved to the wall and leaned back against it. "For two dollars you've got two minutes, Vu—time's runnin'."

Vu punched in a number and, when a voice answered, turned his back to the jailer and spoke in Vietnamese.

After the DEA agents left the *Cassandra,* Clay opened the Plexiglas hatch over the bed in the forward cabin and was lying bathed in the blue moonlight and the cool breeze coming in off the Gulf. At Linda's shout filtering in through the hatch's opening, he swung his legs to the floor and sat on the side of his bed.

"Clay!" Linda shouted again from the pier. He stood and moved from the small bow cabin. Once in the salon, he turned off the alarm before he slid open the dockside door.

Having changed from her cocktail uniform into a pair of loose khaki shorts and an oversized T-shirt, Linda was standing a few feet from the side of the *Cassandra.* She had a brown paper bag clasped in her arms.

"I wasn't going to set the alarm off again," she said, smiling. "It nearly scared me to death last time."

"It's off, now."

When she came through the doorway, she leaned to kiss him on the cheek, then nodded at the paper bag. "Antonio's prints, and three of his friends—two of them regulars, and one man I've never seen before."

She moved to the end table nearest her and set the bag down on the tabletop. Carefully reaching inside the bag, she grasped two glasses at a time, her fingers carefully placed inside the glasses instead of on their outside. Each of the glasses had stuffed inside it a cocktail napkin with a name inscribed on it. One had two napkins stuffed inside.

Linda pointed to it. "That one was touched by two different people. The guy who owns the farm and garden center inland lost all his money and left early. After he was gone this politician from New Orleans who's a friend of Antonio's slid the glass over and finished it off. All the rest were only handled by the ones who drank out of them. Their names are on the napkins." She looked back at him and smiled. "Well, aren't you going to say I did good?"

When he remained silent, her smile faded.

"What's wrong?" she asked.

"I have to ask you something."

"Ask me something?"

"About you and Brouchard."

Her lips tightened, and she shook her head in disgust. "So that's why you've been staring a hole through me," she muttered. He didn't say anything.

She stared at him for a moment, then shook her head again. "I ought to leave, just tell you to go to hell, and leave—but I don't want to." She stepped to the couch and sat down on it, slumped against its backrest, then shook her head once more.

"Everybody thinks that." She raised her face to his. "What good is it going to do me to explain everything to you? You wouldn't believe me if I did—not if you already got it in your mind. Would you?"

"Just say yes or no."

"Okay, I'll say it. No, there isn't any *Brouchard and me*—how's that?"

He only looked at her.

"See," she said. "It's not enough, is it—my word?"

"Linda, I—"

"No, I don't want to hear it." She took a deep breath. "I'm going to tell you how it is. It's up to you whether you believe me or not." She glanced toward the cabinets at the rear of the salon. "You mind if I have a drink?"

She remained silent as he got the bottle of Benchmark from its cabinet, carried it to the galley and fixed the drink.

She began speaking as he handed it to her. "My mother died of cancer two years after I graduated from high school. I didn't have a father. He skipped out for parts unknown two months before I was born, and Mother never remarried, didn't do much of anything but work at the fish factory day and night, always making sure she made enough money to buy me everything I needed. For the longest time when I was growing up I didn't even know we were poor." She sipped the bourbon, and set the glass on the end table next to her.

He walked to one of the easy chairs across from the couch and sat down as she continued.

"She *almost* left me a clean slate when she died. The only problem was a ten thousand dollar second mortgage she had on the house. The first mortgage was only a hundred eighty-six dollars a month—I could make that. But the bank wanted the second paid off right away.

"I talked to my boss at the fast food joint where I worked, and he said he didn't have the money. I knew about Antonio being involved with a lot of charities, so I went to him. Why not? I knew his reputation, but it's not like anybody that talked to him was branded as evil. I've seen your father and Donna eating with him. Last year at the celebration after the fund-raiser they sat at the same table with him. They had been some kind of block chairmen or something and led all the blocks in raising money, something like that.

"Anyway, I told Antonio that if he'd loan me the money, I figured I could pay it back at two hundred dollars a month plus interest. He agreed, but tried to get me to go to work stripping in one of his clubs. Said with my looks I could make a lot of money. Made it sound attractive; said I could earn as much as a thousand dollars a week, according to what I was willing to do after work." She finished the remainder of the bourbon and held the glass out toward him, then changed her mind and set the glass back on the table beside her.

"I didn't see much of him for a long time after that; I always mailed my payments in. But when I took a job at the bar I started seeing him almost every night. And he started back on trying to get me to strip. And he began to flirt, too. More than that, made it plain he wanted to go to bed with me—for money or for fun. But just talk was as far as it ever went, except maybe a pat here and there when he was showing off for his card-playing friends. And I'm a big girl, now. I could stand that so long as the tips were good, and they were. Then I made the last payment I owed him. That was last winter. The next night—it was a night he had been in there playing cards and everybody had left but him and me—he got rough.

"It was like my paying off his loan had triggered something in him. I don't know if paying him off meant to him that I no longer owed him anything, and he gave it his last best try, or maybe he had decided it was time to collect a surcharge for having lent me the money.

"Anyway, he had me down on the floor fighting with him before he stopped. But he did stop. He got up and told me what I could do with myself and stomped out the door."

Linda's eyes up until now had been unfocused but turned in Clay's direction. Now she raised them to stare directly into his.

"I've never told anybody about that until now. No big deal, I guess, my not telling anyone. But by not saying anything about it, somehow I felt like I'd really paid him back some kind of surcharge for loaning me the money. He did save my house for me. For whatever his reason, he did, and it meant a lot to me.

"Anyway, the good news is he quit flirting, hasn't since then, hasn't laid a hand on me. Then out of the blue, a couple months ago he brought me a thousand dollar check with his apologies for when he had gotten out of hand. Guess what? I accepted it. I'm making better money as a cocktail waitress than I did serving hamburgers, but I'm not independently wealthy, yet.

"He told me a few weeks back that his wife had seen the canceled check and had a fit, saying I was a whore and his mistress, and she was making all kinds of threats . . ."

The thousand dollars. If he had already informed her that Jennifer had told him about the thousand, Linda could be attempting an excuse for having received the check. But she didn't know he was aware of it. She didn't know she needed a plausible excuse for receiving it. She was telling the truth—he was almost certain.

She continued. "From the way he was always openly flirting with me in the past, and now that Angela has seen that check and, I'm sure, expressed her opinion of what she thought about it to more people than just Antonio, I'm sure that a lot of people must think I've been sexually involved with him. But I'm not, never have been. That's it—all of it. I hope you believe me."

What difference did it make whether he totally believed her story or not? What difference did it make if, out of pride, she was not quite telling the whole truth about how far she had gone with Brouchard to obtain the money she needed? He glanced at the glasses. *Unless there was a lot more that she wasn't telling.* He needed the prints on the glasses to actually be those of the people who drank with Brouchard.

She was staring into his eyes again. "I hope you do believe me because I don't want to lose you again. I really don't." She came to her feet.

"I'm going to fix myself another drink. Do you want one?"

Her eyes narrowed under her dark eyebrows. "Do you even drink? I've never seen you take one."

"Something with vodka."

She walked to the cabinet, opened it and lifted out the vodka bottle. Then she moved down into the galley where she opened the refrigerator.

Looking back through the lattice divider between the galley and the salon she said, "Tomato juice or orange juice—that's your only choice."

"Either."

Leaning over, he reached under the couch and slid the fingerprint kit from beneath it. Opening the kit, he lifted out the tapes and other materials and placed them on the side of the end table next to the glasses she had removed from the paper bag. He had been practicing on lifting his own prints off glasses on the *Cassandra*.

He put aside the glass Brouchard had used. He wanted to make sure he was properly lifting the prints before he attempted that one.

"Here goes."

Lightly shaking the black powder from the little brush instead of brushing it directly on the glass, he got the first set of prints to stand out clearly. Next, he carefully pressed the clear, yellowish tape over the print. It worked perfectly.

Linda brought the drinks back up into the salon. He glanced at her and nodded at the small, slick, white fingerprint cards. "Hold one of them steady for me."

As she held her thumb on a card, he placed the tape down, and pressed the ends of the print tape firmly to the card.

He smiled a moment at his work, then reached for the glass Brouchard had handled.

The handsome blond-haired man in his thirties stared at the license plate on Linda's Camaro. Then he looked back toward the *Cassandra*'s berth.

He didn't need to have the Camaro's license number run to find out who the woman was who had hidden the car behind the boatyard's small office shed and then walked down the pier. It was the same car the sexy-looking little cocktail waitress had driven away in after the card game at the Beachfront Bar & Inn had broken up. He thought again about her body. Her breasts were smaller than he preferred, but everything was so tight. He smiled and used his hands to slick back the sides of his thick, blond hair.

CHAPTER

14

The telephone rang. The answering machine clicked and started playing Clay's message about the reward notice. When the beep came, the voice was loud and insistent.

"If anybody's there, pick up. I'm not gonna leave a message on this damn machine. I wanna be talkin' to *somebody.*"

Clay sat on the salon's couch. The glasses with the smudges of black fingerprint powder were on the floor at his feet. Linda was at the other end of the couch. She looked at him. The only messages so far had been the one from the kook and the one from the newspaper reporter. Clay felt his pulse quicken. Maybe this time . . . He reached to the end table nearest him and lifted the receiver.

"Okay."

"I wanna talk to somebody 'bout the reward."

He felt a surge of adrenaline. "Go ahead."

"Is this Clay Rodgers?"

"Yes."

"Leave right now. Come down to the Royal d'Iberville Hotel. Circle around behind it. When you get back on 90, turn left and follow the highway across Biloxi Bay. I'll be behind you—I know what kind car of you're in. I'll blink my lights and pass you, then you follow me."

"Which one of the rewards?" Clay asked. But there was no answer. He heard the receiver being replaced.

Linda's brow wrinkled. "What?"

When he had earlier finished lifting the fingerprints from the glasses, he had felt a letdown at the fact that none of them had matched the partial prints Chief Langston had given him. Logically, he had known finding the killer wasn't going to happen so easily, but that hadn't prevented him from hoping.

"There'll be others I'll get," Linda had said, and he had nodded, but still not felt any better. At this moment, though, he felt great.

"Maybe," he said, looking at the telephone receiver in his hand. "Just maybe . . ." He replaced the receiver. "I'll be back as soon as I can."

"I want to go."

He shook his head. "You stay here—where it's safe."

After Clay circled the Royal d'Iberville and turned east on Highway 90, he watched in the rearview mirror for a car pulling out behind him, but never saw one.

On his way across Biloxi Bay from Biloxi to Ocean Springs, he noticed a pair of headlights moving up close behind his car. The headlights blinked twice.

The car passed and pulled sharply back in front of him. The driver appeared to be the only person in the car.

At the far end of the bridge, they turned back to the right and began to follow a narrow, winding blacktop road that ran along the fronts of the homes that sat on the hills overlooking Biloxi Bay.

Most of the houses were older ones, built as summer retreats long before the area developed. From the road, only an occasional residence could be seen, most of them built on the ridge overlooking the Bay and separated from passers-by by stands of squat oaks hung with Spanish moss. To someone unfamiliar with the area it would have looked as if the road was winding through a deserted semitropical forest.

On a particularly dark and deserted stretch of road, the car in front of him pulled to the shoulder and stopped. Clay fingered the handle of the automatic lying on his lap and wondered what to do next.

A figure stepped out and started back toward him.

Clay slid his automatic under his right thigh, but continued to grip the pistol's handle. He lowered his window.

It was unnerving when the figure leaned down wearing a ski mask, but Clay had noticed an instant before that both of the man's hands were empty.

The man glanced in the rear seat before he spoke. "I'm representin' a friend that's ready to do business with ya."

There was nothing noticeable about the man's voice, nothing else for Clay to remember, except for the man being unusually tall. "What's the business? Which reward?"

"Nothin' 'bout your brother. Don't know nothin' from nothin' 'bout that. We're gonna hand you what you want on the drugs— lay it all out plain. But, first off, we gotta take care of some other business."

"What kind of other business?"

"This somebody who's gonna be giving you the info, he's in jail. He's gonna have to be moved over to the feds before he says anythin'. And then he's gonna have to have a guarantee that the charges against him are shucked."

"What's he locked up for?"

"Nothin' that can't be done away with—if you wanna know 'bout the drugs."

Clay forced himself to keep his tone level. "How can I tell you whether I can do what you ask if I don't know what he's charged with?"

The man was silent for a moment. "I might as well be handin' out his name as tellin' you that." He shook his head. "Naw, too dangerous—not gonna."

"I'm after who killed my brother. Knowing who's behind the trafficking might eventually lead me to the killer. There's no way I'd take any chance of anyone finding out who your friend is before I get him to federal custody. But I have to know what he's in for. If I told you I could get him released without knowing what he's charged with, you'd know I was lying." God, don't let it be murder, or something impossible like that. Give me a chance for this to work.

The man nervously glanced down the road, then back in the window. "He got caught deliverin' five kilos—no big deal. He don't have nothin' else on his record."

Clay felt the relief pour through him. "If that's all, then I think I can guarantee you what you want, assuming he gives us what you say he can. I'll have to make a couple phone calls."

"You know Nichols—federal judge?"

"No."

"We'll take his guarantee in writin'. But only his—he won't go back on his word. You tell him the conditions, get him to sign off on them, and you'll get your info."

A pair of headlights came around a curve several hundred feet behind them. The man turned his face away from the lights until the car had driven slowly past. Then he leaned back down to the window and spoke again.

"Tomorrow night, circle the Broadwater Beach Hotel at midnight. This time turn right on 90. I'll pass you again so's you can follow me. Have the guarantee in writin' by then." He turned and hurried toward his car.

Clay looked for the car's license number. The plate had been removed.

He waited until the car pulled from the shoulder and drove down the road and out of sight. Then he made a U-turn up onto the pavement and started back to Biloxi.

Forty-year-old John "Long John" George pulled the ski mask from his face, ran his fingers through his thin brown hair and glanced in his rearview mirror. There was only the darkness of the winding road behind him. He slowed his car and guided it into a gravel driveway where a no trespassing sign hung from a chain suspended between two large oaks. He sat staring back in the direction he had come from. After a few seconds he backed his car from the drive and drove on toward the highway to Biloxi.

Thirty minutes later, having purposely made more than one misleading turn, pulled into driveways and then backed out to retrace his path and make sure no car was following him, he finally drove into the small dilapidated neighborhood where he lived.

After parking under the sagging metal roof of his carport, he moved around to the back of his car and replaced his license plate.

Finished with that, he rose to his feet and glanced back down the narrow potholed street that dead-ended into his neighborhood.

The street remained dark and devoid of any traffic. A smile spread across his face and he clapped his hands. "Damn easy money. Yeah! Come to me you pretty little green ones!" He laughed and clapped his hands again.

He pulled a key from his pocket, stepped up onto the wooden stairs to his kitchen door, and unlocked the latch. Swinging the door open, he stepped inside.

A hard-swung lead pipe crashed into the side of his head above his ear, and his knees bent and he fell forward, the cartilage in his nose crumbling as his face slammed hard into the kitchen's linoleum flooring.

CHAPTER

15

The ship was a freighter of Panamanian registry. Its large stem and stern running lights identified it as a power-driven vessel of fifty meters or more. It plowed slowly through the dark waters of the Coast Guard-maintained Safety Fairway north of the Barrier Islands off Biloxi and Gulfport. At its fantail, a bare-chested Latin wearing only jeans and sandals leaned back against the aft rail and stared toward the bridge.

A small, red light flashed from the bridge, and the Latin signaled to a man standing next to a cargo hatch.

The man peered down the hole and gave a signal of his own. Moments later, two blacks and a white emerged from the hatch. Each carried a pair of black rubberized canisters the size of a small duffle bag.

After hurrying to the stern, the men hung the canisters over the rail and waited for the command.

On the bridge, the first mate monitored the positional Loran.

He suddenly made a quick wave with his hand. The man with the red light flashed it twice rapidly. The crewmen at the rail released the canisters and let them fall into the churning waters behind the freighter's big props.

On the bridge, the first mate peered through his binoculars, centering in his view the small charter fishing boat, darkened and without running lights, moving toward the location where the canisters had been dumped overboard.

On the darkened charter fishing boat, Soung Ming sat aft in one of the two double fighting chairs in the boat's fishing cockpit. He had spent the last half hour gnawing on a slab of barbecued ribs and now dropped the last white bone into a metal bucket beside his chair.

After cleaning his hands on a damp bath towel and dropping the towel on top of the bones, he came to his feet and shuffled to the starboard side of the boat. There, he leaned his heavy bulk over the rail and glanced forward at the freighter's receding lights.

The roar of the charter boat's diesels lessened and it slowed, beginning to ride up and down with the motion of the waves rather than cutting through them. Ming gripped the rail and steadied himself against the pitching motion by spreading his feet wide.

"Dead ahead!" came the captain's shout from where he was monitoring a positional Loran. He quickly glanced at the boat's radar. No other vessel was nearby, and none was coming that way. He pushed a button on an electrical device that looked much like an oversized garage door opener. The ensuing electrical signal from the device triggered into action a small machine sitting next to the starboard rail. The machine sent an electronic signal down a cable trailing in the water behind the boat.

"They're coming up!" he shouted. "Keep your eyes peeled!"

Forty-two feet below and a hundred feet ahead of the charter boat, six rubberized metal canisters lay on the sandy bottom of the Safety Fairway. At the electronic signal, each container automatically released a float, which, trailing a thin line behind it, rushed toward the surface.

Sixteen miles south of the Panamanian freighter, a Coast Guard 41 boat was on special patrol.

The Seaman E-3 monitoring the 41's radar studied the blips on his screen for a moment longer, then looked across his shoulder toward the boat's commanding officer.

"Boat coming in across the freighter's wake, sir."

"Let's go," the skipper ordered, and the helmsman threw the throttles forward, the boat's powerful twin Cummins' VT-403 diesel engines beginning to scream.

On the darkened charter boat, four crewmen, split two to each side of the bow, were standing ready, several foot-long boat hooks in their hands.

"Okay!"

The two crewmen on the starboard side of the boat leaned across the rail and reached with their hooks. They were attempting to snare a pair of bobbing small floats.

There was now similar activity on the other side of the boat. "The current's carrying 'em past!" a crewman warned.

The captain immediately threw the boat's dual gears in reverse, then briefly revved the engines before cutting the power back to near idling speed again. The boat was now moving backwards at the same pace as the current.

In a few minutes, all six of the floats had been snared and pulled to the side of the boat.

The crewmen quickly lifted the floats from the water and detached them from their trailing ropes.

A nylon rope from the boat was used to bind all the trailing ropes together. Then line was played out and the trailing ropes disappeared under the surface once again.

Meanwhile the deflated floats had been stuffed into a metal box the size of a small footlocker, and a diver's weight belt added before the box was closed and latched.

A crew member lugged the box to the rail and pitched it overboard.

"Secured!" one of the crewmen yelled. The captain forwarded the boat's gears. The vessel began to make headway. The watertight metal canisters full of cocaine had not once come to the surface, and now trailed unseen under the water behind the boat.

Soung Ming smiled at the brilliance of the procedure he had fashioned years ago. The leaving of the containers to trail in the water rather than loading them onto a ferrying boat had enabled him for years to ferry drugs to shore without ever having a shipment intercepted. Even when the Coast Guard had boarded one of the ferrying boats, the shipments had remained safe, for there was always the safety valve in the procedure, the resinking of the containers.

"No more than thirty foot of line out!" the captain reminded the crewman standing next to the nylon rope now lashed to the starboard rail.

"Only thirty out!" the crewman replied. A young Vietnamese woman now emerged from the charter boat's steering cabin and walked to Ming. She handed him the barbecue pork sandwich she had prepared. He lifted the top of the bun, stared at the thickly piled meat, replaced the bun and moved the sandwich toward his mouth.

They were moving in the direction of the flashing, six-second white light mounted at Hewes Point, the northernmost part of the Chandeleur Islands.

"Water shallowing!" the captain shouted as he looked up from the boat's depth sounder.

The crewman at the rail pulled in some of the nylon rope. "Twenty foot of rope out, now!" he yelled back to the bridge.

Ming quickly finished his sandwich, then moved back to a fighting chair and plopped down into it. The woman followed him. When she was within reach, he pulled her into his lap, began playfully moving his thick hands over her body.

She giggled, leaned her upper body forward against his, and wrapped her arms around his bulging neck.

* * *

In federal waters, five miles west and the same distance south of Hewes Point, a large shrimping trawler moved slowly through the night. The boat's oversized radar antenna was rotating continuously.

The radar's range was set on twenty miles. The bearded, red-headed crewman monitoring the equipment's scope was watching both the blip of Soung Ming's charter fishing boat and the blip of the Coast Guard 41 moving rapidly toward the charter boat's position. He had been keeping an eye on the Coast Guard boat ever since it had begun its patrol.

The operator looked up at the heavyset, swarthy man standing over him.

"They're going for Ming. Been on a straight course to him ever since they kicked it into high."

"How far apart?"

"Seven miles and closing at over twenty knots."

"Are you sure their course isn't carrying them toward the pass?" the bearded man asked. He wanted to be absolutely sure that the Coast Guard's intended destination was Ming's boat. He didn't want to cause an unnecessary jettisoning of the canisters, then have to face Ming's wrath.

"No, sir. Coast Guard boat's course is a good fifteen degrees off a direct line to the pass."

A second Soung Ming boat, a charter boat similar to the one Ming was in, was fishing the offshore oil rigs. It also contained two men discussing the radar picture they were watching. Their screen showed the same blip closing on Ming's boat.

"If the shrimper doesn't call the jettison order in soon, we will."

Soung Ming's radar operator also watched the closing blip. Like the shrimper's and the other charter boat's radar operators, there was no doubt in his mind about where the Coast Guard boat was headed. But he also wanted to be absolutely positive.

Unlike the ease with which the cocaine canisters were able to be collected immediately after their electronically triggered floats had popped to the surface, when the containers had to be cut loose and allowed to sink to the bottom it would later take divers to find them. Even with an exact navigational fix, there were currents to contend with which, before the canisters settled to the bottom, could carry them as much as a hundred feet from where they were jettisoned. Retrieving drifted canisters was a hard and time-consuming ordeal that kept everybody on edge as the pickup boat's radar swept the seas, and its crew watched wearily for the approach of Coast Guard planes.

But for all the difficulty the retrieving entailed, at the same time the jettisoning procedure was the key to always being able to eventually deliver the containers to shore safely. And there was no problem with waiting until the very last minute to give the order. So long as the boat doing the jettisoning was out of clear binocular range of any Coast Guard boat, what difference did it make? One slash with a knife against the rope lashed to the rail, and the containers would be well hidden again.

The shrimper west of Chandeleur Island was the boat that finally gave the jettison order.

A charter boat fishing the oil rigs, a tug pushing a long line of barges along the intracoastal canal south of Pascagoula and two yachts already in a barrier island anchorage for the night but with their radios still on, all heard the message:

"Anybody tracking west of Chandeleur Island, there's a damn big water-logged tree trunk floating free—about five miles south of the northern tip of the islands in federal waters. Watch out for it."

"Damn" and *"Watch out for it"* meant *"Coast Guard boat"* and *"Coming your way."*

The mention of the tree had nothing to do with the message. The code, now that it had been used once, would be changed before the next retrieving boat went out. The same words would never be used again.

Ming rose to his feet, walked to the starboard rail and looked forward into the distance.

"How far away is the Coast Guard boat?" he asked of the captain who now stood next to him.

"About six miles."

"How much water under our keel?"

"Twelve feet. We can turn back north and be back in over forty feet in eight to ten minutes."

"Do that."

"Turn toward Dog Keys Pass!" the captain shouted to the crewman at the helm.

Ten minutes later, a crewman cut the nylon rope loose from the rail. The canisters, held in a group by the bound ends of their trailing ropes, began to settle toward the sandy bottom, forty-five feet deep.

Ming's captain noted the jettison coordinates on a notepad, though the position where the canisters were cut loose was already stored in the boat's Loran-C receiver. Later, using the receiver's guidance system, they would be able to return accurately to within forty to fifty feet of the spot. Divers would do the rest. A second jettisoning of a shipment had never had to be done before. But there was always that option if after retrieving the canisters a ferrying boat was threatened once again by an approaching Coast Guard vessel.

"Turn on the navigational lights," the captain ordered. The man at the helm threw a switch. The boat's green and red running lights illuminated. They were moving at better than fifteen knots now, a speed meant to distance them farther from the jettisoning point before the Coast Guard boat hailed them to heave to.

"A mile behind us and closing fast!" the radar operator reported. Ming glanced aft. When he could not see any sign of the Coast Guard 41, a smile came to his face. The Coast Guard boat, following standard nighttime procedures by approaching with its running lights off, was attempting to sneak up in the blind spot in the radar that follows boats with low-mounted antennas.

"They're going to surprise us!" Soung Ming announced, and the other men on the charter boat smiled, too.

CHAPTER

16

The jailer at the Gulf City jail hadn't appreciated being awakened from his nap by the fat, happy-go-lucky drunk. So he hadn't been gentle as he had processed the man, roughly pressing the drunk's fingerprints against the card and then pitching him a paper towel to clean the black stain from his fingers.

The curly-headed drunk had looked at the paper towel for a moment, smiled, and then carefully arranged it as a handkerchief protruding from his sport coat pocket.

Being led down the hall toward the cell block, the drunk yelled his greetings at the Vietnamese and the old man who had been brought in drunk earlier in the day. The jailer, his face twisted into a scowl, pushed the drunk inside his cell, slammed and locked the door.

The drunk leaned forward against the front of the cell, and rested his forearms on a crossbar, his hands protruding out into

115

the hall. He spread his palms wide for an explanation. "What's room service like this time of night?" He smiled broadly.

The jailer strode angrily back toward the outer office. He hoped during his next nap he could return to the same crucial point in the sexy dream he was enjoying when awakened by the officers bringing in the drunk.

"Hey, buddy," the drunk hollered after the jailer. "You're not going to get me anythin' to eat? Come on, buddy, I'm starvin'." Getting no response, he added, "There's a hundred in it for you, if I like what you bring me."

The jailer stopped, took a deep breath and shook his head at being tempted by a drunk's ravings. But he turned around, anyway, and walked back to the cell where the man still leaned against the bars.

"What's this about a hundred?"

"When I signed the receipt when you were processing me in, I listed I had seven hundred and eighty dollars on me—really had eight hundred and eighty . . . Go count it for yourself, see if there's not an extra hundred."

"So?"

"So if you can get somebody to whip me up something worth eating, and maybe a couple of beers—"

"Not gonna be any beer."

The drunk nodded. "That's understandable, if regrettable; but somethin' good to eat, anyway. You bring me somethin', and fifty dollars of that hundred is yours."

The drunk turned his head to look through the bars at the side of his cell to the other two jailed men. "Bring somethin' for my friends, too, for all three of us. You do, and the fifty dollars is yours. And, in the mornin', you fetch a good breakfast, and the other fifty's in your pocket, too. Is that a fair and equitable arrangement?"

"I'll see what I can do," the jailer said. "Old man Monk's the only one got a key to the refrigerator, and if he don't want to get up and fix something, he ain't gonna get up. You'd think he runs this place 'stead of bein' a trustee. Son-of-a-bitch is the chief's pet is what he is."

The drunk smiled. "Share, my good man. Give him part of the fifty—an incentive."

The jailer turned and started back toward the door at the end of the cell block.

The drunk pressed his face against the bars and angled his eyes after the jailer. "Roast beef—that's what I want, and maybe some kind of salad. Roquefort dressin'. Don't forget the *Grey Poupon*."

Following standard boarding procedures the Coast Guard 41 approached Soung Ming's charter boat from the rear, then suddenly turned on a powerful spotlight.

Ming held his hands in front of his eyes and turned away from the blinding white light.

The blare of the 41's loudspeaker was startling in its intensity: "CAPTAIN, THIS IS U.S. COAST GUARD. REQUEST YOU HEAVE TO AND STAND BY FOR BOARDING."

The charter boat captain pulled his dual throttles back to idle but didn't cut the engines off completely, leaving himself enough power to maintain control of the boat in the running seas.

The Coast Guard 41, its spotlight still centering its quarry in its bright glow, moved to port and began to inch up alongside the charter boat.

Suddenly the bright light was gone, leaving only the charter boat's running lights to show the Coast Guard vessel pulling alongside.

Standing at the ready, all wearing bulletproof jackets, five Coast Guardsmen armed with shotguns lined the starboard deck of the 41. A sixth Coast Guardsman slowly moved the barrel of the M-60 mounted on the 41's bow.

Two of the Coast Guardsmen, holding spring lines in their hands, jumped across the narrow gap between the boats to the deck of Ming's vessel.

Ming stood grim-faced, no longer displaying the smile that had flashed to his face when the 41 had announced by their "heave to" order that they had slipped up behind their quarry.

The sight of the uniformed warriors had suddenly been too much for him, bringing back all his fear.

As a Viet Cong interrogator he had felt nothing but contempt for the ignorant U.S. servicemen who had resisted him and maintained their arrogant pride. But once he had killed the lanky South Vietnamese officer and acquired his identity in order to make his way to America where he knew he would grow rich, his contempt had begun to turn to fear. Not all of those he had tortured were dead or still held in slave labor in Vietnam. Some, he was sure, had made it back to their country, and made it back with a picture of their tormentor etched in their minds.

A thin, bony man when he plied his trade for the Viet Cong, he had decided on a unique disguise—eating to the point of changing not only his build but his features. And it had worked. He could stand in front of a mirror and know that his mother would not recognize him now. But still his fear had grown, obsessing him. Over the years he had become less and less willing to risk leaving the seclusion of the *Victory*.

Ming's eyes moved to the Coast Guard skipper at the controls of the 41 and his blood froze. The officer, a quizzical expression on his face, was staring directly at him.

Ming, his heart beginning to race, wanted to turn away but feared that to do so would bring even greater scrutiny.

Beads of sweat rolled down the back of his neck. His knees began to weaken. Still the bastard stared. He looked familiar. Graying hair now, but of course it would have been solid brown that many years ago. Ming looked for telltale scars on the officer's face, but in the dim light and shadows cast by the running lights he couldn't tell if there were any disfiguring marks.

The officer continued to stare.

CHAPTER

17

Clay had time to collect his thoughts during the drive back from meeting with the man in the ski mask. The man was for real. If it had been some con man trying to find a way to get his hands on the reward, then he wouldn't have been so adamant about federal custody and the dropping of the transporting charges being the keys to an arrangement going forward. What would happen if the drug ring was eventually busted, and Clay knew nothing more then than he now did about the identity of his brother's killer? Would it be all over? Would he just go on back to Washington?

As he moved down the wooden walkway leading to the *Cassandra,* he glanced up at the wispy clouds racing north across the face of the moon. There was a heavy smell of salt in the increasingly strong breeze coming off the Sound.

Another front was headed toward the coast, the line of

storms close on the heels of the ones that had passed across the area the night Robert had been murdered.

Clay remembered back to when Robert as a child stood on their home's small front porch and smiled up at the storms. Their mother had worried that he would be hit by lightning one day when she wasn't around to make him come inside.

Everything reminded Clay of his brother. Robert was almost all he thought about. It was becoming harder and harder to keep his depression in check. He shook his head as he walked across the gangway and through the *Cassandra*'s open salon door.

Most of the boat's interior lights were now on, but Linda wasn't to be seen.

He glanced to the floor in front of the couch. She had picked up the glasses he had left there. She would have to wash them and then return them to the bar during her next shift. Several glasses disappearing nightly would soon become noticeable.

"Linda!"

She didn't answer.

He moved across the salon and down into the galley, then on to the open door of the bow cabin.

He relaxed. She was asleep, partially curled around a pillow on the same bunk he had lain on earlier. In her simple over-sized T-shirt, with her slim legs protruding from her too-big khaki shorts, and her mussed hair partially covering her face, she resembled both an innocent child and a highly desirable woman; one he couldn't get out of his mind. He smiled and shook his head. The sudden concern he had just experienced when she wasn't in the salon, then his nervousness heightening when she hadn't answered his calling her name—he was afraid he was quickly falling in love with her, if he hadn't already.

He sat on the edge of the bed and she stirred and opened her eyes. A soft smile came to her face when she saw him, and she reached out her hand and clasped one of his.

"Well?"

He shrugged. "I think the guy's for real."

She sat up in the bed, pulled her legs up against her chest and wrapped her arms around them, laying her head sideways against her knees. "What did he say?"

He shrugged off his initial hesitancy at her question. "Said he has a man who's going to be able to prove who the kingpin is."

"Who did he say it was who was going to tell you?"

"I guess we'll find out later—maybe tomorrow night. That's when I'm supposed to meet the guy out on the road again."

She extended her legs and swung them off the bed. "I'm going to fix a drink—you want one?"

"Might eat something."

"I'll fix you a sandwich," she said as she came to her feet. She leaned to kiss him on the cheek, then walked from the cabin into the galley.

At the refrigerator she paused a moment as she held its door open. "I think I'll drink a beer instead of any more bourbon. I've been drinking too much hard stuff, lately."

She glanced at him as he stepped up beside her. "You sure you wouldn't like a beer?"

He felt the cold from inside the refrigerator. It was refreshing. The idea of a cold beer suddenly sounded good. "Yeah, I will have one."

He pointed toward a pack of bologna. "And that, with a slice of cheese and lettuce." He walked to the dinette table across from the refrigerator and slid onto one of the table's benchlike seats.

In a moment she had laid his beer and sandwich before him. She sat down with her beer on the other side of the table.

He thought again of the six-pack still sitting on the chart table. He didn't like what it reminded him of every time he thought of it—how badly his dad was suffering over Robert's death.

He rose and walked up the steps into the salon, and brought the six-pack back with him to the refrigerator.

Placing the beer on the bottom shelf, he stared at the six-pack where Linda had removed their beers. There were only three beers left in the pack.

He spoke back over his shoulder without taking his eyes off the six-pack. "Had you already drunk a beer?"

"What?"

He looked back at her. "Had you drunk a beer—earlier?"

She shook her head.

Somebody had. He moved up the galley steps into the salon and the telephone on the couch's far end table.

Donna's "hello" was full of sleep.

"Donna, what day did you say you brought the beer out to the boat?"

"Clay?"

"Yeah. The beer, Donna—you said you brought some six-packs out to the boat. Didn't you say Friday?"

"I don't—oh, I'm sorry; yeah, Friday."

"Was there any beer already there?"

"What?"

"In the refrigerator—was there any beer already in the refrigerator when you brought the other out?"

"Gosh, I don't know—I'm sure there was."

"How many six-packs did you bring?"

"Let me think," she sighed. "Six—yeah, six; a half a case short of two cases . . ."

He felt a surge of adrenaline. There were only six six-packs there now.

"The convenience store was almost sold out," Donna continued; "didn't have a full two cases left—was two six-packs short. Why?"

"Somebody drank one of the beers. If you brought the beer on board only the day before Robert had the boat out, who drank it? Robert didn't drink."

He heard Donna shift in her bed, the sheets rustling. "Clay, one of the police could have when they were checking over the boat."

"I don't think so."

"Or one of the workmen at the yard could have got it," she added, "either before Robert took the boat out, or since then."

His adrenaline began to drain away.

"Clay?"

"Yeah."

"I really think you should try to stop thinking about it every minute."

"Yeah . . . Okay, thanks. I'm sorry to have bothered you. How's Dad doing?"

"He seems to be resting comfortably. It's just going to take some time."

"Yeah, I guess so. Well, good night." He replaced the telephone receiver, then moved back into the galley and rescated himself at the dinette table.

"You would have known who I was," Linda said, "if I was dating Robert."

Thinking about the beer, he wasn't sure what she had said. "What?"

"You know it's been four days, now," she replied, "and no girl has called to say a thing."

He raised his face to hers. "What are you saying?"

"Think about it," she replied. "Robert was dating some girl from around here, dating her pretty steady from what his roommate told you. How come she didn't come up to you at the funeral and say anything? How come she hasn't called you or Donna to say how bad she felt? If I'd been dating somebody for months and he was killed, you damn well better believe I'd be at the funeral. If it were you that was dead, you could pick me out at the services by the one who kept fainting. If there was some reason I couldn't come to the funeral then I'd certainly come by later and say something to somebody in the family."

He nodded his agreement. "Unless the girl was the one that drank the beer—had been on the boat with him."

"Uh, huh," Linda said, nodding. "And dead, too—wasn't able to come by and pay her condolences."

What about her parents? He shook his head. "No, someone would have reported her missing by now. Her parents would be going out of their minds by now."

"Not necessarily," Linda countered. "The girl could be living alone. I was at twenty—Robert's age."

"You're forgetting the letters I found in Robert's lockbox. I'm almost certain she's a high school girl. Her parents would have reported her missing by now."

"What if she's not missing? What if she was the one who killed him?"

"A high school girl?"

Linda nodded. "It wouldn't be the first time a kid murdered somebody . . . So you have a couple of possibilities; assuming she was the one who drank the beer. A, she killed him and she's not about to come forward and say she was on the boat, or B, she was killed, and *for some reason* her parents haven't reported her missing."

"What reason?"

Linda glanced at the tabletop a moment. "What about if she was a problem kid? Had run away before, or was prone to be gone from home three or four days at a time—it's possible. Or, maybe she's staying at home alone while her parents are on vacation somewhere. I'm sure there's more reasons not on the tip of my tongue—lots of reasons."

"Okay, then, you started this line. Now how do we go about finding out who she is—or was?"

"Too bad it's summer. If she were dead and school was going on, we could call up each principal and ask if any of their female students have been absent from school for the last few days. But what do we do with it being summer?"

Before he could comment she spoke again. "She's bound to have a close girlfriend or two. If she's missing, then her girlfriends would know. If she was a high school kid, then it's logical that her best friend is, too. So we find a girl—high school age—whose friend has been missing the last few days."

"Okay, fine. How?"

Linda shook her head. "I don't know without school in session. If it was it would be so easy. Not only would it be easy to find out if she's missing, but we would even have a chance to find out who she is if she's not missing, if she's the killer. We could put a photograph of Robert on each high school bulletin board and have the principals announce that anyone who had ever seen Robert should come in and say so. As good looking as he was, a girl would be likely to remember him if she had ever seen him, especially a high school girl since he was a college boy. Anybody remembering him would know who they'd seen him with. We'd have her—know who she was." Her eyes suddenly brightened.

"Wait a minute," she said. "There's another way we can use his photo. We can take one around to every place we can think of that Robert and the girl might have been—run one in the *Sun Herald*. If anybody remembers seeing him, maybe they'll remember what she looked like too. Might even know her—there's a chance." Clay nodded.

"We'll give it a shot. I'll get one of his photos first thing in the morning. Have copies made and figure out the best way to start distributing them." He glanced at his watch. It was nearly 4:00 A.M. "I'll walk you to your car."

She smiled. "We've got something else to do before we say good night."

She slid from the booth and started walking toward the bow cabin.

Jesus! "Linda, I don't want to chance it getting back to Brouchard that you've been here. You've got to get your car out of the boatyard before the workmen come in."

"We've got time." She raised her hand back over her shoulder and gestured with a flick of her forefinger for him to follow her.

4:00 A.M. After glancing at his watch, the happy drunk walked to the bars at the front of his cell and glanced down the cell block. The old man was asleep now, as was the Vietnamese, both of them drugged by the chemical added to their bologna and cheese sandwiches.

He turned back from the front of his cell and walked to its rear, to the barred window there. Reaching into his waistband he picked with his thumbnail at a little, knotted thread that protruded from his pants. Grasping the knot firmly between his forefinger and thumb he began pulling on the fine line. Only lightly tacked to the inside leg of his pants, the line slipped loose easily. After pulling it from his pants, the man picked at a second knot.

Several minutes later, six lines, all approximately three feet long, were knotted together into one long line. The man stepped to his window and began feeding the line through the bars.

With only about three feet of string left to feed out, there was a pull on the line. The man fed another foot of it through the window and then waited.

There was another light tug on the line and he began pulling it back to him.

There was a key attached to the end of the line. He removed it and quickly walked to the front of his cell. Being careful not to let the metal bolt clang as his cell door unlocked, he slowly turned the key.

Placing the key in his pocket, he moved to the side of the cell and lifted the single towel from its hook on the side of the wash basin.

He didn't turn on the faucet and allow the sound of running water to come from his cell, but instead walked to the toilet and dipped the towel into the bowl. He then lifted it barely above the level of the water and quietly wrung the excess water from it.

Opening his cell door, he stepped out into the hall and moved toward the cell that contained the Vietnamese.

CHAPTER

18

Clay was still asleep on the starboard bunk in the bow cabin. Linda slipped silently out the door, then quietly through the galley and up into the salon.

There she lifted the telephone receiver and quickly punched in a number.

It was several rings before anyone answered. "Coach McGinnis's office."

"Paul, this is Linda Donetti."

There was an awkward silence for a moment. "Linda, how are you doing?"

"I haven't seen you out at the inn in a good while."

There was another long moment of silence.

"Paul, what I'm calling about, is I need a favor."

He didn't answer.

"Paul?"

"Yeah, how can I . . . what kind of favor?"

"Are you having summer practice?"

"Rules don't allow that. Some of the kids are lifting weights on their own, throwing the ball a little. Things like that."

"How many boys do you have out?"

"About eighty—regular. Have nearly a hundred from time to time. Why?"

"Paul, there's a girl I'm trying to find something out about. She's a high school girl. Might be enrolled at your high school, and might not be. I don't know who she is, but I know a boy she's dated. If I get a photograph of him to you, could you show it around, ask your players if they've ever seen him, see if any of them know if he's been dating a girl from your place?"

It was a way she'd thought of to find out the identity of the girl Robert had dated. Clay wouldn't like her doing it. Too dangerous, he would say. She would tell him what she had done after she'd found out who the girl was. If she was unable to find out, then he would never have to know she had tried.

"Sure, Linda. I'd be glad to show my kids the picture. Sounds cloak and dagger—what's the girl done?"

"Nothing much. It's sort of a personal thing I'm doing for some parents."

"I see. You still working the same shift—nights?"

"Uh, huh."

"Maybe I can get some of my work behind me and come by there one of these nights for a beer."

"I'd like that."

"That's all you wanted—your favor?"

"Well, I was sort of wondering, if none of your players recognized the boy, you think they'd mind carrying a copy of the photograph around if I have a bunch made up? I thought maybe they might ask other kids whether they recognized the boy or not? I mean ask kids from other schools besides yours. Do you think they'd mind doing that?"

"I won't give them any choice. You get the pictures up here, and it's done. You working at the inn, tonight?"

* * *

Clay, on his bunk in the bow cabin, realized he was hearing Linda's voice. Sunlight was pouring through the Plexiglas hatch above him. He glanced at his watch.

Jesus! He threw his covers back and stepped from the bed.

Linda, glancing through the lattice-work between the salon and the galley, saw Clay emerge from the bow cabin. She quickly replaced the receiver.

Clay moved up the steps into the salon. He shook his head in exasperation. "What are you still doing here?"

"Come on, Clay, I called a friend of mine. She picked up the car for me before daylight. You know how I'm getting to feel; running over here, jumping in bed with you, and then gone? Slam, bam, thank you, ma'am. I just wanted to be around you for a while—out of bed. How do you like your eggs?"

"How are you going to leave without being seen?"

"I don't have to go in to work until seven. There won't be anybody left in the boatyard by then. Now, fried or scrambled? I make a great omelet." A broad smile came to her face.

He stared at her for a moment longer. There wasn't much sense in continuing to argue, she couldn't leave now. He would have to make sure that all the workmen were gone before she left. "Okay. I just want you to be careful. An omelet sounds good." He turned to the steering station, flicked on the VHF radio, and tuned it to the weather channel.

Linda stepped to his side. She pointed to the loose wires dangling from the steering station. "That's where things were the guy stole?"

"Yeah, compass, depth sounder, the single side band."

"What's a single side band?"

"Long-range radio."

"Like longer range than a VHF?"

"Talk to a boat off California if you wanted to."

"I've been boating and SCUBA diving all my life," she said, "never saw anybody go farther out than a VHF radio would reach—seems like a waste of money."

"Dad got a good deal on it."

She pointed at the Loran-C. "What's that?"

"A navigational device. It gives you your current location."
He reached to the Loran's power switch and turned it. The
display panel lighted. "Somebody who doesn't know the first
thing about navigation could take this boat to the Bahamas and
back if they simply learned how to operate this little device—it's
amazing really. It'll take you anywhere. All the charter boats
use it to go to good fishing spots."

"You're teasing me—finds fish?"

He smiled without looking back at her. "Finds the spot." He
manipulated a push button on the Loran, and two lines of numbers displayed.

"That's the latitude and longitude. If a charter boat captain
finds a good spot he wants to fish again later, he just turns on
the Loran while he's there and it records his position. He locks
those coordinates into the memory. When he wants to go back,
he pulls up the reading and goes in the direction the Loran
indicates. You really don't even have to have previously been
where you want to go. You just ask a buddy who's been there
and has the coordinates. He gives them to you, you put them
into the Loran, and you go straight to it." *Jesus!—straight to it.*
He felt his pulse quicken.

"What do you want in your omelet?"

He didn't answer. He quickly went through the Loran's memory.

"Clay, would you like—"

"Linda, there're five positions stored in here. If . . ." He
opened a small cabinet to the right of the steering station and
pulled out several folded charts. After laying them on the small
chart table, he opened the first one, glanced at the coordinates
on the Loran and moved his finger across the chart.

He slipped that chart under the others and opened the next
one. He changed the readout on the Loran and began tracing
his finger across the second chart.

"Clay, what are you . . ."

He again changed the readout and looked back at the chart.
"This is it." His heart was immediately knocking, and then as
quickly began to slow. *The location didn't make sense.*

"Is what?"

"Thirty-five to forty miles, Linda. The night Robert was murdered, the boat used enough fuel to have traveled thirty-five to forty miles one way and then back to Long Beach. These coordinates"—he pointed to a spot on the chart—"they're a little over thirty-five miles from here." He shook his head. "But the location is back a quarter mile west of the Chandeleurs, in shallow waters; nowhere near the shipping channel."

"You're going to have to explain," she said.

"If this location was in the shipping channel, anywhere in the Safety Fairway, then it would make sense— a freighter dropped the drugs over and, instead of a boat being there to ferry them on to shore, the drugs were purposely weighted so that they would sink. That way a boat could come back after them at any time. It makes sense. The Coast Guard would be much more likely to search a boat coming directly from where a freighter had just passed, rather than a boat that came from that direction days afterward.

"I had Jennifer call the Port Authority for me. No freighter came in the night Robert was killed; the last one was in Thursday—a Russian ship. I didn't have her inquire about any that might have come in before that. I didn't have any reason to. A few days, a week, it couldn't have been very long since one did." He glanced back at the chart. *Let them sink,* he thought.

He turned away from the steering station and walked to the back of the salon and the cabinets there. He opened the largest one and checked the gauges on both SCUBA tanks. They were full; they hadn't been used since they were refilled.

Walking back to the steering station, he began mumbling his thoughts aloud. "Assume a freighter dropped some drugs over, let them sink and then they were picked up later. Why would they . . ." He nodded at the possibility that ran through his mind.

"Linda, I said the Coast Guard wouldn't be as alert to a boat coming in from where a freighter had passed some days before. They certainly wouldn't be as alert if the boat came in from some location other than where the freighter passed. If the drugs were sunk, or not even sunk, picked up as soon as they were unloaded from the freighter, then taken to a different location and sunk, they would be safe until it was time to ferry them into shore. That's where Robert could have been headed, the location where some drugs had been resunk—stored." He glanced back at the cabinets.

"The only thing," he said. "Both the SCUBA tanks are full. That wouldn't be the case if Robert had used them Saturday night. But he could've been planning to, just never got the chance, was killed first."

He looked at the chart. He knew he was grasping at a straw. The coordinates stored in the Loran could turn out to be the location of a sunken wreck Robert liked to dive; a good fishing spot—the kind of location you would expect to find stored in the Loran. But the distance to the spot and the amount of fuel the *Cassandra* had used that night correlated perfectly. He reached to switch on the big Perkins diesels.

While they warmed he called Donna to explain he had something important come up and he wouldn't be eating lunch with her and his dad. He saw no reason to tell her what he was going to do. All she would do would be to once again ask him to please let the police handle everything and quit putting so much pressure on himself. He told her he would eat with them tonight —maybe they could go out to a restaurant. Then he replaced the receiver.

After moving outside the boat to the pier, he disconnected the telephone and electric lines from their sockets on the side of the *Cassandra,* then cast off the mooring lines.

Beyond the Barrier Islands, on the blue-green waters of the Gulf, several of the area's charter boats were taking advantage of the last few hours of good fishing before the slowly advancing storm front reached the coast. Out in the deep water fifteen miles south of the Horseshoe Rigs, an excited gray-haired couple from Chicago beamed as their grandson, harnessed into a fighting chair in the boat's fishing cockpit, pulled against a rod bent by the strain of a leaping four-hundred-pound blue marlin.

A boat trolling the cut blasted through the center of Ship Island by Hurricane Camille was already loaded with an assortment of red fish, king mackerel and bonito.

On Soung Ming's slowly moving charter fishing boat, despite the fact there was a man trolling a line from the boat's aft fighting chairs, there was no fishing being done. The man and the captain at the bridge carefully searching the sky with binoculars were lookouts.

The quarry this boat sought was lying on the sandy bottom somewhere beneath the craft. A pair of divers had been patiently searching for the canisters for a half hour and now spotted them.

While one diver remained below, the other quickly swam toward the surface.

After his head broke the surface, he floated a few minutes in the gently rolling seas while Soung Ming's boat turned and slowly made its way back to him. Part of any retrieving procedure done during daylight hours was for the charter boat to never stop moving until the last possible moment. A crew of any Coast Guard plane suddenly flying over and seeing a fishing boat stopped over a particular area could conceivably get ideas.

A crewman from Soung Ming's boat handed the diver a thin nylon line. The man turned and, ducking his upper body under the water and kicking his flippered feet into the air, started back down toward the canisters.

The nylon line would serve to not only pull the canisters to the surface and the side of the boat but, if suddenly jerked rapidly twice, would signal the divers the Coast Guard was approaching the area. At that point, the end of the rope would be released over a rail to disappear into the water, and the boat would begin trolling again. The divers would stay on the bottom where they could not be seen. A small explosive device later dropped in the water would signal them when it was safe to surface again.

After the diver returned to the bottom, the nylon rope was quickly tied to the loose ends of the ropes already trailing from the canisters. One of the divers gave a sharp tug on the line. Then both men swam rapidly toward the surface.

In a few minutes the canisters, purposely left suspended a good twenty feet below the surface where they were out of sight of anything but an airplane passing directly overhead, were attached to the boat by a long section of the nylon rope tied to the starboard rail. The charter boat slowly moved forward. The man in the fighting chair played out his trolling line.

There was Coast Guard traffic in the area. In fact, much more traffic than normal. A Soung Ming shrimper moving close to the offshore oil platforms had reported two Coast Guard 51 boats within five miles of the rigs. A Soung Ming charter boat in federal waters toward the nearby Louisiana coast had reported a 41 boarding a fifty-three foot Hatteras bearing a Texas Yacht Club ensign at its stern.

Soung Ming was most concerned about the report of a large Coast Guard cutter, one new to these waters, fifteen miles east of his position and coming slowly up the Safety Fairway. It was reported to be dragging some kind of instrument in the water behind it.

Soung Ming's boat was now moving toward the moderately shallow waters a mile north of the Chandeleur Islands. After reaching that point the boat would turn west toward the delivery point at a secluded spot on the Louisiana coast. They would pass within a mile of where the Rodgers boy had been instructed to pick up a load jettisoned under Coast Guard pressure nearly a week before.

Soung Ming glanced to the charter boat in the distance. It was one of his, too, one of the small fleet he owned—three charter fishing boats and the shrimper, in addition to his large trawler, the *Victory*. He turned to the man at the helm. "Tell them we're clear and to come on in."

The helmsman raised the VHF mike to his lips, reported to an imaginary base station that his clients had already caught their limit for the day and were heading in.

The charter boat in the distance immediately began moving in the direction of the west side of the Chandeleur Islands.

CHAPTER

19

The *Cassandra* was now over twelve miles from the coast and rounding the western end of Ship Island, following along between the markers delineating the shipping channel. Clay, steering from the salon, guided the yacht through the pass and out of the Sound into the clear blue-green waters of the Gulf.

The sky had darkened considerably in the last hour. Lightning could be seen in the distance. Near the western tip of Ship Island and jutting out into the water, Fort Massachusetts was quickly emptying of tourists. A long line of people were filing onto the ferry sitting at the island's dock. The white sand beach on the island's Gulf side was deserted.

Clay glanced through the wide glass windshields and into the distance. "I don't know if I want to be diving in this or not."

"Diving?"

"The only way I'm going to know if there's any drugs there is to go down and see them."

"Even if they were there once, you think they might still be?"

He shrugged. "Whoever killed Robert didn't bring them out —not through Long Beach. Somebody else might have, but they might not have, too." He glanced at the Loran's display. "We'll know in about two more hours." Please God, he added silently, let this lead to something. His brother passed through his mind, and Clay nervously gripped the steering wheel tighter. *I'm trying as hard as I can,* he explained.

Slowly plying the Safety Fairway, the eighty-two-foot Coast Guard cutter had just passed the west tip of Horn Island when the magnetometer drone the vessel was pulling suddenly registered a metallic object lying on the bottom of the fairway.

The skipper gave the orders and the cutter slowed to a stop. Two speedboats, each equipped with a helmsman and two divers, were quickly put over the side.

In a few minutes the divers were combing the sandy floor in the area where the concentration of metal had been detected.

They quickly found the object. It was a steel box the size of a small footlocker, and opened easily. Inside it were no drugs. Instead, it was packed full of small deflated rubber floats and a scuba diver's weight belt, the lead weights obviously used to give the box its negative buoyancy.

As the Loran-C marked down the final mile to the location plugged into its memory, Clay looked through the windshield to the charter boat trolling directly in the *Cassandra*'s path. It was the only boat he had seen in the last hour that wasn't on its way back to the coast. Rain was already falling on the far side of the Chandeleurs.

A few minutes later he cut the throttles to idle, then shifted the gears into neutral, and the *Cassandra,* a small wave building in front of its bow as it settled lower into the water, began to coast to a stop.

The captain guiding the charter boat from its exposed fly bridge station glanced toward them. The solitary figure sitting in the fighting chair continued to fish.

"Are we there?" Linda asked.

"Within fifty feet, in one direction or the other—if the Loran's doing what the salesman said."

In a few minutes they were anchored. Clay retrieved one of the scuba tanks from the salon cabinets and slipped the straps over his shoulders.

As he buckled the strap at his waist he glanced over the stern rail. Protected by the line of islands a quarter mile away, the water was surprisingly calm, the waves not over a couple feet, but it was murky. If there was anything down there he'd have to almost bump into it to find it.

He buckled the weight belt around his waist, raised the gate in the stern rail, then turned and climbed down the short ladder to the swimming platform.

Linda smiled down at him as he eased into the water, then hung by his elbows from the platform as he adjusted his mask and tested the regulator.

"Bring me back a pearl."

Clay's head disappeared beneath the water. She could make out his shape for a few feet, and then it faded into the murkiness. She shook her head. As many times as she had been diving she had never gotten used to murky water. She always had the feeling something was just beyond the limit of visibility—watching her.

Clay's trail of bubbles moved toward the starboard side of the boat and Linda walked to that rail. She glanced at the trolling boat, now passing off the *Cassandra*'s stern by less than a hundred yards.

Then the boat made a sharp turn back to port, a turn that would cause it to pass within a couple hundred feet of the *Cassandra*'s starboard side. She hoped the skipper didn't make his next turn back to port again and cross the *Cassandra*'s bow. If he did, the hooks on the trolling line would run dangerously close to where Clay was.

The skipper was looking at her. She signaled with her hand for his attention, and pointed toward the water, trying to indicate there was a diver below.

The skipper looked away and stayed on course. Then, only a hundred feet in front of the *Cassandra,* the charter boat began to cut back to the left.

Linda strained to see Clay's bubbles, decided it was impossible, and suddenly saw them. The next instant they were gone in the trough of a long swell.

She looked at the man trolling from the fighting chair and worried even more about the angle of his line.

She glanced back where she had last seen the bubbles, couldn't find them for a moment, then saw them again.

Then she saw the other set of bubbles.

Her eyes narrowed, her brow wrinkling. After a moment she turned away from the rail and hurried along the deck toward the salon door.

Inside the cabin she grabbed the binoculars from the edge of the chart table, then hurried back outside to the rail where she brought the binoculars to her eyes.

The new bubbles had been maybe fifty feet to the right of where Clay had been. She couldn't find them. She swung the binoculars back to the left and immediately picked up Clay's bubbles. She lowered the binoculars. She thought she spotted the other bubbles. She raised the binoculars back to her eyes.

Not one but two sets of bubbles came into focus. They were only forty feet from Clay's and moving in a line that would intersect with his.

Clay for some reason made a turn under water and was angling back to the left. The other pair of bubbles stayed straight. The distance between Clay and the other two lines of bubbles widened.

She lowered the binoculars.

She glanced toward the charter boat and the skipper now studying her through his binoculars.

She looked back to the double set of bubbles, a pair of divers diving in shallow, murky water with nothing to see.

A cold chill swept over her.

My God, she thought, and she nearly started crying. No, don't cry—do something.

Her heart racing, she hurried into the salon. She pulled the remaining scuba tank out of its cabinet at the rear of the salon, then grabbed a set of flippers and a face mask. She was so weak with fear that she wondered if she would even be able to don the tank.

You have to, she told herself, and leaned to lift the cumbersome weight.

At the stern rail she laid the tank at the edge of the deck, turned and backed down the ladder to the swim platform.

In a few seconds she had pulled the tank to her, slipped its straps over her shoulders, put on the flippers and adjusted her face mask.

Since coming back out of the cabin she had seen neither the dual set of bubbles nor Clay's, but she remembered the direction in which he had last been swimming. She stepped off into the warm water.

Kicking her flippers rapidly, splaying her arms out in front of her and pulling them back in powerful strokes, she swam as fast as she could. The quicker she could get to Clay the less chance he would have to move very far from where she had last seen him.

But, dear God, had she even kept the right sense of direction? She would have to be within twelve to fifteen feet of him to be able to see him the visibility was so bad.

After a while she lessened her strokes. She estimated she had gone a hundred feet, far enough to be reaching his position—if he hadn't turned in another direction again. Or had she only gone sixty or seventy feet?

She raised her hands. With a powerful stroke she swam toward the surface.

Her head out of the water, she looked for bubbles. They could be only a few feet away and she wouldn't be able to see them from her elevation level with the water. Only when a swell lifted her body could she see the surface more than a few feet in any direction.

Please, God, she begged. At that moment her eyes caught a

line of bubbles ten feet ahead and crossing in front of her. She ducked her head and dove.

The vague shape came into view.

She swam toward it.

Its outline firmed as she neared it.

She reached out a hand to grab Clay's shoulder.

At her touch he turned wildly over to his back. Through his faceplate his eyes widened. He threw his arms dramatically out to his sides, his palms up and his hands spread wide in a questioning gesture. A cloud of bubbles exited his mouth with his loud, unintelligible exclamation.

Linda grabbed for one of his straps and tugged at him, gesturing back toward the *Cassandra* with her other hand.

Through his faceplate his eyes narrowed. He shook his head in confusion and again spread his hands out to his sides.

"Pleeease," she screamed in a burst of bubbles, and pulled on his strap again.

With a kick of his flippers he started to move with her.

She turned and, kicking her legs as rapidly as she could, started in the direction of the *Cassandra*. She glanced back to make sure he was following her.

Twenty feet later she glanced back again. He was falling behind.

She made another frantic gesture with her hand for him to hurry, and he gave a renewed kick with his strong legs, then abruptly stopped, forced his chest back and upwards as his hands splayed out in front of him.

She shook her head in dismay and signaled frantically again.

He tried to shout something, a large cloud of bubbles coming from his mouth. He pointed ahead of her.

She twisted her head around rapidly and her face mask slammed into the white face in front of her. She screamed as the snarling wide-mouthed creature, its teeth bared, rebounded from the butt of her head and came back at her.

Its arms lazily wrapped around her. Her mouthpiece gone from her mouth, Linda screamed again, hit at the figure with the heels of her balled fists, swallowed water, choked, was strangling—she was drowning. She kicked for the surface.

In seconds her head was out of the water, and Clay was beside her.

Coughing, water running from her mouth, she managed to take in a gulp of air, then another gulp, and she could breathe without choking. She suddenly realized what it had been. A body, bloated and pale. The lips not drawn back in a snarl, instead gone from the fishes feeding. She remembered the floating hair. A woman. "It was a woman!"

Clay nodded. "I'd found her a few seconds before you came down. Her feet are tied to an anchor. There's a compass and a depth sounder down there, too. She's going to be the one who was with Robert—the high school girl." He lifted his hand from the water to display a plastic package the size of a sandwich bag. It bulged with tiny white crystals.

"There's several containers down there, all of them packed full of this. Robert *was* here to pick them up. Something happened; something went wrong. When I saw the canisters I knew what they were for, yet I didn't expect them to still have the drugs inside of them. I thought someone would have already been back for them."

Back for them, Linda thought. She glanced wildly at the surface of the water around her. "Oh, God! Quick, get to the boat, Clay!"

"What?"

"They're in the water with us! Two divers!"

Clay felt his throat tighten and at the same time heard the sound of the diesel engines. He looked back over his shoulder at the charter boat a couple hundred feet away.

Linda's eyes were big.

He stuffed his mouthpiece back into place. She dived. He was immediately under the water and beside her on her right, pulling hard in the direction of the boat. She glanced at him. He looked past her at the cloudy curtain a few feet off to their side—and caught a brief glimpse of a shape.

He grabbed her arm, forcing her to angle off to the right. She looked at him, her eyes questioning behind her faceplate. He pointedly looked past her in the direction he had glimpsed the movement. She immediately understood and swam even harder. But they were now angling away from the *Cassandra*.

He tried to remember, to gauge the distance left to swim before they would be in line with the *Cassandra*'s bow, and then they would swim back to its far side. He glanced back in the direction he had seen the shape, saw nothing but the murky water. His eyes playing tricks on him? He had just barely seen it, really more a movement than a shape, maybe only a fish.

Then, a few feet ahead of the spot he was looking back at, there was a slight, cloudy swirl of the murky water and, behind it, the barest glimpse of movement, but too big for a fish.

He turned, swam harder and, out of the corner of his faceplate, he glimpsed another movement off to the right. He grabbed Linda's arm, pulling her to a stop.

She stared at him then glanced in the direction he was looking.

One to each side of them? He thought of the shore of the island. They could backpedal and then swim rapidly in that direction. The divers now to each side of them couldn't see any better than they could. But the shoreline was at least a quarter mile away. Their bubbles would leave an easy trail for the charter boat to follow. And they would have to come ashore exposed, helpless, without any means of defense. Linda, her eyes big, was shaking her head as she stared at him. She glanced in the direction the *Cassandra* should be and back to him.

What choice did they have? he thought. There was no place else to go. Maybe, swimming as hard as they could, they could dart past the two divers and onto the *Cassandra* before they could be intercepted. Given only a second after that and he would have his pistol in his hand.

Past Linda, he glimpsed movement again, there and then gone. She looked across her shoulder and then wildly back past him.

But he wasn't so sure now. The movement had been quick and smooth. Too quick? Too . . .

Ten feet away, the gray shape glided out of the mist, one big eye jutting in their direction. A hammerhead shark, seven or eight feet long—and then it entered the mist ahead of them and angled toward the left.

Linda didn't even look back at him, but instead swam in the same direction the shark had. *And she was right.* Though the sharks were dangerous—especially circling as they were—they were nothing to what the two divers from the charter boat represented. He swam hard after her.

Twenty feet ahead of them, protruding down into the clearer water near the surface, was the faint shape of the *Cassandra*'s hull. They stopped swimming.

The two divers would be coming toward the yacht, too; could already be there, waiting. Squinting, trying to force his sight as far as he could, he could see nothing but the faint, rounded shape of the hull rising and falling on the waves, the rear of the yacht and its propellers stretching back to disappear into the milky whiteness.

His muscles tightened as a long gray shape swam suddenly out of the mist on the far side of the hull, dipped and glided swiftly beneath them, not more than five feet away, then disappeared into the mist to their rear.

Linda looked at him and he nodded, and they began to swim slowly forward, nearing the massive shape of the hull, rising and falling. Her gaze moved back in the direction the shark had gone.

They stopped again, maybe fifteen feet from the wooden swimming platform that stuck out from the back of the yacht.

The faint white, cloudy water was impenetrable beyond the platform. Off to their left, off to their right—in any direction—they could see only a few feet. Their eyes locked for a brief moment and then Linda swam rapidly ahead, passing under the rear quarter of the hull toward the swim platform.

The *Cassandra* rose on a wave and came down hard in the following trough, and the rigid fiberglass hull slammed into Linda's back, her head audibly thumping against the hull.

Her mouthpiece released and her arms splayed out to her

sides. Her body, arched into a bowed-V, began to sink slowly toward the shallow bottom.

He stroked hard toward her, grabbed her arm and reached for her mouthpiece. As he tried to force it past her clenched teeth her eyes began to focus, and she was suddenly grasping for the piece of rubber with her lips.

A long, dark shape suddenly sped past them, and all he had time to do was flinch. And then the shark was gone. He pushed Linda toward the rear of the *Cassandra*.

In a moment she had shed her tank and pulled herself up onto the swim platform.

He glanced in all directions under the water as he shed his straps and then quickly pulled himself up out of the water onto the slippery wood of the platform.

Linda was already over the stern rail, glancing at the charter boat a couple hundred feet away as she ran toward the main cabin.

He went over the rail, slipped on the deck and nearly fell, then ran down the side of the salon toward the door. Linda met him in the door, his pistol in her hand. He took it from her.

The charter boat had stopped less than a hundred feet away. Two heads bobbed in the water next to the craft and then moved around to the ladder at the stern. The boat's captain stared toward the *Cassandra*.

"Coast Guard, Gulfport, this is the *Cassandra*," Linda was saying over the yacht's VHF. "We have an emergency."

On the charter boat, the skipper stared at his radio a moment then turned and looked back at the man at the stern who was now helping the two divers into the boat.

A dorsal fin cleft a swell between the two boats, then disappeared back down into the murky water.

CHAPTER

20

A Coast Guard 41 boat was lashed to the *Cassandra*'s starboard side, the two boats rising and falling on the increasingly heavy swells. Chief Petty Officer Kurt Holston, dressed in tropical blue longs—dark blue pants and a light blue long sleeve shirt—stood next to Clay and Linda at the *Cassandra*'s bow. He was about Clay's size and age, but had the blond hair of his German ancestry. Fifty feet away a Coast Guard 51 boat bobbed over the spot where the body had been found.

Two divers in a rubber dinghy at the side of the 51 were lifting the girl toward the hands of the crewmen on the boat's deck. The crewmen laid her down, then gently slipped a rubberized body bag over her remains.

Clay had already used the ship-to-shore operator to contact Donna and confirm that there had been a spare anchor on the *Cassandra,* a plow anchor, the same type that had been tied to the girl's ankles. In addition to the compass and depth sounder

Clay had seen, the Coast Guard divers had brought up the single side band, finding the long-range radio not far from the girl's body and the canisters.

There was no longer any doubt that the murders were premeditated and that the killer only tried to leave the appearance of a surprised burglar. And, to Clay, neither was there any doubt that whoever headed the area's dope trafficking had ordered the murders.

He looked at the charter boat now moving away from the area. The two who had been in the water had claimed they were taking advantage of their time off work to go spear fishing. The other two said they preferred to troll. The only thing they had seemed worried about was that the man they worked for, Soung Ming, was going to be upset with them because they had taken the boat out without his permission.

Bullshit! They had been there to retrieve the canisters, and Ming had ordered it.

Holston had also been staring at the departing boat. "Maybe they're home free for now," he said. "But at least we know who to keep an eye on. This is the second strike against Ming."

"Second strike?"

"Yes, sir. Man he once employed was picked up out on the interstate a while back. Had a few kilos of cocaine stashed in the panel truck he was driving. We didn't make anything of his previous connection to Ming, but it stands out now."

"Is he in jail around here?"

"Yes, sir, in Gulf City awaiting trial. A Vietnamese named Vu."

The man in the ski mask had said the informant was in jail after being caught transporting five kilos of cocaine. It could be the same man, a man who used to work for Ming. Probably still did, if the truth were known. And if the man was the informant —Clay glanced at the charter boat fading in the distance— strike three, maybe.

It was raining now, and the wind was strong out of the south; a following sea pushed against the *Cassandra*'s stern as the yacht slowly made its way across the Sound and back toward the boatyard. Clay, steering from inside the salon, gave the wheel a turn to starboard in order to pass to its stern a tug pushing a line of barges along the intracoastal waterway. Linda, a beer in one hand, a glass partially filled with bourbon in the other, came up from the galley. She handed the beer to Clay.

"Want to see something?" she asked.

"What?"

She set her glass on the chart table, and walked to the couch for her purse. Bringing it back to him, she opened it and lifted out a small dog-eared photograph. Clay didn't look at it. His eyes remained focused on the snub-nose revolver in her purse.

She saw where he was staring. "I bought it after I started working at the bar," she said. "Some nights I don't get home until three, four in the morning. I can shoot it, too—took lessons."

She held the photograph in front of his face. "This is what I wanted you to see. Recognize the handsome young fella?"

It was a color photograph of him in a boxing outfit—white tank top, blue velvet shorts his father's secretary had cut and sewn for him, and boxing shoes reaching nearly to the beginning of his calves. He smiled. "Where did you find that?"

"In your room. I was by your house one day to pick up Robert. We were going to a concert. He was still taking a shower. There were three or four of these just alike lying on a shelf above the dresser. I stole it."

Clay took the wallet-size photograph in his hand and stared at it a moment. Giving up his senior year of athletics to work at the boatyard had not been the easiest thing he ever did—it left a void. He had soothed that aching somewhat by joining one of the coast's local boxing clubs. It was something he could train for at night, after his morning classes at the community college were over with, and after the last workman at the boatyard had gone home for the day. He had only boxed the one year before transferring to Ole Miss, and his record had only been six wins and four losses, not all that great. But he recalled that he had started off 1-3, and then won five of his last six fights, the single defeat a split decision loss to a boy who went on to win a national AAU title.

Clay handed the photograph back to Linda and she replaced it in her purse. "Stupid of me to show that to you," she said.

"Why's that?"

"Come on, Clay, you know it shows how crazy I was—am—about you. It gives you an edge."

He smiled.

"But I don't care," she said. "I wanted you to see it."

"Off my dresser, huh? I'll remember not to leave my wallet lying around."

Linda walked to the couch and laid her purse on it. Returning toward the steering station she glanced through the galley—and noticed the door to the bow cabin slowly closing.

"Clay."

"Uh, huh."

"The door just shut."

"What?"

"The door down there, it just shut."

He leaned to his left and glanced at the closed door. The *Cassandra* climbed another wave, and the door swung open. He smiled.

As the *Cassandra* tilted forward and ran down the wave, the door closed again. His smile broadened. "Doesn't look like whoever's in there can make up his mind whether he wants to come out or stay."

"It's not funny," Linda said. "I thought it was somebody."

After a last glance toward the door, she looked through the windshield at the rain. "What do we do when we get back to the boatyard?" she asked.

"I'll probably go by and see Langston. I have a couple things I want to talk over with him."

"Like what?"

"The pieces just don't fit together right. Back there when I was watching them bring the girl's body up, I was sure what had happened to Robert. Now, I don't know. He was involved in the trafficking sure enough, no doubt about that. The money in his safe deposit box, his having the coordinates where the canisters were, his going to that particular spot the night he was murdered—yeah, he was involved, and he was coming after those canisters the night he was killed. But I'm not sure any longer that Ming's people had anything to do with his death. I'm not saying they didn't. It's just that I'm having second thoughts after standing here for the last hour thinking about it."

Linda's forehead wrinkled. "I don't understand. What do you mean by the pieces not fitting together?"

"Why were the canisters left there—with the drugs still in them?"

"I guess Ming's people were going to pick them up later," she said. "They were. That's what that boat was there for."

"Why later, Linda? Why not right then while they were there, if Ming's people *were* there the night Robert was murdered?"

"I don't know; there could be a reason."

"Okay, assume there was—why were the coordinates still in the Loran?"

Linda shook her head. "I don't know what you're getting at."

"Okay; if Ming's people killed Robert and the girl and, for some unknown reason, weren't able to pick up the drugs right then, wouldn't they at least have removed the coordinates from the Loran before they allowed the boat to be found? Especially since the drugs hadn't been picked up yet."

She again shook her head. "I don't know. Maybe they didn't think about the coordinates still being in it. Maybe they didn't know they were; Robert wasn't supposed to have entered them."

"There's something else that makes more sense, Linda. If the killer wasn't connected with the traffickers, then that would explain both why the drugs weren't picked up and why the coordinates were still in the Loran—he didn't know about either of them." He paused a moment.

"But why did whoever it was, connected to the drug runners or not, try to hide the girl's body but not care about Robert's being found? There's something in the killer's doing that—there has to be a reason."

*   *   *

Brouchard stood at a window of his living room as he stared through the panes at the rain starting to lessen.

"Please," Angela Brouchard begged from the corner of the couch. "Please, Antonio. I can't stand it any longer."

The big Cajun glanced back at her without saying anything and she dropped her head in her hands and began silently sobbing again.

Brouchard continued to stare at her for a moment then grabbed his white coat off the back of the easy chair behind him and strode from the living room.

CHAPTER

21

It had quit raining. A bright sun now shone down on the cemetery, an old one, its gently rolling grounds heavily wooded with the Spanish-moss-draped, squat oaks common to the Mississippi coast. A particularly big oak cast a mushroom-shaped shadow over the Rodgers's family plot.

Clay had just placed a dozen roses on his mother's grave and now stared at the rain-soaked mound next to her's. He reminded himself to make sure Donna had called about the headstone.

"We found the girl, Robert. We'll know who she is pretty soon. Bet she was pretty if you were taking her out." His eyes moistened, and he had to look away.

Finally, he turned back to the grave. "Dad's not doing so well. I think if the killer could be found it'd be better for him. I —I told Dad not to worry, they'd find him; and don't you worry about it, either. I'm trying to help find him, yet it's so confusing,

so hard. Maybe there's some way you could help me a little . . ." He felt the tears dripping from his chin. He glanced
self-consciously across both shoulders, then raised the back of
his hand to dry his eyes.

"I love you," he said, "both of you." He turned away from the
plot and walked slowly toward his car.

At the service station across the street from the front of the
cemetery, he parked in the full-service lane. While the atten-
dant metered out the gas, he walked to a pay telephone in the
glass enclosure at the edge of the lot.

He punched in the number of the Biloxi Police Station. He
wondered if Langston had heard about the discovery of the
girl's body and how long he thought it might take before a
positive identification could be made.

When an officer answered the telephone, Clay asked to speak
to Chief Langston.

"Chief's over in Gulf City," the officer said. "They had a
prisoner up and hung himself over there last night."

Clay's heart seemed to skip a beat. "Gulf City?"

"Yes sir."

He didn't want to ask. "It wasn't the Vietnamese they caught
out on the interstate, was it?"

There was a brief silence on the other end of the line, and
then the officer said, "Who is this?"

"Clay Rodgers. I'm—"

"Oh, hello, Mr. Rodgers. Yeah, that's the one—a guy named
Vu. How did you know?"

Angel Morales and the two Vietnamese DEA agents stood at
the curb of Highway 90, running above the white sand beach
along the Biloxi shoreline. They were watching the lines of va-
cationing gamblers stream onto and off the big casino boat at
the water's edge. Morales reached into his pocket and pulled
out a quarter. He flipped it in the air, caught it and said, "Call
it."

"What?" the slimmer of the two Vietnamese agents asked.

"Call it."

"Heads."

Morales slowly opened his hand. "Damn," he said, and handed over the quarter. Then he looked back at the casino.

"Well, I can say now that I've gambled in Las Vegas, Reno, Atlantic City and Biloxi, Mississippi." He glanced at the lines of luxury yachts berthed under the arched concrete canopies only a short distance from the casino, and added, "They're never going to believe this back in New York."

With a nod of his head he gestured the two Vietnamese toward their car. "Hit the fish factories, again. See if you can scratch up some information—anything. I'll meet you back here at six." He turned and started toward his rented car parked off to the side of the highway.

On the way to the Gulf City jail, Clay struggled with his thoughts. Maybe he was jumping to conclusions. Maybe the would-be informant and the dead prisoner weren't the same person. He had assumed the man locked up in Gulf City was the informant because he had been arrested for transporting cocaine, and because he had once worked for Ming.

But the informant didn't necessarily have to be in jail on a drug-related charge. A crook's a crook. He could have been locked up for any number of reasons. He . . . Clay shook his head at his wishful thinking. It was going to turn out to be the same man, and he was now dead. Nobody would ever know what he had been ready to tell. Gone, the whole damn thing gone.

The man in the ski mask. There was still him. The informant had put his life in the man's hands by asking him to meet with Clay. The two had to be close—they would have talked. The meeting scheduled for midnight that night could still be important. *Jesus! He hadn't called Judge Nichols, yet.* And what was he going to say when he did? Hey, Mr. Federal Judge. I know you're not used to receiving calls like this, but I have a personal favor I need for you to do . . . There would be more chance of getting a favorable response if the call came from Washington.

There was a service station off to the right. He would call from there. Come on Mr. Vice-President, one more time.

When Clay arrived at the Gulf City jail, the first man he saw was the Biloxi chief of police. Dressed in his full dark blue uniform, Langston was near the back of the lobby and talking with a similarly dressed middle-age man. When Clay walked up to the two, Langston glanced at him, then turned toward him and extended his arm to shake hands. He had a questioning look on his face.

"I called your office, Chief. They told me you were over here. I didn't know if you'd heard yet, but we found the girl who was on the boat with Robert."

"Yeah," Langston said, nodding. "When the Coast Guard gets the girl's body to the morgue, we're going to try and get a reconstructive drawing, get as good a likeness as we can out in the papers and try to find out who she was." He nodded toward the man next to him.

"Clay, this is Eric Ward. He's the chief over here. Eric, this is Clay Rodgers, the one I was telling you discovered the body out at the islands."

The Gulf City chief was of normal height and build, not nearly as stocky as Langston. His brown hair, trimmed at a moderate length and parted to the side, showed little of the gray that Langston's did, although the two police chiefs appeared close in age. He shook Clay's hand. "Glad to meet you, son."

"You, too, Chief. You had a prisoner commit suicide."

"Yeah, hung himself. Tied a towel around his neck and attached it to the bars in his window. Found him just before daylight. Must have just done it; towel was still soaked."

"Soaked?"

"They use a wet towel, or sheet, whatever, so it fits tight. A dry one can gap around the neck and not completely shut everything off."

"He was in a cell by himself?"

"Uh, huh. Only had two other prisoners in the same cell

block, and they were asleep. Even if they'd been awake they might not have noticed. Despite a light we always keep on in the hall, the back of each cell is pretty much in the shadows. That's where he did it; tied the towel to the bars and just sat down." The chief, wrinkling his brow, shook his head. "How somebody can just sit there strangling until they pass out—it's beyond me. All he had to do was put his feet down and stand up." He paused, a reflective look on his face. "I guess they pass out pretty quick. Weight of their body finishes it for them."

"Were there any marks on his body?"

Ward's brow wrinkled questioningly. He glanced at Langston before answering. "None except where the towel bruised him a bit. Why do you ask that?"

If the man had been the informant then there should be other marks, Clay said to himself. No one sits passively by as he's strangled to death—murdered. And if the man was the informant, then he *had* to have been murdered. What man would sit for weeks in jail facing a long term in the penitentiary and then, just as he found himself in a position to know the charges against him were going to be dropped and he was going to receive fifty or maybe a hundred thousand dollars, suddenly decides to kill himself? But was he or wasn't he the informant? Clay glanced at his watch, the second hand turning so slowly. Would midnight ever come?

Ward turned to look at the Vietnamese woman entering the building.

"Excuse me for a minute, gentlemen," he said. "This is Vu's mother."

The dark-skinned woman was short, slightly built, had her thin gray hair pulled into a bun at the back of her head, and was wearing a loose blue cotton dress and sandals.

Ward stopped in front of her, nodded politely and spoke in a low voice.

The woman's stoic expression didn't change as she listened to the chief, or when she spoke.

Ward nodded his head at whatever she said, and the two walked toward the desk in the back corner of the lobby.

The officer sitting behind the desk opened a drawer and lifted out a bundle wrapped in brown butcher paper. He handed it to the woman who clutched it to her chest. Her expression still unchanged, she turned and started back toward the building's front door.

Clay moved to meet her.

"Excuse me, ma'am."

The woman stopped and looked at him with dark eyes staring from the middle of a wrinkled face.

"Ma'am, I'm sorry about your son." She didn't respond.

"I'm Clay Rodgers. My brother was murdered a few nights ago over in Biloxi. I was wondering if I might speak with you a minute?"

He thought her eyes narrowed a bit before she spoke.

"Rodgers?"

He nodded. "Yes, ma'am."

She said no more, only stared an instant longer, then turned away from him and walked toward the exit.

He stared after her.

Chief Ward stepped beside him. "What?"

Clay shook his head. "Nothing. I told her I was sorry about her son."

"What did she say?"

Ward's questioning look bothered Clay. *Jesus! He was starting to be suspicious of everybody.* He remembered Jennifer telling him about the detective who had irrationally suspected the left-handed police officer of murdering his sister. Jennifer had warned Clay that being as emotionally involved as he was, there was no way he would be able to logically investigate Robert's death. She had said, "Everywhere you look you're going to find something that gives you pause for thought." Clay glanced at Ward now walking back toward Langston. Why shouldn't there be a pause for thought? The suicide—the murder, maybe—had taken place in Ward's jail, hadn't it?

The dumb-ass Mexican from south Texas was getting on Charley's nerves. The little bastard had been hanging around the waterfront all day, had been there earlier when it had been raining and now was back again, moving from place to place, constantly asking questions that led in only one direction.

The son-of-a-bitch was trying to find a way to make some easy money; he was obviously hoping to run across somebody to connect him with a ready supply of drugs. Why didn't the bastard just get a job? The factories were always needing somebody, and the shrimpboats—plenty of *honest* work available. Charley walked toward the Mexican.

DEA agent Angel Morales wasn't getting anywhere. The dumb-ass redneck he was speaking with at the moment was obviously the petty crook type. He was talking big, yet it was also clear the loudmouth didn't have the first idea about anybody connected with drug trafficking.

Angel Morales mumbled his thanks and turned away from the redneck to stand face-to-face with the biggest black bastard he'd ever seen. Huge arms hung down from the stretched sleeves of the man's white T-shirt, and the jeans he wore looked like they were about to split at the thighs. The look on the man's face wasn't friendly.

Angel Morales nodded and forced a smile to his face. The big black's expression didn't change. Angel Morales started to step around the man, only to be stopped by the black's quick side-step.

Angel Morales wanted to turn and run, but instead he said, "You have a problem, buddy?"

"You're the one's got a problem."

"You must have me mixed up with somebody else, old buddy. Don't know why your pants are in a wad, but it's none of my doing." He tried to step to the side again and was stopped once more by the man.

A big black hand, attached to the thickest wrist Angel Morales had ever seen, came out and groped for his throat, but he dodged it successfully and backed away. "Hey, man—back off. You got the wrong Hispanic here. We all look alike, right?"

The black wasn't amused. "What I got me is a little dumb-ass

Mexican that's fixin' to head back to south Texas when I get done with him."

Angel Morales shook his head. "I'll go along with the bit about being a little dumb-ass Mexican, if it makes you any happier. But I'm telling you, old buddy, somebody's steered you wrong about me—bad wrong. You haven't any reason to be messing with me."

"Half the kids in my housing project's on shit they got from people like you—my sister's son, even. Filthy, druggy, dope dealin' bastard!" The black's eyes literally glowed red.

Angel Morales turned and ran.

CHAPTER

22

Ben Carson's house, a two-level, stucco contemporary situated on a large, well-landscaped yard, was located in a tranquil wooded neighborhood in Pascagoula, twenty miles east of Biloxi. His red Cadillac was in the garage. Linda parked her old Chevy at the curb in front of the house and moved up the sidewalk to the entrance.

Before she rang the doorbell she undid the top two buttons of her blouse, then adjusted her tight black shirt. She had checked her makeup before she exited her car.

The middle-age man who answered the door immediately smiled. He was big, at least a couple inches taller than Clay, and appeared to be in better than usual shape for his age. He had brown hair, slightly gray at the temples, and was dressed in a beige, short-sleeve pullover shirt left hanging over his tan slacks.

"Mr. Carson?"

"Yeah, what can I do for you, honey?"

"I'm Earline Ashley," she said. "I wonder if I could have a moment of your time?"

She had started thinking about Ben Carson while Clay had stood at the *Cassandra*'s steering station and said that he didn't believe Robert had been killed by the traffickers. Who then had murdered him? A burglar, probably, who dumped the equipment overboard—not to mislead anyone about who had committed the crime, but rather because he didn't want something in his possession that could tie him back to the murder. But Clay wasn't at all convinced of that, either.

The last thing he mentioned when he let her out at her house was that he was still wondering if Antonio could be involved in any way.

She had started to say, "No, I know him too well. He isn't that kind of an individual." But she hadn't. Instead, it had suddenly crossed her mind what she was always seeing quoted in the paper after somebody was charged with a crime. The most surprised statements seemed to always come from coworkers and neighbors, those people who thought they had known the person best: *"I just never would've guessed he was that kind of person. He was always so friendly, so . . .".* How well did she know Antonio?

She had served him drinks no telling how many times; made mortgage payments to him; had him flirt with her, and once get rough; had sat with him at a table in the bar until the wee hours of the morning and listened to him talk. But did she know him? Then she had remembered a man who did know Antonio, Ben Carson, a video machine dealer who lived in Pascagoula. He had been one of Antonio's closest friends until a few years before. And if there was anyone to ask what he thought of Antonio and get an honest answer, it was Carson—the man Antonio nearly killed with a knife after catching him making a pass at Angela.

Linda remembered the man's name well because she had once dated a boy named Carson, Lindsey Carson. He was the good-looking son of a chemical engineer whose father had taken a job in Atlanta and moved the family there about the same time she had fallen in love with the boy. That was when she had been a sophomore in high school, and the time she had been deflowered, so to speak. She still had fond memories of the boy. He was the only one other than Clay who ever passed through her dreams.

Ben Carson continued to smile as he openly ran his eyes down her figure. "Sure," he said, "I always got a minute for a pretty honey like you."

"Well, thank you."

"What you selling?" He deliberately ran his eyes back over her body. "Can I hope?"

She smiled sweetly. "I'm not selling anything, Mr. Carson—doing a survey."

"Come on in."

As he moved aside to let her enter the house, he turned his face just so, and she saw the red scar that started at his left temple and then ran down the side of his face, to end in a jagged upward turn just below the side of his jaw.

When he noticed where she was staring, his smile vanished.

She quickly moved her eyes to his and gave him her best smile.

His returned.

The foyer had a marble floor, and the large living room was tastefully decorated with quality furniture. All kinds of expensive extras were set about: a big built-in TV and audio system, an elaborate treadmill for exercising, a camcorder sitting on top of an ornate desk, and a fax machine attached to the only telephone visible in the room. Carson had a large diamond ring on his finger and wore a Gucci watch. A video machine salesman with money to burn, she thought. He might know more about drugs than she expected. Well good, if she could put him at ease.

He stopped in front of a long couch and gestured with his hand for her to sit there. She would have preferred to sit in a chair. But she also needed to keep him as friendly as possible.

She sat where he indicated. He sat next to her, as she had known he would.

"Now," he said, his face only a couple feet from hers. "What kinda survey?" His breath smelled of cigar smoke.

"Well, Mr. Carson, I—"

"Ben," he corrected.

"Ben, then. I don't like to be formal, myself. What I was wanting to speak with you about—you were involved in a fight with an Antonio Brouchard a couple years back."

His smile was gone. "Wait a damn minute. What is this? You said a survey. Who are you with, the police? No, the damned insurance company. That's what you're here about, isn't it?"

"Well, sort of, in a way."

"Thought so," he snorted. "Money I got from Brouchard was for my mental suffering. Medical bills and all the rest of the shit was rightfully the insurance company's problem. Told that to the man from your company who came by here doing an audit. Shouldn't have even talked to the son-of-a-bitch. Maybe you better be getting out of here now, too." His eyes narrowed. "Which one of the companies are you with?"

"Uh, not with either one of them, really. I'm with an independent consumer organization that checks up on the insurance companies—does follow-up, mainly. That's what I meant by a survey."

"Follow-up? Survey? Dammit, speak where I can understand you, lady."

"We go around and check on things from customer satisfaction to—"

"Well," he interrupted. "Don't be putting me down as that. I'm the furtherest thing from satisfied. I mean, yeah, the companies finally paid, both of them; but they took their damn sweet time doing it."

"Well, Mr.—Ben—we work closely with state regulatory agencies that can handle that, too; maybe file a claim for interest."

"Interest, huh? That's a damn good idea."

"I'll check into that for you."

He nodded. His smile came back as he glanced again at her figure. "Would you like a drink?"

"Well, uh—I'm not really supposed to. I mean when I'm on the job and all."

"Who would I be telling?"

She smiled. "In that case—yes, please. It has been a hot day. A drink would be nice."

"Got about anything you want. What's your pleasure?"

"You have any bourbon?"

"Sure, honey."

"That would be fine—straight up, a little ice."

He smiled and stood. "Be back in a jiffy."

When he returned he held a normal-size water glass in his hand. It was nearly half full of the bourbon and contained only a couple of ice cubes. He had also fixed himself a drink. It was in the same size glass, but not so full, and was diluted with a lot of coke as well as full of ice.

"Thank you," she said. She moved the glass directly to her lips, and drank a full third of its contents.

His smile broadened. He sat closer when he retook his seat.

She held her glass on her lap when she asked her next question. "How long were you in the hospital?"

"Six weeks." He self-consciously ran his hand to the side of his face. "Been back into surgery twice for this." A pained expression crossed his face.

Despite herself, she felt sorry for him, and caught herself giving him a genuine smile. "What was the fight about?"

"What difference does that make?"

His voice was heading toward cold again. She needed to be more careful how she asked her questions; think before she spoke. She smiled again. "You know, I noticed you touching your scar."

"So?"

"I mean I can tell you're self-conscious about it."

"So spit out what it is you're trying to say."

"Well, first place, it doesn't take anything away from you. It's amazing how a birthmark or a mole or something like that scar can give a man that—uh, manly look. Second place, the most important thing to a woman, at least if she's got any sense, is not how smooth a man's face is, but what kind of mind he's got, what he's done with his life." She glanced around the living room.

"Ben, from what I can see, it looks like you've done all right. That tells me you have a good mind." She crossed her legs. She wished she had worn a shorter skirt—she had one in her closet that was ridiculous. But his eyes widened, anyway.

"Now," she said, "what were we talking about? Oh, yeah, I was asking you what the fight was about."

"To tell it like it was, son-of-a-bitch caught me screwing Angela.

Screwing? Linda thought. The story she had heard was Ben had made a pass.

"That's his wife," Ben said, "Angela. Though you wouldn't know he had one the way he carried on. Bastard screwed everything he could get his hands on all the years I knew him."

She had heard those kinds of rumors about Antonio, and, of course, there had been the pass he made at her—but *everything he could get his hands on?* "You were friends, then?"

"I sell video machines to joints all up and down the coast. Don't know how many times I trucked into one of that bastard's places to talk to him about some new machine, and before I could go in to see him I had to wait for one of his strippers to come out—hair all messed up, buttons undone. No getting around they had just been nailed."

She smiled knowingly and nodded.

He paused, a look of genuine reflection coming to his face. "You know," he said, his voice now low and thoughtful, "even though Angela was attracted to me right off the bat, that wasn't the all of it. I think she was getting back at him, too."

Linda nodded again. "What's good for the goose—"

"No, not so much that, honey. In fact, I'm not all that sure she even knew about the other women. I damn sure never let on to her about it. If she would've got onto him, and it came out I was the one who told her . . ." He raised his hand to his scar again.

"No, I believe it was her getting back at him for taking her out of the market, then not being able to deliver the goods himself. Marrying him not only ended her playing around with other men, but he didn't replace it with much. Not as much as she wanted, anyway—that's what she told me.

"I don't mean he was a limpdick or nothing like that when he got on her, I just mean he didn't care nothing about her stuff." He paused. "Funny isn't it, how somebody can be trying to nail everything that walks, then gets married and loses all interest in what he's made permanent."

She nodded again. "Happens quite often—that's why I never have married; I like to keep everything exciting."

He smiled, and once again spoke in a thoughtful voice. "It wasn't just sex he denied her either. According to her he wasn't even sociable to her when they were alone. She figured the only reason he had married her was to have somebody with big tits to show off to his friends." He dropped his eyes to Linda's breasts, more as if he was comparing rather than staring again. She preferred the staring. He took a drink before continuing.

"Fact is—and I already knew this—Angela said he really didn't give a damn about anybody except himself, was a cold-hearted bastard."

Ben held his finger up to make a point. "Except for his mother—Angela said he did care about his mother. Old woman's been dead and rotted away for I don't know how long, but the bastard's got her pictures framed and hanging all over the house. Angela and me, we used the place once when he was on a trip to Chicago. I saw the pictures."

He glanced at Linda's drink. "Taste all right, honey? That shit's good quality stuff."

"Oh sure—fine. It's just that I've had a rough day. Drink's not relaxing me like I thought it would. Got some stuff back at the motel room that will, though." She smiled and winked.

"Pot?" he asked.

"Well . . ."

He smiled. "Don't keep anything around the house any stronger than that, but if that would help any . . ."

She smiled again.

Without speaking further he came to his feet and walked across the living room to the door at its far side, disappearing through it. In a few seconds he was back with two already rolled joints.

She stared at them. She had felt she needed to slip into talking drugs as if she was no prude about them, so he'd be relaxed when she arrived at what it was she really wanted to ask about. But she was surprised he had reacted as he did to her hint. He really hadn't the slightest idea whether or not she was a cop.

He sat down beside her, handed her a joint. "Mississippi Delta grown," he said. "Twenty-three feet of topsoil. If the government would let the delta plantations grow this stuff they could pay off the federal debt in a couple years."

He lit his with a big gold lighter he produced from his pants pocket.

He held the still flaming lighter out toward her.

She hesitated a moment, then moved the joint toward her mouth and leaned forward to let him light it. She coughed slightly, and moved her hand to her mouth. "Excuse me—went up my nose."

He smiled and nodded. She noticed he had gargled with Listerine while he had been out of the room. She was glad. He couldn't be sitting any closer without being in her lap.

She took another drag, held it in her mouth a moment without inhaling, then blew out the smoke. She looked at him, smiled and nodded. She still had her glass in her lap, and she raised it to her mouth and took a drink, trying to erase the taste of the marijuana.

Lowering the glass she turned her eyes back toward his. "You were saying that his wife—Angela, I think you said her name was—claimed he really didn't care anything about her?"

He nodded. "Yeah, honey, like I said, didn't care nothin'. Despite that she warned me to keep my mouth shut about us. Like I had little enough sense to be out and around talking about it. She said that, care anything about her or not, he was some kind of possessive; had slapped her around before just on account of her talking to other men."

Raising the hand he held the joint in, he touched his scar with a finger. Then he moved the drug to his mouth and took a deep drag before continuing.

"Son-of-a-bitch wasn't possessive, he was crazy. But he found out I could handle myself, too. I got the knife away from him. Would have deballed the bastard right then except for a highway patrolman walking in the club."

"You were laying Angela at one of his clubs?"

"Girls Galore—back room. Bastard was supposed to be in New Orleans. I had Angela on top of his desk giving her hell when he kicked the door in. He'd set us up. Was planning on killing me right then—not a doubt in my mind. Maybe the son-of-a-bitch was going to count on his protecting his honor as being his defense. Maybe he was going to put a gun in my hand when he got through—say I came after him with it. But that bastard came to kill me, that's for sure."

He finally exhaled the smoke that he had held in his lungs for so long. She had began to wonder where it had gone.

"I heard he was charged with attempted murder. The charges were dropped?"

He nodded. "Assault with attempt—that's where I got the fifty thousand."

"To not press charges?"

"Right. Had him good, I did. If the bastard had copped a felony conviction he wouldn't have been able to keep running his damn clubs."

She looked at her joint, held it a little farther out on her lap in an attempt to get the smoke to quit drifting up her nose. "Maybe he was messing with drugs."

"What?" Ben asked.

"Why he was so crazy—like you said he was. Maybe he was on drugs."

"No, wasn't that," Ben said, "just pure meanness. He didn't believe for a minute in no drugs. Angela told me the son-of-a-bitch caught her messing around with a few pills one time and got after her good, told her that the stuff would drive her crazy. Hell, I could do a shit potload of PCP and be less crazy than that bastard is."

"I see. I guess I said drugs because I'd heard some rumors about him maybe being involved in moving some drugs. Thought if that was true, he might be using them, too."

Ben nodded. "Yeah, there's the rumors—you got that right. He once talked to me about them. He didn't know how they got started, but said that he'd be crazy to do something like smuggling with the gold mine he already had in his clubs—take a chance on losing it all." He shook his head. "No, he doesn't mess with drugs, using or selling. I'd like to see somebody step up in the bastard's face and blow his damn head off, yet I'll give the son-of-a-bitch credit—he's not stupid. Bastard wouldn't risk what's he got by jumping into something high profile like that." Carson's face took on another reflective look.

"You know," he said, "I sit here and say he's not stupid, and then I think about how Angela feels about him. She wanted to get away from him even back then, but was scared of what he'd do to her if she tried. She's gonna kill him one of these days, you wait and see. And he'll have brought it on himself. Yeah, come to think about it, son-of-a-bitch is stupid."

"But he's not involved with drugs?"

"No, no way. Bastard's clean there. Besides what I already said about him not wanting to take a chance on messing up the good thing he's got going with his clubs, he don't have the personality. Maybe I should put it that his personality wouldn't let him do it."

"What do you mean?"

"Brouchard's an especially arrogant sort. He likes to call the shots—gonna call 'em. Someone into trafficking is gonna have bosses—big boys in Chicago or Detroit. Bastard down here running this end of the operation is going to get rich, but he's gonna have to run the operation like the big boys have told him. Brouchard's not the type could take orders from nobody."

Linda nodded. She had learned about all she could. It really wasn't anything she didn't already know, except maybe for the details. She already knew Antonio stepped out—he had asked her out often enough. He was more abusive than she would have guessed, though she should have known that from the night he had wrestled her to the floor after she refused his final advances. The key thing she had learned from Carson was that she was right in her belief that Antonio wasn't dealing in drugs —he wasn't involved with Soung Ming.

She looked at Ben's smiling face, saw his tongue wet his lips. The trick now was to be able to exit without a hassle.

Let him down easy, she told herself. Don't cut him off too sharply—leave him hoping that if he remains a good little boy there might be more to come. She looked at her watch. "Oh, goodness, I'm late."

His eyes narrowed. "What?"

"I was supposed to meet my boss downtown ten minutes ago. Have to run—don't want to be fired. You listed in the phone book?" She knew he was. That's where she had found his address.

"Yeah, I'm listed."

She smiled sweetly, dropped her eyes just a bit. "If my boss hasn't got me lined up to do something I'm not aware of, maybe I can call you tonight. You're an interesting person to talk to. Maybe we can go out and eat." She dropped her eyes further. "Or something."

His smile was back. "Yeah," he said. "I haven't got nothing going. You be sure and call." His eyes narrowed again. "What if that damn boss of yours does throw out something for you to do?"

She shrugged. "Well then, next time through I'll be sure and call."

"Where do you live?"

"Northeast Mississippi—Iuka." That was as far away from Biloxi as she could think of. She hoped he never happened into the Beachfront Bar & Inn.

CHAPTER

23

The street Clay drove along was lined with old houses, some of them in need of repair. But there was little evidence of trash lying about, and many of the yards had been recently mowed. It was a scene attesting to the fact that though the residents were poor, they also had pride.

The mother of Chung Lam Vu lived in a particularly old house; some of the shingles on its roof were starting to slide. But the windows were spotless, and the blue-and-white-striped curtains hanging in them looked freshly washed.

After leaving the Gulf City jail he had driven back to Biloxi and the boatyard, intent on getting some sleep before taking his father and Donna out to dinner. But Vu's mother had kept coming back to his thoughts. It was unlikely that a son would have detailed any of his prior criminal activity to his mother. Even if she were aware of anything worth knowing, there was no way she was going to speak badly of a dead son; what mother would? Still, Clay had thought, what did he have to lose by paying her a visit?

He parked his car in front of her house, then walked across the yard, damp from the rain earlier that day, and climbed the steps up onto the porch. The warped boards creaked as he moved across them.

He knocked on the door. After a moment, he knocked again. He was about to knock a third time when the door cracked open as far as a safety chain would allow. He saw half the face of the old mother, and one dark eye.

"I'm Clay Rodgers. I met you earlier over at the Gulf City jail."

The woman didn't respond.

"I was wondering if I might speak with you for a minute?"

The eye peered at him a moment longer, then the door closed to reopen wide. The old woman stepped out onto the porch. She had changed from her blue cotton dress to one of all black. A heavy scent of flowers followed her out the door.

"Mrs. Vu, I told you earlier my brother had been murdered."

Expressionless, she gazed directly into his eyes, just as she had done at the Gulf City jail. It was almost as if she were trying to see inside him. He tried to return her look in a friendly way.

"Mrs. Vu, I realize with your son's death—and I'm deeply sorry about that—that this is a bad time to be bothering you. But, I—I want to find my brother's killer. You might be able to help. May I have just a little of your time?"

When the woman looked past Clay, he glanced across his shoulder to see two middle-age Vietnamese men now standing at the bottom of the porch. Both wore khaki pants and both were shirtless, their upper bodies streaked with muscles. A third man, younger and bigger than the two at the bottom of the steps, was walking from the house next door and coming directly toward the porch. A young woman in a black dress and holding a baby stood on the porch of the house the man came from. She was staring Clay's way.

The mother finally spoke. "You are not from here."

Clay pulled his Secret Service credentials from his hip pocket, whipped the black walletlike case open, and held it out so she could read the information imprinted next to his head-and-shoulders photograph.

"I live in Washington, now. I was born and grew up here, but haven't been back for some time." He slid the credentials back into his pocket.

The woman gave a slight nod. "Why do you say I could help you?"

"My brother's death might have something to do with drug trafficking in the area." He looked once more into her piercing stare, and knew he was going to have to be completely open to get anything from her.

"My brother was a good kid, Mrs. Vu, but I think he was working with the traffickers. I found where he had hidden a lot of money, enough money that I don't believe he could have obtained it any way other than through drugs."

"My son was a good man, too."

"Yes, ma'am, I—"

"But misguided."

He nodded. "Yes, ma'am; my brother, too. The traffickers—"

"They hold out hope to the young people," the old woman added. She dropped her eyes and stared reflectively at the porch floor, before raising her face back to his. "A way out of poverty, they tell the youth—a sure way."

"Yes ma'am."

"But your brother, he wasn't living in poverty, was he?"

Before he could answer she spoke again. "They held out vast riches to him, and the temptation was too great."

Clay heard the steps creak. A moment later he sensed someone standing close behind him.

The woman spoke across Clay's shoulder. "This is Mr. Rodgers. He has suffered a great loss, too."

Clay turned to face a pair of cold eyes, as dark as the old woman's. The young Vietnamese man was an inch or two shorter than Clay, but a thick neck bulged from his white T-shirt and his muscled biceps stretched the garment's sleeves.

His eyes didn't leave Clay's when he spoke. "My mother is in mourning."

The mother spoke. "It is all right, son."

The man's look didn't soften. Clay glanced past him at the men at the bottom of the porch, then turned back to face the woman. She had reopened the door and was stepping back inside her house.

Wait a damn minute. "Mrs. Vu!"

Her son stepped around him to the open doorway, barring the way into the house.

Clay glimpsed the woman's form disappearing into the dim interior of her house. He wanted to shout, "Do you know your son was murdered, too; just like Robert? Do you give a damn about finding out who did it?"

But he didn't. He couldn't. How, he thought, could he face himself if he added that uncertain knowledge to the woman's already deep grief? The uncertainties surrounding his own brother's murder were killing him.

He looked toward the bottom of the steps. Four men were now assembled there.

With a last glance at the woman's son, he turned away from the door and made his way slowly down the steps. The men parted and he walked between them and on toward his car. "Son-of-a-damn-shit-damn-crap," he mumbled to himself. *How could she be so coldly uninterested?*

Before driving to his father's house, Clay stopped by the *Cassandra* to check the answering machine. When he did he felt a sudden nervous tenseness. The little screen on the left of the machine showed two calls recorded. He pushed the rewind button. After the tape had rewound he waited a moment, then pushed the play button.

"CONGRATULATIONS! THIS IS JOE, A ROBOTIC DIALING MACHINE. IT IS MY PLEASURE TO INFORM YOU THAT YOU ARE A WINNER OF EITHER A BRAND NEW THUNDERBIRD, OR TWO OUNCES OF PURE GOLD, OR A

TRIP TO FAMOUS HOT SPRINGS, ARKANSAS. ALL YOU HAVE TO DO—"

Clay pushed the fast forward button until the tape had reached the second call.

It was from Washington.

Judge Nichols had agreed to have the informant moved into federal custody as soon as his identity was known. Further, if the informant had only the transporting charge against him and no prior record, the judge would also guarantee that no jail time would have to be served—providing the information given was indeed strong enough to lead to the arrest and conviction of the head of any drug trafficking ring in the area. Nichols was immediately preparing a signed statement containing all the needed provisions. A copy of it would be delivered to the *Cassandra* prior to eight o' clock that night.

Was the judge preparing a guarantee for a dead man, Clay wondered, or would the man tonight still be representing an informant? If the informant was dead, would the man even show up? Clay glanced at his watch.

CHAPTER

24

Donna sat to Clay's right while his father sat across the table from him. Little had been said since they arrived at the restaurant. What was there to say? Small talk was out. Clay certainly didn't want to be speaking about the body he had found that morning or anything else to do with his brother's death. Conversation about the boatyard would be a reminder about the murder, as would anything said about the *Cassandra*.

Not much had been eaten, either, though Fisherman's Wharf was his father's favorite restaurant, and the crabmeat casserole he had ordered was his favorite item on a menu loaded with excellent fare. His father had mostly only picked at his plate, turning his fork first one way and then the other, only occasionally spearing a hunk of crabmeat and moving it into his mouth.

What bothered Clay most was the noticeable redness about his father's cheeks and forehead. There had always been a problem with high blood pressure. The last couple of years the

177

condition had grown worse, only kept under control by strict medication. Clay hoped his father, preoccupied with his grief, wasn't forgetting the medicine. Clay glanced at Donna. When he got a chance he was going to ask her about that.

"When are you going back to Washington?" his father asked.

"I'm not sure. I haven't thought about it."

"Don't want you staying down here so long you get in trouble with your bosses. Donna and I are going to do fine."

"Oh, they don't care if I'm down here for a few days. They said for me to take my time."

His father nodded, and looked at Donna. She self-consciously glanced at her plate and back to him. "I'm ready to go when you two are," she said.

"And you?" his father asked, looking at him.

"Yes, sir, I'm through."

His father pushed his chair back from the table and stood.

Clay worried about what had been meant by the question of when he was going back to Washington. Was his father concerned, as he said he was, that his son was extending his emergency leave too long? Or did his father wish he *would* go on back? By being around, was he only an unwelcome reminder of Robert's death?

When his father stopped at the cash register to pay the bill, Clay accompanied Donna on toward the exit. He glanced back over his shoulder before speaking to her. "Is he taking his blood pressure medication?"

"I don't know," she said. "I asked him that same thing this morning and he . . . He didn't say."

"Resented you asking?"

She nodded.

Clay glanced back at his father. "Pretty rough to live with right now, huh?"

"He's so depressed, Clay."

"Yeah. If he doesn't get better we're going to have to take him to the doctor or find some way to get one out to the house."

"I think he's going to be okay," she said. "As bad as he is, he's better than he was. For the first couple of days he just sat and stared—when he wasn't in bed."

Clay nodded. "I guess it's just that the only way I can picture him is exuberant, so damn full of life." He looked back at his father now walking toward them. "But then there was a period right after Mother's death when he was like this. He got over that about the time I began to wonder if he ever would. We'll wait a couple more days and see."

Linda, passing Coach McGinnis's table as she moved with a tray of empty glasses toward the bar, glanced at him and smiled. He had shown up only a few minutes after her seven o'clock shift started. McGinnis smiled at her and made a little gesture for her to come to him for a moment, as he had done several times in the couple of hours he had been there. She knew he didn't need a drink. He was only on his second beer, and she had brought it to him less than ten minutes before. It had taken him better than an hour to finish his first one.

She nodded at him and smiled sweetly, but hurried on to the bar.

"Two Chivas and waters, whiskey straight up and a glass of Pouilly-Fuisse."

Freddie looked past her to the table of four men she was ordering for. "A glass of what?" he exclaimed.

"He's also telling his buddies how nice it is this time of year in the south of France. Just give him any white wine. He's too drunk to know if it's Drano."

"Where did everybody come from tonight?" Freddie asked, glancing around at the packed house.

"Jackson bankers—some kind of golf tournament. Ten-to-one the guy who ordered the Pouilly-Fuisse will never tee off tomorrow. Also, ten-to-one the bigmouth's lucky if he's ever been farther out of Jackson than south Alabama." She snorted. "France—I'd rather have the kind in here that grab your butt when you walk past."

"Hey, Linda!"

It was McGinnis.

"Be right back," she said to the bartender and headed to the high school coach's table.

"You want another beer?"

"No." He glanced around him, and spoke in a low voice. "You want to get some breakfast when you get off?"

"At two-thirty?"

His brow wrinkled. "—that late?"

She nodded.

"What about lunch tomorrow?" he asked.

She smiled sweetly. "Good idea. Write my number down. It's unlisted."

He quickly fumbled in his pants pockets, then shook his head.

She handed him a pen. He still looked helpless. "Use the napkin," she said.

He was instantly ready, the pen poised. He smiled and nodded.

She gave him her number, transposing the last two digits. She would later look sadly at him and say it was a shame that he had written it down wrong. It would only work one time. She was bound to have to go out and eat with him at least once. Well, she thought, he was a nice guy. And it was still important that he show his kids the photograph of Robert that she had given him. She shuddered as she thought back to the damage the fish had done to the girl's face. It would take an especially close relative to identify her now, if anybody could.

McGinnis smiled, tucked the napkin securely in the breast pocket of his plaid shirt, and rose to his feet. "Guess I'll be going. I've called an early morning practice, uh, workout. Can't have practices." He winked at her.

She smiled. "See you at lunch."

Freddie was signaling for her and she returned to the bar.

Brouchard, dressed in a white suit with a red tie, entered the inn as she carried the tray of drinks back to the four bank executives. He smiled at her.

She returned the smile and began placing the four men's orders before them.

Within a couple of hours, the majority of the bankers had

cleared out. The place now held a normal crowd for eleven o'clock on a Wednesday night. Brouchard had only drunk one Scotch and water but now signaled for a second one.

Freddie was busy preparing another waitress's order, so Linda fixed Brouchard's drink and carried it over to him.

He handed her a ten. She knew she was to keep the change, yet went through the routine of counting out on the table what he had coming back to him.

"You keep it, honey."

"Thank you."

Brouchard smiled his greetings toward somebody behind her. She caught a whiff of an unusual cologne. She looked. *Lionel.* She smiled at him, though he made her skin crawl.

It wasn't his looks. He was quite handsome, in fact, and a sharp dresser. But something about him had immediately bothered her when she met him the night before.

He had shown up at the card game, the only player who wasn't a regular.

Brouchard had introduced him to her as a new man now on the payroll. He was: "Back from California. Tired of big city living—good to be back home in the South, again." His accent was pure northeastern Yankee.

Lionel politely returned Linda's smile, then pulled one of the table's chairs around close to Brouchard's and sat down.

"Bring Lionel a Scotch and water."

"Please," Lionel added.

When she returned to the table with the drink, the two men were coming to their feet.

Brouchard handed her another ten and paid no attention to her beginning to count out his change. Instead, he pointed Lionel toward the door to a back office in the inn and followed him in that direction.

Linda stared after the two for a moment, then moved back toward the bar.

"Freddie, I've got to go to the back for a minute—must be something I ate. Have Lori catch my tables for a while."

"Yeah, your eyes are red, too. Maybe you haven't been getting enough sleep."

Linda hurried toward the employees' rest room, which was off the short hall at the back of the inn.

Inside the bathroom she reached for the wall switch and turned off the bare overhead bulb. It and the exhaust fan were wired together, and the light couldn't be on without the rough sound of the fan's vent blades. She needed quiet.

She leaned to the wall over the toilet and pressed her ear against the paneling.

The wall abutted the small office where Brouchard and Lionel had gone. The group of local entrepreneurs who had originally built the bar and inn hadn't wasted money on insulation between inner walls, and it was easy to hear through the thin paneling nailed to the two by fours.

"He's meeting her at the club at three," she heard Lionel say.

"You're positive she's okay?"

"Yeah, Peg's reliable. I've used her before."

Brouchard must have said something Linda didn't hear, or else made some sort of facial expression, because she then heard Lionel add, "Don't worry about it, Antonio. All she knows is she got her hands on a thousand just to shack up with him last night, and gets a thousand more for meeting him there Friday night. She'll ask him to meet her in the garage at three o'clock, and then she'll be gone—praying we'll need her services again."

Brouchard had to be speaking softly, or mostly thinking, for again she didn't hear him say anything and then Lionel was speaking once more.

"You sure you don't want me to handle it for you, it'd be a pleasure."

"No," Linda heard Brouchard say. "I have to do it, myself. It wouldn't be right any other way."

Handle it, Linda thought. *Do it myself.* They could be talking about anything from a business deal to a—a murder. Brouchard's voice had been low level, but there was something in his tone. Linda felt a tightening in her stomach.

The door suddenly swung open behind her, and she bumped her knee hard against the commode as she whirled around to face who was entering.

"What in the hell are you doing in here with the light off?" Freddie asked.

"What in the hell are you walking in on me for—told you I was going to be in here."

"If you wanted privacy you shoulda locked the damn door. Besides, I thought you were already out." He switched on the light and the fan blades filled the small room with their rough sound. "Well, if you're through, mind if I take a crap—by myself?"

Linda couldn't have responded to his remark if she had wanted to, for her throat had tightened at the sudden realization of what had just transpired.

The fan off and Freddie shouting his question, and her yelling back at him—Brouchard and Lionel would have heard every word and would be wondering now if somebody had been listening to them. She felt her hand tremble. Perspiration formed on the back of her neck.

She quickly moved out of the bathroom past the bartender and down the hall. Maybe they didn't recognize her voice. Had Freddie spoken her name? She couldn't remember. Hell, they could just ask him who had been in the bathroom. Her stomach tightened, again.

Halfway to the bar she glanced back over her shoulder to see Brouchard and Lionel emerge from the back office. They stared at her a brief moment, then Brouchard smiled and nodded. *Like he always did when he caught her eye,* she thought. He didn't know somebody had been in the bathroom, or, if he did know, didn't realize that the shouting voices he heard could have also overheard his. She felt a shiver run down her back anyway.

Lionel said, "How much more you gonna let that bitch get away with before you let me do something about her?"

Brouchard thought for a moment, then looked at Lionel and nodded.

CHAPTER

25

Clay, not only wearing his usual attire of slacks and an open-neck dress shirt, but also a sport coat to hide the pistol holster at his waist, made sure he arrived at the Broadwater Beach Hotel at precisely midnight. He drove slowly down the side of the hotel, circled behind it and back out to the exit onto Highway 90.

He paused at the exit long enough for the stoplight to turn green a second time, then pulled out onto the highway and drove west.

Several minutes later, having crossed into Gulfport without any car behind him signaling by blinking its lights, he pondered what to do next.

Another mile farther, he crossed over into the eastbound lane and drove back to the Broadwater. Circling the main building once more, he drove even slower than before. He blinked his lights twice to draw attention to his passing.

Back on 90 he was once again nearly in Gulfport before he
was sure he still wasn't being followed.

Damn, he thought, *where in the hell is he?* Or, as Clay had
earlier worried, was the informant dead and there was no
longer any reason for the man to show up? Clay guided his car
into the left lane, made a U turn at a NO U TURN crossing and
then headed back toward the hotel. Beads of perspiration were
beginning to form on his forehead.

This time he stopped his car in front of the guest cottages
directly behind the main hotel building. Leaving his parking
lights on to draw attention to his car, he stepped from it and
walked around the west side of the hotel to the large, two-tier
swimming pool next to the ground floor lounge.

He could see through the glass windows several people enjoying themselves. Off to his right a couple in their twenties was
sitting next to the pool. On its far side, a man in a business suit
laughed loudly as he waved a wad of bills in front of a woman
who returned his laughter; he had likely been to the hotel's
casino across the highway at the yacht marina.

Clay looked toward the marina. He worried for a moment
that the caller had said circle there instead of the actual hotel.
But, no, he had said the hotel. Maybe the man had meant for
him to circle the entire complex behind the hotel rather than
the main building? The drive he had entered not only led to the
throughway directly behind the hotel but also meandered for
several hundred yards through the heavily wooded area of individual cottages, motel-type units and tennis courts to the rear of
the hotel. He felt a nervous sensation at the possibility he *had*
misunderstood the instructions and that the caller might be
growing tired of waiting for him to arrive—might be preparing
to leave. Clay turned and walked hurriedly toward his car.

As he opened the driver's door, he thought he glimpsed
movement in the cab of the pickup truck parked between a pair
of the two-story cottages a hundred feet away.

It was as if somebody had been watching him, then had
ducked behind the dash when he glanced in that direction. He

shut the car door and walked slowly down the pavement toward the pickup.

He saw the movement again, a brief glimpse of somebody's head, then the cab appeared empty again.

He stopped and stood in thought for several seconds. After reaching to reassuringly pat the butt of his automatic, he walked toward the driver's side of the pickup.

It was a couple, low against the far door and embracing. The woman's eyes were closed and her hand was at the back of the man's head. Her eyes opened, locked on Clay's.

"Homer! A Peeping Tom!" The man's face twisted toward the window. Clay turned quickly away from the truck, and started back across the pavement toward his car.

The pickup's door opened. An empty beer can fell out of the cab, bounced, and rolled across the pavement.

Clay stopped and turned around.

The man, dressed in a plaid long-sleeve shirt, jeans and cowboy boots, was in his middle thirties. He had shoulder-length blond hair held in place by a sweatband around his forehead— and he was big.

The woman hopped from her side of the truck and hurried around its front. "Get him, Homer!" she shouted. "Damn pervert!"

The man started forward.

Clay reached into his hip pocket and pulled out his credentials, opened them and held them up in front of the man's face. "You have the right to remain silent. Anything you say can and will be used—"

"What's this shit?" the man exclaimed, coming to a stop. His eyes narrowed as he looked at the credentials.

The woman, a skinny, frizzy-haired blonde with a low-hanging bustline, hurried up beside the man. "What's he saying?" she asked.

Clay moved the walletlike case in front of her face. "Secret Service. You're under arrest."

She leaned forward to study the credentials. Her eyes widened. "My Lord!" she said. "He is the Secret Service."

"You're both under arrest. You have the right to—"

"Wait a damn minute," the man said, "what for?"

"You're not entitled to that information."

"We wasn't doing nuthin'."

"Maybe not. That will be for the Justice Department to decide. My only function is to arrest anyone I find in the secure area."

"The what—"

"Mister, really," the woman said, her voice now low and polite. "We really wasn't doing nuthin'."

"You entered the secure area quite knowingly, ma'am."

"No, sir—I mean we didn't know."

"Didn't know?"

"No, sir. Honest to God."

Clay glanced across his shoulder to the cottage on his right. "You telling me you didn't know about him being here?"

Both the man and the woman looked at the cottage. "No, sir," the man said, shaking his head. "Swear we didn't."

"How old are you two?"

"He's thirty-two," the woman said. "I'm going on thirty-five."

Clay shook his head. "That's bad." The man and the woman glanced at each other, then back to Clay.

"Bad?" the woman said.

Clay nodded. "Yeah, real bad." He looked toward the cottage, and back to the two. "I hate to see you all in such a mess." He shook his head, glanced back at the cottage again, and back to the couple. "Damn. I just hate it." He dropped his gaze to the pavement, thought a moment, then raised his face back to the two. "Okay, I'll take a chance. If I let you go can I have your word you won't say anything about"—he glanced to the cottage again—"him being here."

"Swear to God," the woman said.

"Okay. Get out of here fast before my supervisor comes by."

"Thank you, mister," the man said.

The woman was already on her way to the truck. She glanced back over her shoulder. "Dammit, Homer, come on—'fore his supervisor gets here."

* * *

"For you," Freddie said, holding the telephone out toward Linda.

She placed the receiver against her ear. "This is Linda."

"Caller didn't show up."

Clay's voice sounded drained.

"He'll call again," she said softly.

"I started thinking maybe he meant for me to circle back through the whole complex, not just around the main hotel. When I didn't, maybe he got tired of waiting and drove off."

"What if he did? Your reward's still there. He'll call again."

In the back office, his hand cupped over the mouthpiece of the telephone, Lionel listened intently.

"Clay," Linda said, lowering her voice and glancing across her shoulder to make sure Freddie wasn't paying any attention to what she was saying. "I heard something a while ago that scared me. Antonio and that new guy I told you about from the poker game, Lionel, were talking about somebody in New Orleans Friday night. It almost sounded like they were talking about—I don't know, something about *'handling'* it. The way they were talking, it gave me cold chills."

Clay was silent a moment. "Could be anything. But it's time you got out of there, anyway The Coast Guard saw you out at the islands. Your name will be in the morning's paper. I'm going to stay here a while longer—maybe the guy was detained for some reason. I'll meet you out at your house when you get off work. You can pick up some clothes and then we'll go back to the boatyard. You're going to stay with me from now on."

She laughed. "I don't know about that. I'm really going to have to think about it." She laughed again.

After getting Freddie's attention, and handing the telephone receiver back across the bar to him, she glanced at her watch. There was almost nobody left in the bar. She turned back to him. "If you don't mind, I'm going to check out of here. I've got some things I need to do." She would be packed and waiting when Clay arrived at her house.

Freddie nodded.

In the back room, Lionel, having replaced the telephone receiver, continued to sit a moment, thinking, then he rose to his feet and walked to the door.

He looked toward Linda. She was leaning over the bar going through her receipts. After a couple of minutes she picked up her purse, glanced inside it, then turned and walked toward the exit.

CHAPTER

26

Linda lived in a quiet neighborhood located on the south shore of Back Bay. Her house was wood siding, painted white, and contained a little over twelve hundred square feet of living area. It had gone up several thousand dollars in value since so many Northerners had begun moving to the area to take advantage of the temperate climate and the low living costs of the Mississippi coast. But she would never sell it. It was the home she had grown up in; the one she had barely managed to save from the bank through Brouchard's loan.

As she parked at the curb in front of the house, she noticed the porch light was out. The house's entrance was cast in a darkness made creepy by the tall hedges beginning at each side of the door. She would have to remember to get around to trimming them next spring.

At the front door she opened her purse, removed the house key and inserted it in the lock.

Nothing happened.

She turned the key back to the left, and again to the right.

There was still no sound of the lock releasing. *"Damn!"* She had been having trouble with it for weeks. Sometimes it had taken her several minutes of jiggling the key, turning it again and again before everything would be lined up just so, and the lock finally release. And, after releasing, sometimes it didn't want to lock again.

She finally heard the sound of the bolt retracting. She opened the door.

As she walked into the house and shut the door behind her, she left the key in the lock. Now that the key was inserted just so, she didn't want to remove it and have to fumble with it again to lock the door when she left with Clay.

She moved across the small living room/kitchen combination to the counter dividing the two areas. There she laid her purse on the counter, opened a cabinet and removed a bottle of Jack Daniel's. After fixing herself a drink, she retrieved her purse and started toward the short hall at the back of the living room.

Her room was off to the right. The bedroom directly across the hall was no different in size, but hers had a direct opening into the house's only bathroom, while sleeping in the other room meant having to walk across the hall to the bath.

She set her drink and purse on top of the chest of drawers, then walked to the double closet. She opened the doors, lifted out her suitcase and carried it to the bed.

After returning to the closet, she selected her nicest dress, a couple pair of slacks and several blouses, and placed them on the bed.

After a trip to her chest of drawers for lingerie, selecting only those bras and panties that weren't frayed, and leaving one set on top of the chest, she returned to the bed and finished packing. Finally, she removed another pair of slacks and a blouse from the closet and laid them over the back of a chair. She retrieved her drink from the chest of drawers and started toward the bathroom.

Hearing a noise from the living room/kitchen combination, she stopped.

There was no further sound.

Deciding the noise had come from the icemaker, she moved on toward the bathroom, unbuttoning her blouse as she walked.

After she undressed, she moved to stand in front of the full-length mirror attached to the back of the bathroom door.

She stared a moment, then turned sideways. She wished her breasts were a little bigger, but, overall, she looked okay.

She moved her gaze to the reflection of the white lines left by her bikini, and she shook her head. In past years she hadn't had those. But last summer she'd noticed her neighbor, old Mr. Bullard, peeking through the hedges between their houses, and she'd had to start leaving her bikini on when she lay out in the backyard. She moved on to the tub at the back of the bathroom.

After adjusting the shower spray to just the right temperature she stepped into the tub. She pulled the heavy plastic shower curtain emblazoned with jumping dolphins closed behind her.

Clay parked behind Linda's car and moved up the walk to the darkened entrance of her house. The ragged hedges leaning from each side toward the entrance made him uneasy. They didn't look like they'd been trimmed in years. The door was standing partly open. The key was still in the lock.

He pushed the door the rest of the way open, and stepped inside. A table lamp next to an easy chair in the living room and the light over the counter dividing the living room from the kitchen area were both on. Down the short hall at the back of the living room, the illumination of another light shone from an open door.

"Linda!"

He reached back to the lock for the key, had to tug on it for a moment before getting it loose, then shut the door.

"Linda!"

Still no answer.

He moved through the living room.

As he neared the hall, he heard the sound of a shower.

Inside the bedroom, he moved toward the partially closed bathroom door. He pushed it open and stuck his head inside.

Through the shower curtain he could see Linda's form, sideways to him as she stood in the tub—her back turned to the shower spray, her hands busy working the soap out of her dark hair. Steam was rising above the curtain.

He knocked on the inside of the door.

She started, then jerked the shower curtain back. "Scare me to death," she said. "I wanted to freshen up." The steam enveloped her in a misty cloud. She resembled some kind of nymph in a surrealistic painting.

She smiled at his staring and pulled the shower curtain back across her body.

He turned away from the door and moved back into the bedroom.

"Did he ever show up?" she called after him.

"No."

"He'll call again. You want a drink?"

"No, thank you."

"Anything else?"

He smiled. He would actually rather just get some sleep. He glanced at the key in his hand, and directed his voice back through the bathroom door as he walked toward the bed.

"You have many visitors when you're taking a shower?"

She turned off the water. "What was it you said?"

"Do you have many visitors when you're taking a shower?"

"Not lately."

He sat on the edge of the bed.

A yellow towel wrapped around her body, Linda appeared in the bathroom door. "Why?"

"Well, I know this isn't New York, yet I don't think I'd be leaving my front door open while I was in the shower." He held the keys up for her to see.

"Lock doesn't want to unlock or lock," she said. "The door was standing open?"

"It was."

"Warped—it does that sometimes when I don't lock it. Snake

got in once. Hole in the bottom of the counter is where I shot at it and missed. Scared it though, thing slithered right back out the door."

Tucking the towel tighter around her, she stepped from the bathroom door and started across the bedroom toward the hall. "If you don't mind I'm going to fix myself a quick drink."

"Fine."

He turned and propped his back up against the headboard, and rested his eyes.

Linda dropped the yellow towel to the floor, and quickly slipped on the bikini-like panties and push-up bra she had left on the top of the chest of drawers. She turned back toward the bed. "You sure you don't want anything? There's a couple of beers in the icebox."

He didn't answer; he was already beginning to breathe heavily.

Linda smiled and walked on into the living room/kitchen combination. The front door was standing open again, and she moved to shut it.

CHAPTER

27

In Washington, D.C., four men sat around a dining table near the back of the second floor of a three-story walkup within a few blocks of the Capitol.

Two of them, swarthy, heavy-set brothers in their fifties, both with dark thinning hair and similarly attired in hand-sewn silk suits, had said very little that night. They sat across the table from each other.

At the near end of the table was the man who had done most of the talking. In his early seventies, he was white-haired, slim, and dressed in house slippers, a pair of dark, wool slacks and a turtleneck sweater. It was his home the four were meeting in.

"Gulf Coast operation's finished," he said. "Feds know how the shipments been coming in, and they know it's Ming."

"Ming's what's bothering me now," the man sitting at the far end of the table said. "Lot more than losing the route." He was in his early sixties, had his slicked-back hair dyed coal black, wore tan slacks, and a beige silk shirt. "So what are we gonna do with him? He ain't from no Colombia or Nicaragua; he ain't got no place to go back to. And he can't stay in this country, they'll pull him in sooner or later."

The white-haired man nodded his agreement. "Good chance they will, but let's not jump to no snap decision. We got the feelings of our other importers to consider. We take him out and they might get to thinking that if they ever got busted they'd be safer with the feds than us." He stroked his stubble-covered cheek as he thought.

"Here's the way I see it," he said when he finally spoke again. "I think for right now we send one of our best people down there and have him keep an eye on everything. If Ming's picked up, we do him then, say he was gonna talk. Other importers would know we had to handle him if he started talking."

The one at the far end wasn't so sure. "What if the feds grab him so fast our man can't get to him; then he really does start running at the mouth?"

"His connection only goes to his sister. So that happens we'll take her out. That way there'll be nobody down there knowing nobody up here. The chain will lead to a gap if anybody tries to come up it, no way to trace nothing." He glanced at the brothers at each side of the table. They quickly nodded their concurrence.

The man at the end of the table shook his head. "I don't know. Guess if we can keep a finger on where his sister is at all times, it'd be okay until we make up our minds for sure about Ming."

"Want to make sure we know where she is until then," the gray-haired man said. "Let's reward her with a vacation—send her to some little island where there's not much room to get lost." He glanced at the brothers again. "So we're all agreed?"

The two nodded their heads simultaneously. The man at the end of the table did, too.

"It's settled, then. Now let the women back in here." He looked back to the man at the end of the table. "What's the filly with the big ass's name?"

"Patty."

"You sure she's clean?"

The man at the end of the table smiled and shook his head in amusement. "Come on, Uncle Jack. I've been popping her, myself—you know I'm gonna make her get a clean bill of health before I'm popping her."

"You ready?" Clay heard Linda say. He opened his eyes. She had her hair pulled back and braided into a thick tail. She was dressed in white slacks and a light blue blouse, and held her suitcase in one hand while she clutched a paper bag filled with toiletries to her chest with the other. Her purse was tucked under her arm.

He had been asleep. He came up off the bed and reached for the suitcase.

Linda had a big smile on her face. "Promise I'll leave you alone when we get to the boat," she said. "You need to get some rest—me, too."

Clay let Linda drive his Taurus from her house, and he fell asleep again, awakening as she guided the car off the highway and into the boatyard. She stopped at the walkway leading to the *Cassandra*.

Once on the boat he carried her suitcase and paper bag to the small bow cabin where he laid them on the port bunk.

He nodded toward the only hanging locker in the cabin. "You can put your things in there. My stuff, what's not dirty, is in that drawer. There's not much; you can make room for what you need. There's an empty drawer under the sink in the head if you need more space."

"I can leave most of my things in my suitcase—put it under the bed."

CHAPTER

28

The telephone began ringing. Each time it rang, there would be a click and the answering machine would begin its message. When it was time for the caller to speak, all that could be heard was the dial tone. Moments later the telephone would ring again.

Clay, next to Linda on the starboard bunk in the crew's quarters, opened his eyes. He heard the telephone ring, and the silence as the answering machine took over. He pushed back the covers and slipped from the bed. As he walked to the salon he heard the sound of a dial tone.

There were no messages on the machine.

The telephone rang again. His reward message started playing. He lifted the receiver and placed it against his ear.

"Hello."

"Clay Rodgers?"

"Go ahead."

"I'm calling about the reward—the drug smuggling."

The voice wasn't that of the man he was supposed to have met at the Broadwater. "I'm listening."

The caller quickly explained where he wanted to meet—describing a secluded wooded area five miles north of Biloxi. Then he hung up. He had exhibited a noticeable Vietnamese accent; Clay was positive of that. He replaced the receiver.

Linda, attired in one of his T-shirts that hung midway down her thighs, came up the stairs into the salon. "Who was it?"

"About the drug smuggling. It wasn't the man I was supposed to have met."

"Is he wanting to meet with you?"

He nodded.

"Clay, can I go?"

He shook his head. "You shouldn't have gone to Carson like you did, shouldn't have been hiding in a bathroom eavesdropping, either. I have enough to worry about without you playing detective."

"What about your playing detective?" she asked. "Somebody could be mad about losing their canisters. You don't know who made that call."

"I know. I'll be careful. But I can take care of myself a lot better if I don't have to be worrying about taking care of you, too."

He walked to her and hugged her. "I'll show you how to set the alarm. Then you keep that big old revolver of yours close at hand."

"God," she said. "You trying to scare me to death before you leave?"

More than an hour had passed by the time Clay had made a stop at a local motel and driven to the heavily wooded area north of Biloxi. The final mile was a long gravel road.

He sat a moment after parking his car next to the handmade gate he had been told to look for.

"We there?" Angel Morales asked from the floorboard of the backseat.

"Yeah, I think."

"See anything?"

"A lot of pine trees. There's a logging road on the other side of the gate—like the guy said."

"Are the trees close enough for me to get into them without being seen?"

Clay looked off to his left. "Go out my side. The fence is about ten feet, trees right against its other side."

"You know you don't have to do this. Anybody wanting the reward bad enough could meet you at a spot of your choosing. What Linda said was right—this might not even be somebody interested in the reward. You could be making it easy for them."

"Could be the break I'm looking for, too."

"Well then, old buddy," Angel Morales added, "about all I can promise you is if I hear a big bang, they won't get out this way."

"Yeah, thanks."

"That was meant to remind you to be careful."

Clay slid between the strands of barbed wire in the gate and followed the muddy logging road into the thick stand of pines.

A hundred feet down the road, he pulled his automatic from its holster. He nervously checked the clip, though he knew it was full. He heard a twig snap. He raised his head.

Fifty feet ahead of him two shadowy figures moved from the trees out into the middle of the road. They started slowly toward him.

Twenty feet from him, their faces became clear. It was the Vietnamese woman and her son. Chung *had* talked to her of what he did. He lowered his automatic, but didn't holster it.

The old woman stopped directly in front of him. "I was a maid on Soung Ming's boat," she said. "That is where my son Chung first met Ming, and that is what I have to bear."

She glanced toward her son. "This is Hong. The reward will be for him to continue his education. Chung was a good son, too, but easily distracted toward easier ways to make money than through an education. I explained to him what kind of fate he was fashioning for himself, but he thought my words only those of a scared old woman.

"Ming is an evil man, but smart. It is commonly spoken of in our community what he does, but there is no proof. Except, I believe, somewhere on the *Victory.*"

"What kind of proof?"

"Every month his sister arrives from New York. She never stays more than one day, and while she is present no one is allowed in the lower lounge. She is an accountant, yet never brings anything with her, and never leaves with anything."

"An accountant—you think she keeps up with the drug profits?"

"Everyone answers to someone, Mr. Rodgers. Ming has to keep his superiors informed."

That was the same thing Linda had told him Ben Carson had said—that whoever was running the operation on this end would have to take orders from the big boys up north. That was one of the reasons Carson was so sure Brouchard wasn't involved in the smuggling; said he wasn't the type to take orders from anyone.

The old woman had spoken again. He hadn't caught what she said. "I'm sorry, what did you—"

"I asked if you found records, would that be enough for the reward?"

He nodded. "Yes. But you never saw a set of books?"

"I cleaned the lower lounge every day except when Ming's sister was visiting. If there are books, as I believe there must be, they are not in the lower lounge or above it."

A set of books would be better than a cache of drugs. Records would detail the scope of the ring. "What's below the lounge?"

"Three cabins, the crew's quarters and the engine room."

He voiced his ever-present thought. "Mrs. Vu, my brother worked for Ming, didn't he?"

"I'm not aware he did. But there are many who work for Ming other than those who man his boats. That is why I elected to meet you here rather than speak with you at my home where eyes might have been watching."

"And Robert's murder—you don't know anything about that, either?"

"Nothing."

Halfway back to his car, Clay heard the bushes rustle off to his right. Angel Morales stepped from the pines.

"Welcome back to the world of the living. Glad your trip wasn't permanent. How did it go?"

"It was Vu's mother and brother. She thinks Mlng has a set of books hidden on his trawler."

"He's a gone sucker if he does. Wait until Becker hears about this—he'll wet his pants."

CHAPTER

29

Something bumped!

Linda, lying on the starboard bunk in the bow cabin, opened her eyes, rolled them up to stare past her forehead at the closed cabin door. After a few seconds she moved her gaze back to the overhead, and looked through the Plexiglas hatch. There was a wide cloud moving across the face of the moon. The sky darkened until there was only a faint glimmer of light. Then that was gone, too. *That's what Mrs. Bushbee had seen—the light fading.* Linda wished she hadn't thought of that.

It had been about a year ago. The old widow woman had returned to her house after eating dinner with her daughter and son-in-law. She had watched the ten o'clock news, changed into her nightclothes, creamed her face and gone to her bedroom.

Once in bed, she had lain propped up on her pillow against the headboard as she read her Bible. Then she had placed the Bible back in the drawer of her nightstand and reached for the light. The sliding doors to her closet were only a few feet from her bed. As she turned off the light the widow recalled the room not becoming suddenly dark, but instead remembering a brief instant when the light seemed to fade. In that fading light she had glimpsed a man with a knife raised over his head stepping from the closet.

She had survived, but only after several hours of major surgery. The man, an escaped mental patient from the John H. Douglas State Mental Hospital in Davis County, was apprehended two days after the attack. He had still been in the house, hidden in a big cardboard box in the attic.

Linda shuddered and reached to turn on the light mounted against the bulkhead above her head, then swung her feet to the floor and sat on the edge of the bed. She was wearing one of Clay's large T-shirts over her panties.

Where, she wondered, *had the killer been hiding when Robert and the girl came aboard?*

She reached for her revolver, stood and opened the door. The remainder of the boat was well lit by a fixture over the dinette table in the galley and by one of the brass end table lamps in the salon.

She stepped from the crew's quarters and wandered slowly through the galley up into the salon, where she stopped and looked out the pier-side windows.

The cloud had cleared the face of the moon. The moonlight now bathed the walkway in a soft, dim glow. Beyond the pier the boatyard was dark and appeared forbidding. Just past the boatyard an occasional car moved up and down Highway 90.

She turned away from the windows and looked toward the door leading down into the master stateroom—where Robert had been murdered. She had never seen the door open. She walked toward it.

She hesitated a moment with her hand on the doorknob, took a deep breath and slowly opened the door.

The cabin was dark, but just inside the door there was a light switch, and she flicked it on.

The sheets had been stripped from the mattress on the

queen-size bed. She saw the curved line of small black dots on the light blue wallpaper above the headboard. There was a stale odor in the room, and the stench of something else. She moved down the two steps.

Opening the door just beyond the foot of the bed, she looked into the small head.

Towels and washcloths hung on the rack above the toilet. The curtain was pulled back displaying the undersized porcelain tub. She closed the door.

Looking back between the dressing table and that side of the bed, she saw the round black stain on the floor. She felt a disturbing sensation sweep over her. She started for the steps up out of the stateroom.

Reaching them, she hesitated a moment to glance at the hanging locker. It was not quite the size of a house closet, being both a few inches shorter and narrower, but big enough to hide a man.

Raising the revolver, she slowly opened the locker. It contained some ladies' casual outfits and a couple of men's pants.

After moving back into the salon, she looked at the cabinets covering the aft bulkhead. They were each too small for anyone to hide inside. Nevertheless, she walked to them and opened one. It was mostly full of books.

She noticed a thick dictionary. She sat cross-legged on the carpet, laid her pistol beside her and reached for the book, *The Reader's Digest Great Encyclopedic Dictionary.* She opened it in her lap.

Clay had told her his father had named the *Cassandra* after a legendary Trojan princess. She wondered if he had in fact once known a girl by that name. She knew a banker in Moss Point who had named his bass boat after a prostitute.

It was listed. Cassandra *was* a princess, the daughter of Priam. Linda looked at the last line of the definition: "Anyone who utters unheeded prophecies of disaster."

Unheeded prophecies of disaster, she said to herself. The *Cassandra,* an unheeded prophecy of disaster? She thought back to the marijuana leaves Clay said he had found in the cabinets.

Was it environment or heredity? She wondered. Clay, mature and settled ever since she had known him, had ended up working to fight crime and terrorists and the bad things in the world. Robert, a great person to be around, loving and happy, but also irresponsible, had eventually become involved in drug trafficking. What was the difference?

Maybe the *Cassandra* was the difference, at least in one way. Maybe the yacht indeed had been a prophecy of disaster for Robert. She had once seen a yacht named *Daddy's Toy*. She had heard the old saying that the only difference in men and boys was the price of their toys. But Robert hadn't been a man when he had first been given free use of the *Cassandra*. He had taken her out on it when he was only fifteen. He'd never had to work, had been able to do much as he wished since he was eleven; his mother dead and his father working long hours at the boatyard. He had never paid any attention to what Donna said.

Clay, on the other hand, by circumstance forced to work hard ever since he was in high school, had been left no choice but to be responsible. Who had, when all was said and done, really had the best childhood? Simple, she proclaimed silently, the childhood that had shaped a man with character.

Linda smiled. The first time Clay ever mentioned how rough his early years had been, she was going to explain to him how really lucky he'd been. She should have been a psychiatrist, she thought. Then she thought of the definition again. *Prophecy of disaster—the* Cassandra. She glanced over both shoulders, then placed the dictionary back in the cabinet and came to her feet.

As she shut the door she noticed the roses, wilted brown and drooping, in the yellow vase on top of the cabinet. After picking up her pistol, she removed the dead flowers and carried them to the galley, disposing of them in a wastebasket under the sink. Then she looked around her. Was there anyplace else she needed to check before she went back to bed?

There was no room to hide in the small hanging locker in the crew's quarters. Looking back to her left, her gaze fell on the small, cabinetlike double doors behind the two steps leading up into the salon; the doors marking the entrance to the engine compartment.·

She walked to the steps, removable to allow access into the compartment. Grasping the lightweight metal frame the steps were built into, she lifted it, detaching it from the brass holding brackets bolted to the bulkhead.

She moved the frame to the side, knelt, laid her pistol on the carpet and opened the doors.

The lamp fixture over the dinette table cast some illumination into the compartment. But the light was no more than enough to display the very beginning of the wooden walking platform over the bilge and show the general shapes of the two big diesel motors sitting one to each side. The back three quarters of the compartment was in total darkness.

She leaned forward, felt inside the opening to its left. She couldn't find a light switch. She felt to the opposite side of the opening. There was nothing there, either.

She leaned farther forward, sticking her head inside the compartment.

Even after waiting several seconds for her eyes to adjust to the darkness, the back of the compartment was still cast in blackness. She stood. Where did she remember seeing a flashlight? The cabinet to the right of the sink.

Moving to it she found the flashlight and lifted it out, then went back to the engine compartment opening, where she knelt and shined the light inside.

The engines glistened a bright reflection against the white fiberglass bulkheads to each side. The air conditioner compressors, even the metal piping and brass seacocks, reflected the light. The small amount of water under the spaced one-by-fives of the wooden walking platform gave off an oily shine. The only place she couldn't see were the spaces at the rear corners of the compartment, the areas between the end of the engines and the far bulkhead.

Sitting down on the floor, she grasped a bracket at the top

corner of the opening, slid her legs inside the compartment then slowly lowered her feet until they touched wood.

She walked down the platform, slowing as she neared the rear of the compartment.

Shining the light first behind the port engine and then behind the starboard engine, she saw a pair of spare batteries bolted securely in place behind one, and a toolbox behind the other.

She marveled at how clean and neat everything was. She thought back to the untrimmed shrubbery at the entrance to her house, and was embarrassed that Clay had seen it.

She turned and started back to the other end of the compartment.

She heard a swallowing sound, and froze in her tracks. It was behind her.

For a terrible instance she couldn't make herself turn around.

She heard it again and whirled in its direction. She saw nothing. She quickly shined the flashlight to the other side of the compartment. Nothing.

Wide-eyed, playing the flashlight from side to side, she began backing toward the entrance.

Back to her left an air conditioner compressor kicked on, startling her.

Outside the *Cassandra* a building swell swept into the starboard side of the hull, gently tipping the yacht to port.

Inside the engine compartment, the noise sounded again—to her left, low. She shined the light on the bilge pump as it sucked air, then cut off.

Her muscles seemed to sag with her relief. She took a deep breath and released it audibly, then turned toward the opening back into the galley. She only then realized how hard her heart was pumping. She had heard of people dying of fright, and now she knew how that could happen. She had thought she was going to pass out.

As she neared the opening her light shined on a small box at the top of the entranceway. It was the light switch.

She switched it on and the compartment was suddenly bright

with the illumination of two overhead lights covered with heavy metal grids.

She shook her head at her ignorance. Her heartbeat was slowly returning to normal.

She first stuck her arms through the opening. Then she raised her left knee to the lip of the galley floor. Holding tight to the sides of the entrance, she pulled herself from the compartment.

A heavy weight coming down on her back slammed her face hard into the galley's carpeted floor.

A gloved hand grabbed her pistol and jerked it from her grasp.

She looked wildly back over her shoulder into the masked face. She was so terrified she couldn't scream.

CHAPTER

30

The eastern horizon was beginning to glow red as Clay parked at the edge of the pier, opened his car door and stepped from the Taurus. He looked at the dark clouds again gathering overhead.

Jesus, he thought, would the rains ever stop, get over with and be gone? Would what he was doing ever get over with? If it came down to it would he be able to stop and go on back to Washington with his brother's killer still unknown?

Crossing the gangway he noticed that the salon door was cracked open. Then he saw where a piece of wood was broken off the door next to the latch.

A cold chill swept his back.

He jerked his pistol from the waist holster, slid the door the rest of the way open, and stepped quickly into the salon.

Linda stared at him from the couch. Her revolver was tightly clasped in both her hands and pointed toward him. Her hair was disheveled and there was blood caked on one side of her mouth. She still wore his T-shirt, but now it was grimy, stretched at the neck and ripped up one side.

She lowered the revolver. Her lip trembled, and her eyes filled with tears. "Somebody—somebody . . ." Her voice broke and she shook her head.

His stomach twisting, he hurried to the couch. "What?" He sat beside her and clasped her forearms.

She shook her head again. "Somebody—he said it was just for fun. If I didn't leave Biloxi, it wouldn't be—wouldn't be for fun the next time." A tear ran down her cheek. He wanted to cuss and yell out his anger, but he only tightened his jaw.

He gently removed the revolver from her hands and placed it on the end table. He saw the bruise on her neck and his teeth pressed together harder. *Some son-of-a-bitch was going to pay.*

He put his arms around her and pulled her to him. She buried her face against his shoulder. Her silent tears began to dampen his shirt.

"He didn't—I—he didn't rape me." He closed his eyes in his relief for her. "But he—his hands, his fingers . . ."

He held her tighter. "Do you know who . . ."

She shook her head against his shoulder. "He had on a ski mask. His voice was like—like he was speaking through something. He—he had a knife." She shook her head again. "I didn't know what he—I thought he was going to kill me. I . . ."

Her body convulsed with a choking sob. He stared past her to the far bulkhead. *Son-of-a-bitch was going to pay.*

A moment later he felt her move her face again, could tell she was trying to quit crying.

"There was this cologne," she said.

Less than fifteen minutes after Clay telephoned, Becker's dark form stepped through the passageway into the *Cassandra*'s salon. "It damn sure wasn't any of Ming's people," he exclaimed, his voice even huskier than normal, his words coming fast. "They would've either stayed as far away from here as possible, or they'd have killed her. And if they had, they'd have waited for you to come back, too, Clay. I'd say the same thing holds true for this Brouchard you talked about. So maybe he found out she was working with you—so what? What did he have to gain by having her worked over? If he is into something and thought she'd found out about it, he'd have had her killed, not slapped around and felt up. Besides, you said yourself she was only guessing it was the guy who worked for him—based on smelling a cologne. I don't want you going off half-cocked. Where is she?"

"In the bow cabin."

"Asleep?"

"She can't. I told her to try and relax."

"You want us to get something to help her sleep?"

"She doesn't want to go to sleep—she's afraid to. She'll calm down after a while. But I promised her she wouldn't be alone."

"Angel will stay with her."

"Let me tell her. I'll be right back."

"We'll be waiting at the cars for you."

When Clay and the DEA agents came down the pier, the lookout on the bow of the *Victory* turned and ran through a forward passageway into the trawler's superstructure.

A sullen looking, broad-shouldered man in deck shoes, jeans and a tight T-shirt met them as they came up the gangway.

Becker flashed the search warrant and shouldered the man aside. One agent moved toward the bow and a second the stern. Becker, the other five agents and Clay moved inside the trawler.

Though one of the *Victory*'s crewmen ran ahead of them into the lower salon and announced their presence in a loud voice, Ming was still sitting in his big chair at the aft end of the cabin when the boarding party came through the door. He didn't move, only raised his face and stared.

Like an overstuffed turtle, was Clay's first thought. Wearing an open shirt, his big rounded belly protruding, his knee-length shorts split at the ends to give his massive legs room, Ming on the street would be more pointed at than feared. Yet he was worse than any mass murderer, the poison he traded in not only destroying many of those who used it, but countless innocents falling victim to the muggers and murderers attempting to obtain the money they needed to sustain their habit.

Clay moved his gaze to the bulkheads covered with the garish imitation gold leaf. Every few feet the leaf was overlaid with brightly painted Vietnamese figures. The furniture in the lounge was expensive, but much of it was mismatched, and all of it in loud colors more suited to the home of a pimp than a trawler's salon. There was a faint smell he couldn't quite fathom —maybe some kind of incense.

Becker, through speaking with the other agents, gestured with his hand toward the aft entrance to the master stateroom. Then he nodded his head toward the passageway leading forward and down into the bowels of the trawler. An agent sped in each direction.

Without further direction, the remaining agents and Becker began searching the salon—opening lockers, tapping on bulkheads for hidden compartments and carefully checking each piece of furniture.

Clay looked again to Ming, noticed the tightness of the man's face and the sweat on his upper lip.

The Vietnamese wasn't just resigned to the intrusion and waiting for it to be over; he was noticeably scared. *Maybe, please God,* Clay thought, *there were books to be found.*

In a few minutes, an agent who had moved lower into the trawler came back up, escorting three crewmen and a slim, young Vietnamese woman into the salon. Becker nodded toward the passageway leading out to the deck, and the agent took the four in that direction.

Twenty minutes later, the agents had finished searching the salon thoroughly except for the floor. They began to pull back the carpet, rolling it aft.

As they progressed, they lifted up pieces of furniture and set them back down, until they reached the big easy chair where Ming sat.

He didn't move, nor did he raise his face to the agents standing in front of him. If it hadn't been such a childish thought, Clay would've bet there was a trap door in the flooring under the chair.

"Excuse me," one of the agents said in a cold voice. Ming's head raised. Using his hands against the arms of the chair to help move his great bulk, he slowly rose to his feet and stepped out of the way.

The chair itself was quickly searched, and moved. The agents pulled the rug back.

There was nothing underneath except for the teak flooring.

One agent remained in the salon with Ming while Becker and the others moved forward down the passageway lower into the trawler. The Vietnamese still hadn't spoken, and no one had said anything else to him. He slowly sat back down in his chair, glanced at Clay, then quietly dropped his gaze to the floor.

After an hour of further searching, Clay's hopes began to diminish. Two of the agents came out of one of the cabins and reported to Becker, shaking their heads.

Becker walked to Clay. "We'll wait on the drug dogs, but that's only routine. I didn't really expect to find any contraband. But the books—after what you were told, I was hoping we'd find them. All we have left is the engine room."

Clay nodded. As Becker and the other agents moved toward the engine compartment, he walked to the passageway to the crew's quarters and stepped inside the cabin.

The agents hadn't been dainty. Mattresses lay on the floor. Every locker was open, their contents spilled on the cabin floor. The lone picture in the quarters had been taken down and left lying on a bunk.

Twenty feet from the last cabin was the entrance to the engine compartment. Clay moved to it, meeting the agents as they came out of the passageway. Becker shook his head.

Stepping through the doorway, Clay moved down the steps to the wooden platform over the bilge.

The compartment was the least likely place for anything to be hidden, the engines, compressors, generators and other machin-

ery, along with the pipes, wiring and conduit running from
them, all in plain view. There was a faint odor and it took him a
moment to realize it was the smell of urine. He looked down at
the water under the walking platform.

Someone servicing the engines had been too lazy to walk fifty
feet to the nearest head and had used the bilge as a latrine; not
the first time that had happened on board a ship and not the
last time, but still amazing how crude some men could be.
When as a youth working at the boatyard for his father, he had
once helped clean literally dozens of cigar butts from the bilge
of a four-hundred-thousand-dollar yacht they were refurbishing.
His father had remarked that it would serve the owner right if
his bilge pumps someday became clogged with the butts and the
yacht sank.

Then the trawler rolled slightly from the wake of a boat entering or leaving the marina at too great a speed. The water in
the bilge sloshed, the odor of urine seeming to grow stronger
with the movement. Clay shook his head, glanced a last time at
the welded steel plates of the hull, then turned and walked back
to the steps, climbing up them out of the compartment.

After moving back to the trawler's main deck, he walked to
the starboard rail and looked out across the marina.

Becker walked up to the rail, his dark face tight with his
irritation. "Struck out, didn't we?" he said.

Clay nodded. "How long until the dogs get here?"

Becker glanced at his watch. "Already should have. I don't
look for them to find anything."

Clay nodded again and turned to lean back against the rail.
He thought of the detective in Indianapolis. *Was there something
they were overlooking?* He looked around the deck.

The one mooring line that could be seen was coiled perfectly.
The small amount of brightwork visible was polished. There was
no evidence of rust anywhere, though in a marine environment
keeping steel plates from showing evidence of rust was almost
impossible. The captain was a tough taskmaster—had developed a disciplined crew. *But not so disciplined that they hadn't
used the bilge for a latrine.*

Clay's brow wrinkled with his thought: A boat where the deck was so clean you could eat on it, but where you wouldn't even want to touch anything in the bilge? Touch anything— You wouldn't want to— Clay turned back to Becker.

"Richard, I've got an idea. Only a wild guess, but it won't take but a little while to check out."

"I could use a good idea," Becker said.

"If we can find a screwdriver and a set of wrenches . . ."

Reentering the engine compartment, Clay looked for the bilge pumps; saw two.

An agent hurried down the steps to Becker and handed him two screwdrivers and a set of wrenches found in a locker in the crew's quarters. Becker walked to Clay and handed the tools to him.

Clay knelt next to the nearest pump, stared at the oil slicked water, the foul odor drifting up from it. He wished he had a pair of gloves. Then he moved his hands to the side of the platform, and, using a wrench, began loosening the pump.

Finished, he lowered the pump into the dark water. Nothing happened.

He glanced over his shoulder to Becker who had moved back to the end of the platform. "It's not turned on. Its control will be in the main circuit panel at the steering station."

Becker turned and climbed up the steps out of the compartment.

Clay moved down the walkway to the next pump, knelt and began loosening the bracket that held that pump so high.

After the pumps were switched on, they rapidly began emptying the bilge of its excess water.

In fifteen minutes the intake valves were sucking air, the last couple inches of water in the bilge unable to be drained. But it was enough. Clay smiled as Becker knelt beside him.

Near the very bottom of the hull, grit was cracked in a thin slit outlining where a lid to a false section in the steel plates didn't fit quite perfectly against the plate abutting it. There was no sign of a latch or handle, yet it was obvious the false plate covered a hidden compartment.

Becker rose to his feet and looked over his shoulder to the agent standing in the doorway at the head of the steps. "Get some crowbars down here," he said. "If that doesn't work we'll get some damn acetylene torches."

Ming and his crew were handcuffed while the false plate was being pried back, and officially put under arrest after it was.

The books were there, as well as dozens of plastic bags stuffed with currency of all denominations—hundreds of thousands of dollars.

CHAPTER

31

"Ming's scared to death," Chief Langston said as he and Clay stood in the small darkened room, looking through a two-way mirror into the adjoining interrogation room. "His ass is drawn so tight that you couldn't drive a railroad spike up it with a sledgehammer. You should have seen him earlier when he made his decision to cooperate—his knees got so weak he started to collapse."

Orange coveralls straining to contain his great bulk, the big Vietnamese sat in a cushioned wooden chair, his arms resting on the chair's padded armrests. A soft, black cuff encircled his right bicep, recording fluctuations in his blood pressure. Wires ran from small metal electrodes attached to the first and third fingers of his left hand. Like the tube from the blood pressure cuff, the wires also ran to the polygraph instrument, recording his galvanic skin response. Bands around his upper and lower chest recorded changes in his breathing rate and lung expansion and contraction.

The examiner, a slim middle-aged, sandy-haired man with a narrow, pleasant face, sat at a desk next to the polygraph instrument. He wore spectacles and was dressed casually in khaki slacks and an open-neck sport shirt. He had already covered the preliminary questions, asking Soung Ming to state his name, age, place of birth and current residence. Then he had gone on to the main body of the examination, the questions he was now asking. A set of pens on the polygraph instrument was busy recording Ming's responses on a chart.

"You could almost feel sorry for him if you didn't know what he represents," Langston continued. "After his captain turned on him, told us about him ordering the murder of the Vietnamese at the Gulf City jail, think of the choices he faced. Adding the murder count on top of us having the goods on him regarding the drug running, he could refuse to cooperate and get the death penalty or cooperate and face the prospect of his bosses in New York putting out a contract on him. I'm glad it was him and not me faced with a decision like that."

Clay looked at the beads of sweat glistening on the Vietnamese's forehead. His chest was expanding and contracting noticeably.

Not knowing how efficient the insulation was between the two rooms, Clay leaned close to Langston and spoke in a low voice. "How can the examiner differentiate between the fear and a response brought on by deception?"

"You don't have to whisper," Langston said. "They can't hear you in there, short of your screaming something out. A good examiner won't miss a beat. And Dick Carruthers there is as good as they come. It doesn't make any difference to him whether the subject's totally relaxed or damn near panicked. In simplest terms, if the subject is about to pee in his pants when the examination starts, he still draws up tighter when he lies. You can't use those machines in court without both sides stipulating to it because you have some examiners don't know what they're doing. Yet, when you hand me the conclusions of a polygraph administered by a top-notch examiner, I have as much faith in the conclusions as I do the accuracy of a fingerprint."

Inside the interrogation room, the examiner glanced toward the mirror. He cupped his hand over his mouth as if to stifle a yawn.

"He's giving us the signal he's ready to get into the questions you wanted answered," Langston said. "Most of them were what he'd already asked this morning after Ming first decided to cooperate, but Carruthers's going to ask them again for your benefit."

Langston reached to flick a switch next to a speaker recessed into the wall next to the mirror. Carruthers's voice was clear.

"Did you kill Robert Rodgers?"

Clay felt his muscles tense, though he had already been told how the fat Vietnamese had answered the same question earlier.

"No," Ming answered.

"Did you hire anyone to murder Robert Rodgers?"

"No."

"Did you have anything to do with the murder of Robert Rodgers."

"No."

"Do you know who murdered Mr. Robert Rodgers?"

"No."

The examiner glanced at the two-way mirror as he paused in his questioning.

Langston turned his head toward Clay. "There's been a little waver shown up on the instrument with the response Ming just gave," the chief said. "Doesn't necessarily indicate deception. I told Carruthers to touch his hand to the side of his head if the instrument should register a clear sign of Ming's lying. If it indicated possible deception but he wasn't sure it was, he was to glance this way. He'll follow up on the question, now."

Clay caught himself leaning closer to the two-way mirror.

"Mr. Ming," the examiner said. "You answered no, that you don't know who might have killed Mr. Rodgers, is that right?"

"I don't know."

"Have you thought about who might have committed the murder?"

"Yeah."

"When you thought about it, who passed through your mind?"

"I heard the cops—police—thought it might have been some-one on the boat to steal something."

"Then, Mr. Ming, other than the possibility the police have suggested—that Mr. Rodgers and the young woman came upon someone looting the *Cassandra*—you don't have any idea who killed Mr. Rodgers?"

"No."

The examiner nodded.

Langston turned toward Clay again. "When Carruthers origi-nally asked Ming if he knew who murdered your brother and he said no, he was telling the truth. Yet he had heard it might have been a burglar and that passed through his mind. The instru-ment registered his doubt, his hesitation. Carruthers giving the nod you saw was a signal to us that the response has been cleared up now. There was no deception."

So now Clay had heard it for himself—somebody other than the drug traffickers. He again thought of Brouchard. But why him, if he wasn't connected to the drug ring?

"Did Robert Rodgers work for you?" the examiner asked.

"Yeah."

"He ferried drugs to shore for you?"

"That night, he was going to."

"He did other things for you?"

"No . . . Well he used his boat on the radar screen, once."

"But he mostly ferried for you?"

"Two times before."

"You said this morning that he started working for you during the holidays. Is that correct?"

"Yeah."

"Did he come and ask for a job?"

"No. He was talking big on the docks. Was saying what he would do if paid enough."

"You then offered him a chance to make a delivery?"

"Yeah."

"To transport some drugs?"

"Marijuana."

"To Florida, right?"

"Yeah."

"You said it was just a small amount. The trip was meant to see if he really would make a delivery."

Ming nodded.

"Please answer the question," the examiner said.

"Yeah. To see if he would."

"You said he made one more land delivery."

"Yeah. A locked satchel. He was told it was cocaine."

"It wasn't?"

"We wanted to be sure of him."

"And after that you let him make his first pickup. You said this morning it was of a load that had been jettisoned."

"Yeah."

"The question before—when you answered you said *we* wanted to be sure of him. Was he working for you or for you and someone else?"

"For me."

"You personally?"

"He dealt with me only through one of my men."

"Through Chung Vu, the Vietnamese killed at the jail?"

Ming hesitated a moment then nodded.

"Please answer the question."

Ming nodded again, then said, "Yeah, through Vu."

"Were you having any trouble with your territory?" the examiner asked.

"Trouble?"

"Is there any chance the murder could have been committed by other drug runners?"

The same thought had also passed through Clay's mind.

"No. Territory was ours, alone. It was controlled and protected."

The examiner looked at his sheet of questions. "Do you know Mr. Antonio Brouchard?"

Clay again felt his muscles tightening.

"Yeah," Ming answered.

"Have you worked for him?"

"No."

"Has he worked for you?"

"No."

"Have you two worked together in any way?"

"No."

"Did Mr. Brouchard kill Robert Rodgers?"

Clay again leaned closer to the glass.

"I—I don't know."

"Did anyone who worked for Mr. Brouchard kill Mr. Robert Rodgers."

"I don't know."

"Do you have any personal knowledge as to Mr. Antonio Brouchard being involved in any way with Mr. Rodgers's death?"

"No."

"Do you have any reason to suspect Mr. Brouchard might be involved in the murder?"

"No."

Clay's muscles sagged with a mixture of relief and disappointment. Neither Ming nor any of his people had murdered Robert. Brouchard couldn't be involved in the drug trafficking without Ming's knowledge. There was no dispute with a rival gang of traffickers. What was there? Who? Why? *Would the truth ever be known?*

When Clay and Langston stepped from the viewing room, the chief was the first to speak.

"From the polygraph we administered earlier, we know the ring's real bosses are in New York. While Ming doesn't personally know any of their names, his sister does. We have an AP bulletin out on her now. If she's half as cooperative as Ming's being, we'll have it made." He paused a moment. "You know there's something going through Ming's mind more than just the trafficking and murder charges—I mean that has him so scared of us. Maybe it's some kind of flashback from when he was in Vietnam—what he saw there during the war. When he was being booked, he kept asking the jailer what we were going to do to him. You know, like we were going to torture him. I've placed a special suicide watch on him. Nothing's going to happen here like it did in Gulf City—guarantee that."

A young, medium-built police officer with light brown hair came down the hall to stop in front of Langston.

"Got an attorney asking to speak with Ming," the officer said.

"Who is he?" Langston asked.

"Never seen him before."

"Send him to my office. I'm going to try and find out who sent him."

A small smile appeared on the officer's face. "Chief, he isn't—"

Langston interrupted by nodding his head several times. "I know," he said. "He isn't going to tell me diddly squat. But I want to see him in my office, anyway; look him in the eye." The chief looked back at Clay. "He's going to be out of New Orleans—a mob attorney hired by those thugs out of New York. That's an even bet without my ever talking to him." He faced back to the officer.

"I'm going to have to let him see Ming. Before he goes in I want him to have proved to you he's a lawyer—not just take his word for it. I mean proof. And search him from head to toe. He's going to bitch, but tell him that's the only way he's going to get in to see Ming."

The officer nodded, and moved back down the hall.

Langston looked after the man for a moment, then turned toward Clay. "Becker told me you think somebody working for Mr. Brouchard is the one who roughed up Ms. Donetti."

"Lionel."

"Clay, don't want you going off half-cocked."

"That's what Becker said—I'm not. But when I know for

sure . . ." He finished the rest silently—the bastard's going to pay.

"How's Ms. Donetti doing?"

"She's going to be okay."

"Good."

"Chief, do you have any kind of identification on the body yet?"

"We've had a composite drawn up. At least the best the artist could do; her face was eaten up something bad by the fish. Composite's at the printer's now. I'll send a copy over to the boat when we get it back."

"Thank you. I'd like to see it. It's all we have left, isn't it? But what's it going to tell us? The name of Robert's girlfriend— what will that add?"

"Nobody's reported her missing yet. That's strange."

When the telephone rang Linda reached to answer it from the salon couch. Angel Morales sat in one of the easy chairs across from her.

"Hello. Is Clay there?" It was a woman's voice, sweet and syrupy.

"No, he isn't," Linda said.

"Well, darlin', could you tell me where I could find him?"

The woman was using the kind of accent Linda couldn't stomach—a put-on Southern accent with long drawn-out words. The woman must have strung together four or five *n*'s in her *find,* had even somehow managed to draw out the word *him.*

It was an accent that could only be found in the movies or, occasionally, spoken at a local society party by some aging matron who *thought* her great-granddaddy had spoken like that.

As Linda thought instead of answered, the woman spoke again.

"Darlin', did you hear what I was askin' you? Who am I speakin' with, anyhow?"

Linda smiled, and answered back with the same fake voice. "Why, darlin', this is Linda, and who might I be speakin' with?"

Angel Morales raised his eyes.

"I'm Jo Anne Wilkins. I'm sure you've heard the name. My granddaddy served ten years in the state senate."

Well haven't we got a lot in common, Linda thought, *my granddaddy served six years in Parchman.*

The syrupy voice came back. "You said Linda, darlin'?"

"No, I said Linda Donetti—the Biloxi Donettis. You might have heard of my mother. She was in the fish business for quite a while."

"The fish—oh, yes," the voice came back. "I've heard they're doin' that now. Have just loads of catfish plantations in the Delta, don't they? I really don't like those things. Cotton was so much more romantic, the little ole boll weevils and all."

"Well I'm sorry, Mrs. Wilkins, but Clay isn't in, and I don't know when I'll be expecting him."

"Expectin' . . ." the woman said. "This is his yacht, isn't it? I've had a just awful time callin' around tryin' to find Clay. No one was at home at his father's, so I telephoned the police station. The darlin' officer there gave me two numbers. I wasn't sure I was callin' the right one."

"You sure 'nuff got the right one, darlin'." There were several seconds of silence. Angel Morales was smiling now.

"Well, darlin'," the woman said, "would you mind writin' down my number and givin' it to Clay?"

"Certainly. Be glad to give him your little ole number. Wait a minute and let me get a pencil." She sat there for several seconds.

Angel Morales's smile broadened.

"Okay, Mrs. Wilkins, I found a pen and just the cutest pink pad. I wish you could see it." She smiled. "It goes with my eyes."

It was several seconds before the woman spoke again. Her voice was now cold. "If you will, please," she said, "just write down my name. He knows the number, any old how."

Linda half expected the woman to add, "So how do you like those apples?" But she didn't.

Linda spoke in the syrupiest voice she could muster. "Writing you down right now, darlin'. There. Anything else?"

"No, thank you." The line disconnected quickly. Linda replaced the receiver and looked at Angel Morales. He winked at her.

In less than a minute the other line was ringing, the one to the answering machine.

"Ten to one she's calling back to leave a message," Angel Morales said. "She knows you're not going to tell Clay she called."

Linda reached for the receiver, hesitated, then picked it up. "Hello."

"Is this here where you call 'bout the reward?" It was a woman, but not the same one. This one's voice was shrill and high pitched, her words coming fast. "I say, is this here the place you call 'bout the reward?"

"Yes, ma'am."

"This here is Hattie Lou Farmer. Me and Horace done seen the killer. We laid our eyes right on him—weren't no more than thirty, thirty-five feet away when we done it. Whadda we do now?"

CHAPTER

32

As Clay, returning from Ming's polygraph session, neared the *Cassandra,* Angel Morales and Linda crossed the gangplank from the yacht to meet him.

The Mexican had a broad smile on his face. "You got another call about the reward. This time it's about your brother."

Clay's heart jumped.

Linda hugged him. "Honey," she said, "it was a woman. She said she saw the killer when he brought the dinghy to shore. She wants to meet with you right away."

"How are you feeling?"

"Oh, I'm fine," she answered. "Excited for you."

He couldn't keep a smile from coming to his face. "Where does she want to meet?"

"Here."

"Here?"

"She's coming to the boat, Clay. She should be here any . . ." Linda smiled and nodded across his shoulder.

He turned to see an old, blue three-quarter-ton pickup pulling to a stop at the end of the pier. He had the urge to start toward it.

Both doors of the pickup opened, a man climbing from the driver's side and a woman from the passenger's side. They started down the walkway.

The man wore bib overalls, was short and balding. The woman had on old-fashioned spike heels, tight black slacks and a sleeveless white sweater. Her pink-framed sunglasses disappeared into the gray hair pyramided like a beehive on top of her head.

"Mr. Rodgers," she said as she stepped up to Angel Morales and extended her hand. "I'm Hattie Lou Farmer." She had to be in her late sixties at least. The man appeared a few years younger.

Angel Morales shook her hand, then nodded toward Clay. "He's the one you're looking for, ma'am."

"Oh," the woman exclaimed and stuck out her hand to Clay. Her fingernails extended almost an inch past the ends of her fingers and were painted silver. Long, glittering earrings hung down her wrinkled neck nearly to her shoulders.

Clay shook hands with her. "Mrs. Farmer, you're the one who called about the reward?"

"Sure am," she said and smiled broadly, a gold tooth glinting in the noonday sun. "Aren't you goin' to ask me aboard your fancy ship there?"

"Of course."

He stepped to the side and she strolled past him across the gangway and into the salon. The little man followed close behind her. He walked with a slight limp.

Clay glanced at Morales, and then Linda, who winked at him. They followed the couple onto the *Cassandra*.

"You ain't got a bar on this ship?" the woman asked as Clay came through the door. She went down the galley steps. In a moment she was opening the cabinets and looking inside them.

"I'll fix you something," Linda said, entering the galley. "Bourbon and vodka are all we have."

"Take either one. My preference runs to the bourbon, though. Won't you join me?"

"I will," Linda said and grinned back over her shoulder at Clay.

The man held out his hand, pumped strongly when Clay took it. "I'm Horace, Horace Little. Name sorta goes with the size, don't it?"

Clay nodded politely.

The man took a seat on the couch, stretched his arms above his head and rubbed his back against the cushion, then hooked his thumbs in the straps of his overalls and crossed one leg over the other. "Nice boat you got here." He glanced through the lattice divider toward the galley. "Fix me a little 'un, too, honey."

Angel Morales chuckled under his breath as he took a seat in one of the easy chairs across from the couch.

Clay was having a hard time maintaining his patience.

While Linda was preparing the drinks, the old woman walked into the crew's quarters and looked around.

In a few seconds she strolled back through the galley, took her drink from Linda's hand without stopping—"Thank you, Honey"—and continued on up the stairs into the salon. "What's in the back of this here ship?"

Clay forced a polite smile to his face. "Linda will show you around after we talk, ma'am. Would you tell me what it is you know? You said you saw the killer."

Horace nodded. "Sure did—both of us."

"But the reward's mine," the woman said sternly, turning to stare with suddenly narrowed eyes at Horace. "We agreed."

Horace nodded. "Don't need the money—it's yours." He looked back at Clay. "Don't need the money cause I got savings. Saved every nickel I ever made when I was young. Not like today's young'uns spendin' everythin' they've got; spendin' everythin' before they get it—what they ain't got. Savin' pays off in the long run I tell 'em. Did for me—house paid for, little tree farm paid for. Between the interest I get—tax free, you know—between that and the little bit the government sends me in Social Security each month, got it made. Medicare deduction's gettin' high, though, just barely tolerable. You're from Washington, ain't you? That just came to me. You might need to be a talkin' to some of your senator friends about the Medicare premiums. I wrote some letters—"

"Shush, Horace," Hattie Lou said. "My Lord, he gets to goin', don't he?"

She walked to the back of the cabin, opened the cabinets there and started looking through them.

Clay felt his exasperation rising. "Ma'am, can we talk now?"

She turned toward him and smiled, "Sure we can, honey." She shut the cabinets, then walked to the couch and sat next to the man.

"Now what do you want to hear?" she asked as she removed her sunglasses. She handed them to Horace.

"Whatever you were going to tell me—what you saw, anything you know."

"Well, right off—to lay the groundwork you know—Horace here, and me, when we saw your ad about a reward notice in this mornin's paper, we was sorta hesitant to come on in and talk with you. You see, that night we'd been out dancin' and my husband don't know nothin' about that." She glanced at the man next to her. "Don't know nothin' about Horace here no kind of way. That's gonna have to remain our secret." She quickly glanced around the room and added everybody up. "The five of us, okay?"

"Of course."

"I'm gonna be takin' your word; don't have to raise your hands or nothin', but it's gotta be between us."

She looked at the smiling Angel Morales, and he raised his hand, palm out. "Between us," he promised.

She nodded and turned back toward Clay. "Okay then, Mr. Rodgers. As I was fixin' to say, Horace and me had been out dancin' and were headin' in. We still had a little time before dawn—my hubby don't get up 'til an hour after dawn; you can set your watch by it. I don't ever have to be in until just around the crack. Anyways, Horace and me don't like to waste any time —never know how much you got left at our age. So we figured it down that we had maybe forty minutes to pull off the side of the road and . . ." She looked toward the man in the overalls and jabbed him in the ribs with her elbow, before turning back to finish her sentence.

". . . to do a little sparkin', you know. Anyways, we were sitting here by the side of the beach under this palm tree, dark night and all, nobody could see us. We couldn't see nothin', neither. Then this bunch of lightnin' shot off up over our heads. I remember I fairly jumped at the racket come after it, and then several more of those bolts shot out. Horace said 'looka there at that fool.'

"I looked down at the beach at some damn fool Yankee—it had to be a Yankee, least from north Mississippi; nobody down here'd be stupid enough to be out in a little dinghy like that in the kind of weather we was havin' that night. Lucky he didn't get his you-know-what fried.

"Anyways, there's a man beached this dinghy and hopped out of it and came up across the sand. Course we didn't know it were no man at the time. Was able to first tell that when he strolled by the pickup. Went right by us." She looked at Horace. "Would you say thirty, thirty-five feet, Horace?"

The man shook his head. "I'm not much good at distances, Hattie Lou; but if I was to estimate I'd say come near being twenty-five, twenty-five and a half."

The woman turned back toward Clay.

"That's what I'd of said if I had somethin' bet on it. Is that good enough?"

"Yes, ma'am—that's good enough."

"Anyways he come right by us. Lightning went off again somethin' terrible." She held her hands in front of her and vibrated them.

"Like that, you know. Just a quiverin'. Sort of reminded me of those disco lights they've got at that club we were at. You know black, white, black, white—enough to tell it was an old man, white-haired as all get out."

"An old man?"

"Yeah, even older than Horace, here."

Horace responded. "Yeah, older than me, Hattie Lou—about your age."

She slapped at the side of his head. "Hush up. Anyways, I saw him good. An old man; tall, too. His hair was maybe a little above middle-of-his-neck length, maybe a little higher, 'bout like Horace's hair—except he had some in the front, too. Good lookin', too."

Horace shook his head. "Weren't good lookin', he was ugly as hell. She thinks everybody's good lookin'—men, anyway."

"Were too good lookin'. Had this prominent Indian nose, high cheekbones, but he weren't dark-skinned, sorta white. Not as white as his hair mind you, but he weren't tan, neither. He was slender, tall. How tall would you say he was, Horace?"

"Told you I wasn't good at estimating stuff like that—about five-eleven and a half, if I had to say."

She nodded. "That's what I would have ventured if you'd asked—'bout five-eleven and a half."

She was suddenly silent, as if she had finished.

Clay glanced at Linda, and back to the woman. "Ma'am, you said about five-eleven?"

"And a half," Horace said.

Clay nodded. "Okay, five-eleven and a half, medium length gray hair . . ."

"White," Horace said, "more like white."

Clay nodded again. "And slender?"

"Skinny," Horace said.

"What else?"

Horace looked at Hattie Lou. She looked back at him and shrugged before she answered. "Not much else, Mr. Rodgers; 'ceptin' he never saw us . . ." She turned her head to Horace. "Probably did see us, didn't he?"

"Probably saw the pickup—doubt he saw us in it."

"That's what I'd have said, too, if you'd asked me."

"Ma'am, did you see where he went, if he had a car parked on the highway?"

"Didn't have no car," the woman replied. "The last I seen of him he was walkin' down the highway, sorta fast like, almost . . ." She glanced to her side. "What do they call it, Horace?"

"Jogging."

"Yeah, joggin', that's what I was fixin' to say. Then he went on off and we never saw hide nor hair of him again."

"Would you recognize him if you did see him again?"

"I would," Horace said. "She wouldn't."

"Now why do you say that, Horace?" the woman asked, a frown coming to her face. "I would too recognize him if I saw him again."

"Mrs. Farmer, you think either one of you saw him well enough that you could give his description to a police artist?"

The woman laughed. "Be a waste of time to do that."

"I don't understand, ma'am, I—"

"Horace here don't like to admit it," she said glancing to her side. "Likes everybody to think he made his money tree farmin' —gentlemanlike. But he didn't, he made his money drawin' pictures of Yankee tourists and sellin' 'em down on the street. He can draw you a picture of the man that'll be a closer likeness than a photograph."

CHAPTER

33

Horace sat at the *Cassandra*'s galley table carefully detailing the face he had drawn on poster paper Angel Morales had gone after. He had at first worked with incredible speed, outlining the man's facial structure, hair and ears in a matter of seconds. He had slowed his work as he filled in the nose, eyes and mouth, then worked even slower as he did his final detail work. Yet, overall, he had completed the drawing in less than fifteen minutes.

"What do you think?" he asked, leaning back in the booth.

Incredible—if it was possible that Horace had indeed seen the man in such detail. It was an old man with his hair cut full. He had a narrow angular face, a prominent nose that Horace had drawn leaned slightly to one side, as if the bone had been tilted that way by a roundhouse punch and then never repaired, and, on his right cheek, an unusually wide, black mole.

"What did I tell you?" Hattie Lou asked. She finished her

drink, then leaned over and kissed the beaming Horace on the side of his forehead.

Angel Morales leaned over the table and studied the drawing closely. "You have a fingerprint and now what amounts to damn near a photograph of him," he said. "Give it three, four days after you get this circulated, and his ass is yours."

Clay hoped so. "Unless he's out of the country."

"Why would he be?" Morales asked. "He doesn't know about this, doesn't know about the fingerprint—the police not putting it in the paper." He glanced at his watch. "Wish I could stay around for the lynching. However, I can't—Becker will be waiting at the motel. Enjoyed meeting you." He held his hand out to Clay.

Clay grasped it and the two shook hands.

The Mexican glanced at Linda. "Ma'am," he said, smiling and bowing gallantly.

Linda returned his smile. "If you're ever down this way—" she said.

"Sure will." He turned toward the salon. "Yip, Yip, and away," he mumbled to himself, and chuckled, and he moved up the stairs toward the salon door.

The telephone rang, the personal number. He stopped by the end table to answer it. "Yes?"

He tilted the receiver away from his ear, and rolled his eyes exaggeratedly. "Just a moment," he said. He held the telephone receiver out toward the galley. "Clay, it's for you. Be careful, she'll burst your eardrum."

When Clay took the receiver the Hispanic nodded a last time and winked, then stepped out through the salon door.

"Hello."

"Clay! Oh God, Clay! He's had a stroke!"

The first light of the morning sun shone through a hallway window on the second floor of the Memorial Hospital in Gulfport. Clay, sitting between Donna and Linda on the hard plastic chairs lining the wall across from the intensive care unit, stared for a moment longer at the dim glow, then turned back to look once more at the ICU door.

Donna bit her lip and shook her head. "What's happening to us, Clay? Why?"

He laid his hand on her forearm.

He shouldn't have skipped the lunch with his dad. He swallowed and took a deep breath. *He should have been staying at the house instead of on the boat.* His fingers trembled against Donna's forearm and he pulled his hand back into his lap.

Out of the corner of his eye he noticed Linda staring at him. Her hand slipped around his back and she gently patted him on his shoulder. Then he saw Becker and Morales coming down the hall. He came to his feet and met them a few feet from the chairs.

"Sorry, man," Angel Morales said. "How's he doing?"

"The doctor says he's going to make it, but beyond that . . ."

Donna stepped to his side. "He's going to be all right," she said. "I know he is. The doctor even said he would be."

"Yes, ma'am," Angel Morales said.

Clay glanced at her.

She lowered her eyes. "Said he *might* be all right—but he will be, I know it."

Clay looked back at the DEA agents. "I thought you all had to be back at your home office by this morning?"

"The others left," Becker said. "Angel and I decided we'd stay around a little while longer. You need anything?"

"No. No, thank you." He felt Linda's hand on his back as she stepped up to his other side. Angel nodded at her.

"Hi, Angel . . . Richard."

Becker smiled at her. "We were just asking Clay if he needed anything—do you?"

She glanced down at her wrinkled skirt, touched her hand self-consciously to the side of her hair. "Gosh—if you wouldn't mind."

"Sure—what?"

"I left my purse in the salon last night. If I had it where I could touch up my makeup a little bit, I'd feel a lot better."

Clay noted the tiredness in her voice. Donna was staring at the ICU entrance. He turned back to Linda. "Why don't you and Donna go get some sleep?"

"Yes, ma'am," Morales said. "You look like you could use some. We'll stay with you so Clay here won't be worrying about you."

Gerald Shelton looked for the hundredth time at his copy of the drawing of the killer. Then the muscular, six-foot-two-inch Mississippi highway patrol sergeant leaned back against the seat of his cruiser and stared absentmindedly out the windshield at the few vehicles traveling Highway 49 just after dawn.

He knew the face—but from where? The prominent nose tilted to one side, the wide nearly disfiguring mole on the right cheek, the full hair indicated on the drawing as white—he should have instantly recalled where he had seen the man before.

He shook his head and glanced at the picture once more. Before he had decided his life was too boring and had joined the Highway Patrol, he had taught at Hinds Community College. There, he had gained a wide reputation as a man who never forgot a face. A week after any semester's classes had started all he had to do was look over his assembled students to know who was cutting classes—the missing faces. He looked again at the drawing. *He would remember.*

An hour after Linda and the others had disappeared through the swinging doors at the end of the fifth floor hallway, the chief neurologist came out of the ICU and joined Clay.

"Your father's vital signs have stabilized, but he remains semi-comatose. With your permission I'm going to order him moved to a private room. I'd like to have him in a situation where you and the rest of your family are close to him. Maybe if he can hear you talking, realize someone familiar's in his presence, he'll respond."

*   *   *

Sergeant Gerald Shelton sat at a table in the Howard Johnson's Restaurant off Highway 49 in Hattiesburg. Half of his eggs and bacon still lay uneaten on the plate before him. In one hand he held a cup of coffee, while in his other he held a copy of the drawing done by Horace Little.

"Hey, Gerald," the waitress said as she walked by. He smiled and nodded before looking back at the drawing of the killer.

It was the third woman to acknowledge his presence since he had sat down to eat breakfast. With his thick, dark hair, and his muscular build trim under his snappy uniform, he was always attracting women's attention.

A mole that prominent, he thought; *a nose like that; he should be able to instantly recall the face.*

A mole, he thought further, a creature that hid in dark caves in the ground. Where was this mole hiding?

Come on mole, where are you?

CHAPTER

34

"Fore!"

Sergeant Gerald Shelton raised a hand to his forehead to shield the sun from his eyes as he watched his golf ball rocketing up into the sky, then beginning a long arch back toward the fairway. The ball hit at the edge of the green, took one big bounce, two successively smaller hops and began to roll toward the flag, stopping a foot from the cup.

Clapping came from off to his right and behind him. He turned and nodded toward the attractive brunette who was waiting with her husband as Gerald played through them. Her husband said something to the woman. She frowned, reached to her cart and began selecting a club from her golf bag.

Gerald hoisted his bag to his shoulder and moved toward his cart. His thoughts were back on the face Horace had drawn.

He knew he had seen it before. He shook his head in disgust.

This wasn't like him. If he didn't remember who the man was, he should at least remember the area in which he had seen him.

Angela Brouchard had been extremely nervous ever since hearing on the radio about the discovery of a female's body west of the Chandeleur Islands. Her face was drained of color as she followed the stocky, white-coated medical examiner across the tile floor of the morgue. Twenty feet ahead of them, lying on a gurney placed next to the stainless steel autopsy sink, was the sheet-covered body of the unidentified female.

To Angela's right was another gurney. The body on it was that of a man's, and was completely exposed except for a sheet draped across his midsection. He had been unusually tall in life, his bare feet—a tag on one of his big toes extended a full foot off the lower end of the gurney. His eyes were open. Angela thought they closed them. There was a small, plastic block supporting his neck. His thin brown hair hung down to touch the metal surface of the gurney. She saw the jagged, star-shaped hole above his right ear.

"Suicide," the medical examiner said as he noticed her staring. "That's the side the bullet went in. There's a lot bigger hole on the other side."

She immediately turned her eyes away. The examiner reached the unidentified female's body, and walked around to the far side of the gurney. He looked into Angela's face. "Remember," he said, "I told you there's a problem with the face. In addition to the decomposition, there were the fish, and, from the looks of it, I think maybe a turtle, too."

Angela nodded nervously, her hands slowly reaching for her throat where they moved nervously. She could smell the odor.

"Okay?" the examiner asked.

She tightened her fingers on her throat, and nodded.

The examiner reached to the sheet and pulled it back.

Angela's eyes widened immediately, and she began to scream, and scream, and scream.

* * *

The four men at the small round table in the clubhouse were playing cards, and talking.

"Left-wingers getting control of everything!" the chubby red-haired forty-year-old man said. Dressed in a white short-sleeve dress shirt and bright blue slacks, he was a dentist and an authority on most things. He wore glasses but now held them in his hand and was thumping them on the table to emphasize each of his phrases. "Can't have prayers in our schools (thump), burning the flag's okay (thump), criminals receiving more rights than ordinary folk do (thump)."

Sitting directly across the table from him was a slim, blond-haired young lawyer. Dressed in a white short-sleeve cotton pullover and brown slacks, he was nodding his head every time the dentist's glasses hit the table.

To the dentist's right, and attired in a drab brown business suit complete with a vest, was a prematurely gray fifty-year-old professor who taught in the nationally recognized polymer science department at the Hattiesburg-based University of Southern Mississippi. Rather than nodding at the dentist's words, he was shaking his head solemnly.

The fourth man, attired in a pair of casual khaki slacks and a white cotton pullover identical to the young lawyer's, but with his muscular upper body filling the shirt much more admirably, wasn't paying attention to the dentist's words. He was Mississippi Highway Patrol Sergeant Gerald Shelton, and he was again deeply absorbed in his thoughts.

The dentist's blood pressure was up, his fat cheeks noticeably red as he continued to speak.

"Did you see the paper this morning—Judge Nichols's latest gift to the poor mistreated little things locked up at Parchman?" He shook his head and thumped his glasses a little harder against the tabletop.

Before either of the two men listening had a chance to answer, the dentist continued.

"Prison officials have to add more living space, now (thump). Each prisoner has to have more room (thump). I forget the exact amount. An editorial in the paper said it was more space than the Defense Department required for soldiers living in a barracks (thump). Can you believe what we've come to in this country? (thump, thump)."

The professor shook his head solemnly, and spoke. "I married Lucille when I was twenty," he said. "We went to Mexico on our honeymoon. You know, the usual week-long tourist visit: Mexico City, Taxco and Acapulco. When we were driving through the mountains, went through a little town populated by Indians. They were eating these iguanas—big ole ugly lizards. Eating iguanas while chickens were running all over the place— something about their religion.

"Our driver stopped and climbed out of our car to go in a restaurant and get some cool drinks for Lucille and me. I remarked on whether it was safe for us to sit out there like we were going to have to do while we waited on him. I mean those Indians were starving. I figured no telling what they might do if they started thinking about us rich Americans sitting out there by ourselves and all. I figured they'd do anything to get their hands on a few dollars.

"Driver told us we could take a five dollar bill and put it under a rock on the sidewalk. When we came back through it would still be lying there. Said it was because Mexico's laws were so strict and that their prisons were used for punishment rather than vacations.

"That got him going about the prisons here in America. He said he had read in the paper that our prisoners not only have cells with toilets, but aren't required to work; receive three good meals a day, get to watch television and are even allowed magazine subscriptions. He said that just wouldn't work in Mexico. Said what he had just described was a better life than most Mexicans could ever expect to have.

"I remember his very words. He said if Mexico had a prison system like we did, that there'd be people killing somebody just to get locked up. It just wouldn't work. What he was also saying, in a polite way, was that our system wasn't working, either. Too soft—not much of a deterrent."

"You said twenty years ago," the young lawyer interjected.

"Times have changed. Mexico's having their problems with crime now just like we are."

"Maybe in some respects," the professor said. "Because they have drugs down there, too, now. People doped up don't think about what kind of prison system they might end up in; only think about whatever it's going to take to get enough money to buy some more stuff to sniff up their nose. But the normal everyday criminals, they still don't have as many of those as we do."

The dentist shook his head. "Fact of the matter is, whether you want to say it's dopers or regular criminals, Mexico has a worse problem than we do; actual higher per-capita-crime rate than right here in America—if you can believe that. I read that in the paper just yesterday. You combine that with the devil worshipping they have going on in a lot of places down there— I'd just as soon stay here and complain about the good old U.S.A. Still can't beat it, overall."

The professor nodded and said, "Amen."

The young lawyer spoke again. "I'm not so worried about how they're having to treat the prisoners up at Parchman, if they'd just keep them there."

Both the dentist and professor nodded repetitively. The dentist thumped his glasses twice against the table. "Hear, hear," he said.

"Put a candy kiss on their pillow each night," the lawyer added. "That's all right by me. But quit turning them out quicker than the cops can book them—quit paroling them."

Paroling them, Sergeant Gerald Shelton thought. *Parole. That's it!* He suddenly stood.

The others looked at him. "Excuse me," he said. "I'll be back in a minute." He turned and walked rapidly toward the exit out of the card room. There was a pay telephone hanging in the hallway outside.

The reason he had such a difficult time recalling where he had seen the man was that he had never actually seen him. He had seen only his photograph in the newspaper. It was the year before, during the controversy raised over the parole board deciding to release the man, a hired killer convicted of a contract murder less than a decade prior.

The family of the killer's victim had hired their own lawyer in an attempt to keep the parole board from releasing the convict, but it had done no good.

"We believe we have reached a sound and proper decision here," the head of the parole board was quoted in the paper as saying. Jeffcoat had been a model prisoner—not to mention that he claimed to have been truly born again.

CHAPTER

35

Clay was applying glycerine to his father's lips when the telephone on the bedside table rang.

"Hello."

"This is Langston. The girl was Brouchard's daughter."

Soung Ming's sister was not all that attractive, her face plain, her shoulders and hips a little too wide for her short height; but she loved men. So when she had noticed the handsome young black face turn her way to stare at her when he had driven past her beachside cottage on New Providence Island, the Bahamas, she had boldly returned the stare. A few minutes later, when he had driven back from the other direction, slower this time, she had waved. And now he was in the small cottage's living room.

"You sure you don't want a drink?" she asked again.

"No, mum, I don't have the time," he said, and pulled the silencer-equipped automatic from inside his sport coat, then shot her twice in the face.

Brouchard was at Girls Galore, his original club, a metal building with a bare concrete floor, a rough-built wooden stage at its center, a rather ordinary structure to be netting three quarters of a million dollars profit each year.

He was at a desk in a small back room, otherwise furnished with two chairs in front of the desk, a single filing cabinet off to the side of the room, and, hanging on the wall behind him, an oil portrait of a dark-skinned, middle-age woman with long black hair. He didn't rise when Clay and Langston stepped inside. Lionel was standing beside the desk. He made a last low comment to Brouchard and walked from the desk toward the door.

As the long-haired blond moved past him, Clay caught the scent of the subtle cologne.

"My condolences," Langston said, stopping at the front of the desk.

Expressionless, Brouchard nodded.

Clay wondered if the portrait was of Brouchard's mother. Carson had told Linda there were pictures of the mother hanging all over Brouchard's house.

"Hate to be asking you questions at a time like this," Langston said. "But you understand."

Brouchard nodded again.

"Do you mind?" Langston asked, pointing at the chairs in front of the desk. Brouchard nodded for the third time.

Clay had expected Brouchard to ask Langston why he brought somebody with him. Yet so far he hadn't even acknowledged Clay's presence with a glance.

After seating himself, the chief scooted his chair a little closer to the desk, and leaned forward to slide a copy of Horace's rendition across the desktop. "We believe this is what the killer looks like," he said. "Every law enforcement officer in a hundred miles has one of those now."

Clay moved to the desk and lowered himself into the chair next to Langston's. He felt uncomfortable at being there, but he couldn't imagine why Brouchard hadn't reported his stepdaughter missing. He wanted to hear the explanation. He glanced at the portrait again. She'd been a very attractive woman; reminded him of Sophia Loren.

Brouchard lifted the copy of Horace's drawing from his desk and looked at it. He was still expressionless. After a moment he laid the sheet down, raised his face back to the police chief's, and spoke in a low, level voice. "You told me on the phone you wanted to ask some questions."

"Well, first, Mr. Brouchard, it's been nearly a week since the murders."

"I thought she'd run off," Brouchard said. "That's family business. I take care of my family's business in my own way."

"What was your reason for thinking she'd run off?"

"We been having some arguments over her doing things I didn't like—staying out too late, other things. She been threatening her mother with running away if I didn't leave her alone. Like I said, thought she had."

"You said she'd been doing 'other things'—like what?"

"Things I didn't like."

Langston was silent for a moment, but showed no trace of irritation at the way his question had been answered.

"You were in Florida the night of the murders?"

"That's right, Miami."

"When did you come back?"

"Sunday night. Angela called me that morning. She had gone to New Orleans Saturday to shop, and spent the night with a friend of hers there. When she got back Sunday Karen's bed hadn't been slept in."

"Did you know that Karen was seeing the Rodgers boy?"

Shifting only his eyes as he did so, Brouchard finally looked at Clay. "I knew she had been with him before, but I thought she had stopped. He was too old."

"That was one of the things you argued about?" Langston asked.

Brouchard moved his eyes back to the chief. "No, I told you I thought she had stopped seeing him."

"You've heard about the drugs that were out there?"

Brouchard stared a moment, still expressionless, then nodded.

"And that we think—pretty well know—your daughter and the boy were there to ferry the drugs to shore."

Brouchard didn't respond in any fashion.

"I guess that's enough for now," Langston said, and stood, surprising Clay.

"Sorry to have bothered you like this," Langston added, "but, like I said, I'm sure you understand. Later we're going to have to get a full statement from you and from your wife, too."

Sergeant Gerald Shelton was back on the telephone. As good as he was at remembering faces, he was terrible with names. So he had given his district office enough time to ascertain the man's name from information in their files. Then he had called them back.

The name was Jeffcoat, Johnny Jeffcoat. He lived in Louisiana now, in Gretna. His parole officer had just departed for a two-week vacation at Gulf Shores, but it didn't matter, Jeffcoat's current address was a matter of record.

The Mississippi Highway Patrol's main Jackson office was even now contacting Louisiana authorities. Jeffcoat would be in custody within a half hour. A satisfied smile crossed Gerald's face as he replaced the receiver.

A nice-looking woman passing by the telephones returned his smile and nodded. She glanced back as she moved on down the hall between the card room and the pro shop.

Outside Girls Galore, Clay turned to Langston. "Chief, staying out too late, drinking—that's a big difference from running off for several days."

Langston nodded. "Yeah, there's more. Figure Mr.

Brouchard and Angela were having a lot of trouble with the girl. But you could see how it was bothering him to answer. I figure I could talk to him about it again later, after some of the shock has passed."

The two shook hands before the chief climbed into his white cruiser and guided it away from the curb. After getting into the Taurus, Clay continued to sit for a moment.

Brouchard had remained expressionless even when he looked at Horace's drawing of the killer. Grieving, Clay could understand—grieving, being depressed, not demonstrative. But there should have been some reaction upon seeing the killer's face for the first time, if only the tensing of the jaw or a wrinkling of the brow—something.

Six days. Brouchard might prefer to keep family matters private, but a daughter missing for nearly a full week and he'd done nothing?

Clay looked back at the front door of the club. No, six days was too long. Brouchard had done something; a hundred to one he'd done something, sent people looking for her, at least. That would be more like it, more normal—what Clay would have expected of him, of any father.

Brouchard would know how to look, too. A man doesn't run strip joints for over twenty years and not know his way around —know the streets. He would have known the right people with the right resources. In some ways he could have done as good a job of searching as the police and still kept family matters private.

Clay nodded slowly at his next thought. Looking for his stepdaughter might not have been the only thing Brouchard had done. He could've put people to working on finding the killer, too. There would have been no reason for his expression to change if the picture wasn't news, if Brouchard already knew what the killer looked like.

I take care of my family's business in my own way, he'd said to Langston. Clay thought of the oil portrait hanging behind the desk, and he thought of the time that Brouchard had used a shotgun on his stepfather. Brouchard had certainly taken care of his own business then.

Linda had said she overheard Lionel and Brouchard talking about something to handle. At a club in New Orleans, Friday night—*tonight*—at three A.M.

CHAPTER

36

Pat O'Brien's on Bourbon Street might be the singular attraction on a street noted for its attractions. Actually, the entrance to the well-known watering spot is not even on Bourbon Street, though the exit—a wide, brick-floored passageway spotted with tables and lined with clumps of greenery and small fountains protruding from its walls—does lead to the famous street.

In this passageway, Antonio Brouchard sat at a wrought iron table next to a small fountain lit with flaming gas. He was staring at an old white-haired man and a woman sitting at a table in the middle of the corridor.

The man, around sixty and with thick white hair, was dressed in loafers, baggy khaki slacks and a loose white cotton pullover worn under a blue sport jacket. The most noticeable things about his angular face were his large nose, tilted noticeably to one side, and a wide mole on his right cheek.

The woman, in a chair pulled to the same side of the table as his, was much younger and nice looking, though her image was cheapened somewhat by her bright makeup and the overly tight sweater vividly displaying her heavy breasts. She leaned and kissed the old man on the cheek, then moved her lips to his ear and whispered.

He nodded. She faced back to the table, drained the last of her drink, and stood. After a last buss of the old man's cheek, she made her way through the thick crowd toward the exit, her swaying walk attracting the attention of most of the males in that section of Pat O'Brien's.

Brouchard's gaze remained fixed on the man's face. After a few minutes the old man raised his wrist to glance at his watch. He quickly finished his drink, slid his chair back and started in the same direction the woman had gone. Brouchard didn't bother to rise right then; he knew where the old man was headed.

Fifteen minutes later and several blocks from Pat O'Brien's, the old man started up an inclined driveway toward the third floor of a dimly lit parking garage.

Though he was becoming short of breath by the time he neared the second floor entrance to the elevator, he didn't even consider getting on it; he had a terrible fear when it came to elevators. He took a deep breath and started up the last ramp.

On the third floor, Antonio Brouchard stepped off the elevator and hurried between the rows of parked cars to his Lincoln. Once there, he didn't climb inside the car, instead walked around to the front of the hood and waited.

The old man appeared around the last curve leading to the third floor. With an audible sigh of relief, an anticipatory smile crossing his face, he made for the Lincoln.

Alert, due to the type business he was in, he immediately noticed the Harrison County, Mississippi, tag, and stopped short. If the Lincoln was the woman's he had talked to in Pat O'Brien's, it should be sporting Louisiana plates.

And why, it suddenly occurred to him, *couldn't he have waited for her on the ground floor?* Even if she had heard her estranged husband was in the area looking for her, and even if her husband did happen to see her walking toward a parking garage where an old man stood, how could that cause any suspicion?

The man reached quickly toward the inside of his coat, but was too late. Brouchard, a silencer-equipped automatic in his hand, rose from where he crouched behind the hood of the Lincoln.

"Get in—it's unlocked."

Brouchard's dark Lincoln moved down the ramp, pausing at the exit from the parking garage before turning right onto the narrow, brick street.

Across the street and half a block away, Clay reached for the ignition and started his car. He pulled away from the curb and began following the Lincoln.

Brouchard had left Biloxi shortly before midnight, carefully observing the speed limit on his way to New Orleans and the parking garage.

When he had driven into the facility, Clay had circled to the far side of the building and parked a few hundred feet from the garage's exit, waiting in his car until he had seen the elevator door open and Brouchard step out.

Clay had tailed him to Pat O'Brien's, then walked around to the Bourbon Street exit and lingered there until Brouchard had emerged nearly an hour later.

Walking more hurriedly than he had on the way to the club, Brouchard had made his way back to the parking garage where he had taken the elevator again.

Clay had noticed somebody else sitting in the passenger seat when the Lincoln pulled from the garage, yet nobody had gone up the elevator since Brouchard had, and the one man immediately preceding him had just left in a red Corvette.

There was considerable traffic on the causeway over Lake Pontchartrain leading away from New Orleans, and on Interstate 10 going east. But when Brouchard turned off onto a rural highway the traffic became sparse. Clay allowed his car to drop well behind the Lincoln.

He pulled over to the shoulder and stopped completely when

Brouchard turned off onto a gravel road. When the Lincoln's taillights disappeared over a hump a quarter mile away, Clay doused the Taurus's lights and pulled out onto the gravel road.

He never saw Brouchard turn off the road. Rather, in passing a dirt road that intersected the gravel one, he noticed taillights fading from view down the dirt road. There were no lights on the gravel road ahead.

Once on the dirt road, spotted with mud puddles from the recent rains, he followed Brouchard's taillights until he saw them suddenly brighten and the Lincoln turn off to the left. Clay guided his car to the side of the road.

The headlights of the Lincoln shown on an old house. Then the lights went out. Clay opened his car door and climbed outside. After a moment, he started forward on foot.

A hundred feet from the house, he moved off the side of the road and knelt in the high weeds next to a barbed wire fence.

Brouchard's Lincoln was parked close to the front porch of the house, really more of a tin-roofed, wooden shack than anything.

Two front windows, one to each side of the front door, were darkened. There were two other windows on the side of the house Clay faced, light dimly glowing through a pulled shade at the one nearest the back. The entire yard was knee-deep in weeds, but otherwise open.

Clay glanced at the full moon. It was a hell of a time for everything to be so bright and well lit. He glanced around to see if he could spot a sign of anybody else's presence.

In the pasture to his left there were the shapeless forms of a few head of silent cattle standing a couple hundred feet away, and his nose told him there was a chicken house close by, but he noticed nothing else. He angled across the yard toward the window showing the dim glow.

There was a narrow crack between the side of the shade and the window facing. He peered through it.

The light from a bare bulb at the center of the ceiling showed the room he was looking into to be empty, the hardwood floor bare except for a cardboard box, two empty paint cans lying on their side, and a newspaper spread out near the far wall. Brouchard suddenly walked into view.

He moved to the far side of the room, gathered the spread-out newspaper into his hands and, wadding it, disappeared from sight to the left.

Clay moved to the other side of the window and peered through the crack there.

He looked directly at a large, old-fashioned fireplace. Sitting on the fireplace's brick stoop, his arms awkwardly above him to his right, his hands working at something up in the flue, was a slim, white-haired man. The back of his head was toward the window as he stared at the newspaper Brouchard was stuffing into a pile of kindling already in the fireplace.

As Brouchard moved back toward the center of the room, the man began tugging at something in the flue, finally frantically jerking his arms, and Clay realized the man was not reaching up into the flue of his accord, but that his hands were secured there.

As Brouchard came toward the fireplace again, the man started glancing wildly around the room. Clay saw the face for the first time. A cold chill swept across him.

The tilted nose, the wide mole—it was Horace's drawing to the last detail.

Brouchard did have his own resources. They had paid off for him. The man who killed Robert—and Brouchard's stepdaughter—was now being brought to justice in Brouchard's private manner. There would be no chance of acquittal, and no parole.

Clay glanced across his shoulder toward the road in front of the house. All he had to do was turn away, walk silently from the window, and go on back to Washington. The search for Robert's killer was finally over.

Brouchard reached into his pocket for a match, struck it on the brick stoop, then touched its flame to the paper stuffed into the kindling.

The old man again began jerking his arms frantically.

Brouchard stepped back from the fireplace and stared as the fire began to catch.

The old man began to wail, started pleading. Clay couldn't understand what he said.

Brouchard bent to fumble at his sock. When he stood he held a switchblade in his hand. He flipped it open. The blade glinted the reflection of the blaze.

Clay felt a sudden dryness in his throat. The fire wasn't going to be the only punishment.

The man now came to one knee on the stoop. Twisting toward the fireplace, he kicked into it with his free leg, scattering burning paper and kindling across the stoop and out onto the floor.

Brouchard moved forward. He grabbed the man's thick white hair and yanked him around, slamming the back of his head into the brick over the fireplace. Reaching forward with the knife, Brouchard slashed a deep gash in the man's pale cheek.

The old man, seemingly oblivious to the cut and the pulling of his hair, kept kicking wildly back at the fire, continuing to scatter the burning kindling.

Clay shut his eyes for a moment. When he reopened them he reached to pull his pistol from the holster at his waistband.

All he had to do was walk away, but he couldn't.

He turned toward the door.

At that moment the cold barrel of a pistol pressed into the back of his shirt. He froze.

There was a scream from inside the house. Clay smelled the cologne. Anger and fear immediately intermingled within his stomach.

A hand reached around in front of him to take his automatic away. He was pushed face first against the wall.

Another scream rang out, louder and shriller. Clay closed his eyes.

The hand was back again, searching him now for any other weapons. A moment later he was yanked away from the wall and shoved stumbling toward the front of the house.

There was another scream, changing abruptly to a blood-curdling choking sound—trailing off into silence.

When Clay hesitated at the front porch the pistol jabbed into his back and started him up the stairs.

At the entrance to the house the pistol again jabbed. He opened the door and was prodded inside the dark living room, as bare as the room he had seen through the window.

"Antonio!" Lionel called.

A door opened off to the far left of the room, and Brouchard appeared in the illuminated doorway.

He walked forward to stop a couple feet away.

Clay noticed the knife, blood on its blade, in Brouchard's hand. His lips grew dry.

Brouchard looked at Lionel. "Anybody else?"

Lionel shook his head.

"You figured it out from what Linda overheard," Brouchard said. "Why did you come alone?"

"I didn't."

Brouchard again looked at Lionel, and the blond man once more shook his head.

Clay did his best to make sure his voice was steady. "I left two DEA agents in New Orleans. One was in the club and one was in the garage. They saw you with the old man. I didn't have time to wait on them or I would've lost you; so I followed you alone. But they know where I went, and they'll know what had to have happened to me if I don't come back."

Brouchard stood silent, expressionless, staring.

Clay spoke again. "I'm a law enforcement officer. If I don't come back they won't stop until they get you. If you let me go, you have a chance at a trial. The old man was a killer. He'd murdered your daughter. A jury would sympathize with you." He glanced at the knife, thought of the last choking sound that had come from the old man. Beads of perspiration dotted the back of his neck.

Brouchard finally spoke. "You would've done the same thing," he said.

"I don't know. I would have been hoping he'd try to run. I would've hoped that."

Brouchard, quiet again, stared a moment, then, as if agreeing with some thought that had passed through his head, slowly nodded. "You would have killed him," he said. "You would have killed him whether he ran or not—it was your blood he murdered. But you're also a cop. Secret Service, cops; you're all in the same bag, and you've seen me here." He glanced aimlessly at the floor for a moment, then raised his eyes back to Clay's.

"It's a chance I must take," he said. "Isn't it—like a game? The agents, Linda—if you don't come back. But I'm not going back to face any kind of charge. The scum in there isn't worth it." He stared deeply into Clay's eyes and his words came slower now.

"You're not going to tell anybody what you saw, because if you do I'm not only going to have you killed, I'm going to have Linda killed, too. I swear that before Almighty God.

"If you say nothing, go back to Washington, what's the harm in that? Nobody paying for a thief and a murderer being done away with—what difference does it make? I'm gonna take your word on what you're going to do, knowing that to save your hide you'll agree to anything. But if you lie, you've buried yourself—and Linda."

Clay felt his racing pulse begin to slow. "Why did he kill Robert?"

"A thief—a burglar like the cops figured. Your brother and my daughter came up on him and he killed them. Now, say it; say it whether it's a lie or the truth; you're not going to tell anybody what you saw here."

Clay nodded. *What other choice did he have?*

Brouchard looked toward Lionel. "Take him back to Biloxi. Use his car."

Lionel's eyes narrowed. "Antonio, he—"

"The old man murdered his brother. I think he will stick to his word." He looked back at Clay.

"Remember my oath," he said, "and think about whether my paying for that scum's death is worth Linda dying." He turned back toward the doorway he had walked from, then suddenly stopped.

Without looking back he said, "Hold him here a minute." He moved on through the doorway.

Minutes passed, and he emerged again. He had a torn remnant of newspaper page in his hands and was folding it.

"Here," he said. "The old man's fingerprints. I want there to be no doubt in your mind that it's the right person."

Clay took the folded piece of paper into his hand.

Brouchard nodded at it. "My prints are on there, too, if you wanna check them again."

Again. Clay glanced at Lionel and the blond man smiled.

Brouchard's brow suddenly wrinkled in thought. He glanced over his shoulder back toward the illuminated doorway. He turned back to Clay. "How long were you at the window?" he asked.

"For a couple of minutes."

"What did you see?"

"I—I'd just got there—I—"

Brouchard spoke sharply. "What! What did you see?"

Clay took a deep breath. "The old man with his arms up in the flue, you lighting a fire, you cutting his face."

Brouchard looked past Clay.

Lionel nodded.

Brouchard turned his eyes back to Clay's, and phrased his words carefully. "I'll tell you what happened after you were gone from the window. The bastard broke loose and ran out the back door before I could get a hold of him. Maybe I'll find him again. Maybe I won't. But all that you need to remember is that I didn't kill him. Wasn't going to in the first place. Just wanted to make him suffer for what he did to Karen. So assault is what I'd be tried for if you go back on your word. Most I'd cop out of that would be probation. But you would still face my oath. Linda would, too."

CHAPTER

37

And kidnapping, Clay added silently to himself as he drove along the gravel road on his way back to the rural highway and the interstate to Biloxi. Brouchard at the bare minimum would at least also be charged with kidnapping, and he knew it. But there had been no need for him to mention any other charge when he said that all he could be tried for was assault. And there had been no need for Clay to mention it.

Brouchard had only been making a point. There would never be a body found—that was the real message. Brouchard was attending to that now. It was doubtful the farmhouse would even be standing after tonight.

If it came down to a trial, it was Clay's word—which would be accepted by almost any jury—that Brouchard had taken the old man to the house and tortured him. But what more could Clay swear to, no matter the obvious truth.

The defense attorneys would harp on "what was seen." He

269

had not been an eyewitness to the very end. And there would be no body—the man *could* have escaped.

Even if that line of defense failed, the attorneys—and they would be the best ones money could buy—would detail to the jury exactly what the old man had done to Brouchard's stepdaughter. That would so mitigate what Brouchard had done that it would be hard to sustain a murder conviction; harder still to get a judge to impose a life sentence if there were a conviction. There would most certainly be no charge of capital murder; however, that's what it was. Without being convicted of capital murder the most time Brouchard would ever serve in prison would be six, seven years.

Robert was dead. Brouchard's daughter was dead. But Linda was still alive. Should she have to look over her shoulder forever, or until someone Brouchard hired tracked her down? What about his father and Donna? Brouchard hadn't mentioned them, but maybe only because he hadn't thought of them at the time he was making his threat. They could be added later.

A car wreck a couple of years from now, an accidental drowning, a fall from some high place; even if the deaths were suspicious, how could anything ever be proved?

Clay shook his head in disgust with himself. What kind of law enforcement would there be if every time an officer or his family were threatened, the officer backed off? But, then again, to risk danger, especially danger for a loved one, shouldn't there at least have to be some worthwhile purpose for the risk?

How was it worthwhile to force Brouchard to stand trial for killing a man who had murdered his stepdaughter; murdered Robert? Clay knew, had he been the one to reach the old man first, that there was a good chance the old man would still be dead. Not tortured, but dead nevertheless. Or would he be? His thoughts confused, his frustration mounting, Clay shook his head again.

Then he once again caught the scent of the cologne. He glanced toward Lionel sitting in the passenger seat, a snub-nosed revolver held in his hand and pointed loosely in Clay's direction.

Brouchard had said if you want to check my fingerprints *again*. Lionel had smiled at that. Clay felt his hands tremble on the steering wheel. He had sworn somebody was going to pay.

He turned back to stare over the steering wheel and down the gravel road. The intersection with the rural highway was just ahead.

He touched his foot gently to the brake and lightly pumped it, gradually beginning to slow the Taurus as it neared the intersection.

Reaching the highway, he released the brake, let the car begin to move onto the pavement, then suddenly jammed down hard on the brake.

Lionel was flung forward hard against the dash, the side of his head slamming into the windshield. Clay was across the seat in an instant, his hand gripped firmly around the wrist of the hand that held the revolver. He swung with all of his strength at the blond man's jaw, caught it squarely just above the point—a boxer's perfect punch. Lionel, his eyes rolling back in his head, dropped the gun and slumped in the seat.

Clay grabbed the steering wheel and jammed hard on the brake, stopping the car just before its wheels went off in the ditch on the far side of the pavement.

He threw the gear into park, then reached past Lionel's slumped form and opened the door. Lionel toppled out onto the grassy shoulder. Clay climbed out the same door.

He didn't know what to do about Brouchard, but he did the blond man. Clay leaned over and grabbed him by the shoulders and began dragging him down the slope toward the water collected in the ditch.

Reaching the bottom of the ditch, he released Lionel's limp form, the blond man's face splashing into the water. Clay stepped on the back of Lionel's neck. The thick blond hair, beginning to float, spread out just under the surface of the water.

After a moment Lionel's body jerked. Bubbles came up. He started writhing, his hands splashing in the water. He yanked his head out from under Clay's foot and rolled to his back. Groggy, his eyes wide, he coughed one time, and moaned.

Clay backed up the slope and moved to the car. He found the snub-nosed revolver on the floorboard.

He walked back to Lionel who had rolled to his stomach and was now on all fours.

Clay cocked the revolver.

Lionel looked across his shoulder in the direction of the sound.

Clay pulled the trigger. The revolver roared, jumped in his hand, and the bullet sent a spray of dirty water into the air.

Lionel shrieked and rolled to his back.

Clay smiled. "Get your kicks roughing up women?" He pulled the trigger again and a hunk of soft mud exploded from the ground beside Lionel's head.

"Pleeease don't!"

"Going to beg, huh? Come on, I want to hear you beg."

Lionel slowly lifted his back from the ground. "Please." He held his hands out in a pleading gesture. They were trembling. He looked like he was about to cry.

Clay stepped forward and kicked hard into Lionel's face, knocking him backwards sliding to the bottom of the ditch again. His head submerged once more, and he didn't move.

Clay stared at the limp form for a moment before he leaned over, caught the man's ankles and dragged him far enough up the bank that his face was no longer under water.

He climbed back up to his car and opened the glove compartment. Finding an old gas ticket and a pen, he took the piece of paper to the flat hood of the car and scribbled a message, using his left hand and printing in block letters.

Brouchard,
This doesn't change our agreement. This was personal.

He slid the piece of paper in a gap between the buttons of Lionel's shirt, checked to make sure the man was breathing okay, then walked around the front of the car to the driver's door.

After slipping inside the Taurus, he leaned across to grab the passenger door and shut it. Lionel, still on his back, was now moving his head from side to side.

Clay put the car in reverse, backed it out onto the highway, and dropped the gear into forward.

The Ford, wheels squealing, leaped forward, leaving a cloud of black smoke floating above the pavement.

Lionel moaned and rolled to his stomach, raised his head to look after the car speeding away. He shut his eyes in pain and slowly shook his head back and forth.

"You're dead," he mumbled.

CHAPTER

38

When Clay opened the door to the hospital room, Linda sat up in the bed next to his father's, swung her feet to the floor and hurried to him.

"Oh, I've been so worried," she said as she threw her arms around him and hugged him. She was wearing a set of his pajamas, the legs of the pants rolled up above her ankles. Her hands were hidden by the long sleeves.

"Your father came out of the coma twice last night. He didn't talk, but he definitely knew what was going on around him. He even nodded his head when Donna spoke to him. The doctor says he can't guarantee anything, but he thinks he'll soon come out of it permanently."

Clay nodded. "I telephoned the neurologist at his home last night—he told me it was looking better. Where's Donna?"

"She wanted to go by her church for a while—she said she had to." Linda glanced over her shoulder at his father.

Clay walked to the side of the bed. His father, breathing quietly, looked more relaxed than he'd been since Clay first arrived in Biloxi.

"What happened in New Orleans?" Linda asked.

"Nothing."

"Nothing?"

"Nothing."

Clay turned away from the bed, walked to the window and looked out.

"Clay, what is it?"

He shook his head. "I'm just tired."

"Clay, something's wrong . . . What did happen in New Orleans?"

He didn't answer.

After a moment he turned away from the window and walked back to his father's bed.

"Clay?"

He turned to face her. "Why do you keep asking me what happened?"

She stared at him for a long moment. "I wasn't," she said. "I was going to ask you if you wanted to go get a cup of coffee."

He was silent a moment, then shook his head. "I'm sorry."

She nodded and stood, started toward the door to the room. He moved to her, caught her by her elbow and turned her around to face him. "I'm sorry. It's just that I'm so damn tired of trying to think like a detective."

She looked at him a moment, then leaned forward to kiss his cheek. "What about the coffee?" she asked. "The nurse said she'd keep an eye on your father if I wanted to get out of the room for a little while?"

He nodded. "Fine."

She turned toward the small bathroom. "It'll just take me a minute to dress."

"Linda."

She turned back around. "Yes."

"Brouchard tracked the killer down."

Her eyes narrowed. "That's what he was talking about with Lionel—the something he had to handle personally."

Clay nodded. "Brouchard followed him from a bar, drove him into the country and killed him in an old farmhouse."

Linda's mouth gaped open. "Killed him? Why do you . . . How?"

"I saw it."

"Saw it?"

"I'd followed Brouchard. I came up to a window at the house when it was happening. Never saw him actually kill the man, but he did."

"I don't understand."

"Doesn't matter. What matters is I know he killed him, and I don't think I'm going to say anything about it."

"Not say anything about it?" Her forehead crinkled in puzzlement. She spread her hands out to her sides. "Will you please explain where I can understand?"

"There's nothing to understand. He killed him. The guy got what he deserved. I don't think I'm going to . . ." He made up his mind. "I'm *not* going to say anything about it."

Linda was silent for a moment. "You're sure he was the one who killed Robert?"

"Horace couldn't have drawn a picture that looked any more like him." He reached into his shirt pocket and pulled out the folded scrap of newspaper. "His prints are going to be on this, too."

"Where did you get it?"

"Brouchard gave it to me."

"Who was he? I mean why did he kill them?"

"Brouchard said it was like the cops thought at first—a burglar."

Linda shook her head. "No. He threw the equipment overboard."

"He didn't want to be fencing anything that might trace him back to the murder."

"Clay, why didn't he just let it sit on the boat? Why did he go to the trouble to throw it overboard?"

"Maybe he was worried about fingerprints."

"He had gloves on."

"I thought about that. He tore one, remember."

"But he—"

He didn't let her finish. "Linda, please. Can we just leave it alone for a while?" His words had come out sharper than he had meant them to be.

She stared at him for a moment, then nodded. "Sure," she said. "I'm sorry." She turned toward the bathroom. "It'll just take me a moment to get dressed."

Linda raised the doughnut to her mouth and took a bite, laid it back on her plate and reached for her coffee cup. Clay, sipping his coffee as he sat across from her at the cafeteria table, was lost in thoughts created by her questions in his father's room. One thing was obvious. If the old man Brouchard had killed hadn't been a burglar, hadn't been on the *Cassandra* to steal something, then there was an obvious conclusion—he had to have been there specifically to kill Robert, or the girl or both of them. Why? The killing had nothing to do with drugs. Ming's polygraphs had proved that beyond a shadow of a doubt. What then did it have to do with?

He raised his face to Linda's. "Okay, if the old man wasn't there to rob the boat, but instead came with the specific intention of murdering Robert and Brouchard's stepdaughter, he either had a personal grudge against one or both of them or was hired by someone who did."

She stopped the doughnut on its way to her mouth. "Clay, let's not even talk about it. You said he's dead. What difference does it make if he was a burglar or not? I shouldn't have been running my mouth up in the room. Go ahead and drink your coffee. Then I want you to go back to the boat with me. Your father's doing all right, and you have to get some sleep—a little at least, or you're going to fall over."

"I don't think we need to go back out to the boat. Part of what I did last night was beat the hell out of Lionel."

"What—how did you—"

"Brouchard wanted me out of there, and he wanted to make sure I stayed gone, at least gone long enough for him to dispose of the old man's body. He had Lionel ride back to Biloxi with me. I jumped him."

A worried expression coming to her face, Linda was silent for a moment. "I'm pretty sure he was the one on the boat that night," she finally said, "yet I'd rather you'd just left well enough alone."

"I wish I had, too, now that I've had time to think about it. To be safe, I'm going to get us a motel room under an assumed name. We'll stay there until we go back to Washington."

Linda's eyes narrowed. "We?"

"Yeah, you're going with me."

She stared at him a moment before speaking. "I guess this is the time to ask some probing question, however I'll make it simple. Give me ten minutes' notice and I'll be packed and ready."

The middle-age woman with a name tag that read "Manager" leaned to refill their coffee cups. "Ten minutes is not very long to pack," she said. "I guess it's the old Rodgers charm."

Clay looked into the woman's smiling face. "You don't know me, do you, Clay?" she said.

"Sorry."

"I used to work at the Hook, Line and Sinker. Your father ate in there a lot, and your brother, too. They were two of my favorite customers. I never actually met you, but I'd heard about your father's being upstairs. When you walked in the door, I knew who you were right off—the family resemblance. For what it's worth I heard the doctors talking. They think your father's going to come out of his coma in pretty good shape. I hope so."

"I appreciate that."

As the woman moved away from the table Linda spoke around the piece of doughnut in her mouth. "That was nice of her." She held up the last of the doughnut. "Sure you don't want a bite? It's good."

"No, thank you." He noticed a hospital security guard stop at a table a few feet away. The guard briefly engaged in conversation with the young couple at the table, then moved on toward Clay's table.

"I'm looking for a Mr. Rodgers."

"Yes."

"There's a Chief Langston, Biloxi Police Department, on the line for you. I can have the call transferred to the receptionist's desk right down the hall."

At the desk Clay lifted the receiver to his ear. Linda stood a few feet away.

"Hello."

"Clay. They've found the killer."

"Found him—?"

"Yeah. A creep named Johnny Jeffcoat. He lives in Gretna. Louisiana authorities have his house staked out now."

"Yeah, well, thank you."

"Thank you?" Langston roared. "Is that all you're going to say? I thought you'd scream so loud you'd burst my eardrum. Thank you . . ."

"Yeah, well—God, that's *great* news."

"Clay, you sick or something? Oh, your father—I wasn't thinking about him. How's he doing?"

"Better—I think."

"Glad to hear that. Only thing tempers my enthusiasm over knowing we're going to get the killer is that he shouldn't have ever been out in the first place."

"Out?"

"He was over here—in Parchman. He was convicted of murder a little over ten years ago. Damn parole board let him out last year. I don't mean they just let out a killer; I mean they let out a damn cold-blooded one who killed for money, a hired killer. Should have known a bastard like that would kill the first person who stepped in his way. Shit, cops in this state put four thousand bastards a year in Parchman, and parole board lets four thousand out. What sense does that make? Well, I have to run; just wanted you to know. I'll call when they arrest him."

After Langston was off the line, Clay stood for a moment with the telephone receiver in his hand.

"What?" Linda asked.

He shook his head. "God, I'm doing it again."

"What?"

"The guy who killed Robert. He was out on parole from a murder he had committed several years ago."

"The police found his body?"

"No, I didn't even think to ask Langston how they found out who he was. I guess the palm print matched up with one in the files, or maybe somebody recognized him from Horace's drawing. When I was listening to Langston talk the only thing I could think about was he said, *hired killer.* It scared me to death."

Linda's eyes narrowed questioningly.

"Hired killer, Linda. He killed for money. I started thinking —did somebody hire him to kill Robert."

"No, Clay, come on. Don't start again. Accept he was on the boat to steal something."

"I don't—"

"No, listen to me, Clay; even if he wasn't a burglar, he's dead. Okay? What difference does it make what he was?"

"The difference it would make is whoever hired him is still out there."

"Clay, it's one in a million that somebody hired him, that he wasn't just simply there to steal. But if he was hired what good is it going to do you to agonize over it? With him dead there's no way now to find out who hired him, if someone did. Get your mind on something else, please. You're going to end up in bed right next to your father."

Clay took a deep breath and exhaled it audibly. "Yeah, okay. You ready to go back upstairs?"

She glanced back toward the cafeteria. "We better pay for our coffee first."

CHAPTER

39

As Clay waited for the cafeteria's cashier to ring up his bill and return his change, he noticed the manager who had spoken to them a little while earlier. She saw him looking in her direction and she smiled. He returned the smile and looked away.

After a moment, he moved his eyes back to her. The family resemblance. "That's the same thing Langston said."

Linda, counting out the candy mints she had lifted out of the big jar sitting next to the cash register, looked over at him. "What?"

"When the manager came over to our table she said she knew me right off because of the family resemblance. When I was in Langston's office to pick up the fingerprint he said he recognized me from the family resemblance. That same day, when I went over to Jennifer's office, she said we were 'like peas in a pod'—all three of us, especially Robert and Dad."

Linda nodded. "You all do look alike. The only reason anybody would have thought Robert looked any more like your dad than you is because they were built the same; about the same size."

His heart was suddenly racing. "Come on, Linda."

"What?"

He was already heading for the doorway and the bank of pay telephones across from the cafeteria.

Reaching them, he quickly punched in Jennifer's office number. After the secretary answered it was only a few seconds until Jennifer's voice came over the line.

"Clay, it's not your father, is it?"

"No. He seems to be doing better."

"Good. When my secretary informed me you were on the line—"

"Jennifer, you said the boatyard wasn't in all that great a financial shape, didn't you?"

"No different than usual. It's always had cash flow problems."

"Does Dad owe anybody any money on it, other than the bank?"

"Nobody else I'm aware of. Why do you ask something like that?"

"I've started worrying—what if the person who killed Robert had really meant to kill Dad?"

"Meant to kill your father?"

"Yes. They're the same size—look a lot alike at first glance. What if the killer was waiting on the boat for Dad, and—and— hell, I don't know. Maybe when he came out of hiding and saw it wasn't Dad but Robert, he didn't have any choice but to go ahead. Robert had seen him. The girl, too. I don't know. It'd take forever to explain all the things I've been through this past week, but I haven't found the slightest reason for anyone to want to kill Robert. I was wondering if someone might have a reason to be after Dad. He hasn't mentioned anything about any problems he'd had with anybody?"

Jesus! Only a few days before he was asking the same thing about Robert. Only a few hours before he had thought it was all over, that the killer had been a burglar, plain and simple. Now here he was back to not being sure of anything again.

"What problems would your dad be having with someone, Clay? He gets along with everybody."

Clay turned and leaned back against the wall. "You've been his lawyer all these years. Is there anything you can think of, anybody he's had trouble with in the past? Everybody makes enemies."

"Clay, the only thing important at this point is that the police apprehend the murderer. What difference does it make whether he was after Robert or meant to murder your father?"

Meant to murder your father.

Meant to, but hadn't—had failed. The killer was dead now, but if he had been hired by someone, then the one doing the hiring was still around—the job unfinished.

A chill ran up Clay's back, tingled at his shoulders, and he literally shook.

"I'll call you later, Jennifer." He quickly replaced the telephone receiver. "Come on," he said to Linda and started toward the elevators.

Linda stared after him. "Clay?" She shook her head, then hurried after him.

At the elevators he slipped into a nearly full one, and impatiently began jabbing the fifth floor button. Linda barely made it inside before the door closed.

When the door opened on five, he was the first one out, pushing past a nurse.

Donna, having only a few minutes before returned from her solitary visit to her church, was standing by his father's bed when Clay burst into the room.

"What?" she asked as he came to the side of the bed and looked down at his father.

Linda entered the room, and walked up beside him. She looked at Donna, saw the questioning stare. "He's started thinking somebody might have been after his father and killed Robert by mistake."

Donna's eyes narrowed, and she shook her head. "I don't understand."

Clay looked at her. "You all were going out on the boat last weekend, right?"

"We do nearly every Saturday and Sunday," Donna answered.

"Some kind of business came up in Jackson."

"Yes."

"What kind of business?"

"Gosh, Clay, I don't know, just business."

"Was it unusual for business to come up like that, suddenly?"

"There's always somebody in a hurry, wanting him to get on something right away."

"Do you know who it was he went to see, who it was that wanted him up there?"

"No." Her brow wrinkling, she shook her head. "Clay, you have me going in circles. Linda just said you've started thinking somebody might have been after your father instead of Robert. Now you make a comment like, 'want him up there,' like you're suggesting there was some—something behind your father's going off to a last-minute business meeting. You're not making sense. If somebody were trying to kill him, why would they call him to Jackson, then mistakenly kill Robert on the boat here?"

He shook his head. "I know what I'm saying is confusing. I'm confused." He looked at his father. "I started thinking how much he and Robert looked alike. For the life of me I can't come up with any reason for anybody to have wanted Robert dead. So I started wondering if maybe . . ."

"Why would anybody want your father dead?" she asked.

"Yeah, Clay," Linda said. "It was a burglar; what the police have thought from the beginning. Why not? That's what you say Antonio said, too. If he knew enough to track . . ."

Donna waited for Linda to finish, then looked back at Clay when he spoke.

"Donna, would anybody at the boatyard know who Dad met in Jackson?"

"Probably Rosemary, his secretary. She was by here to visit not an hour ago."

"I'm going to go talk to her. If she doesn't know maybe one of the workmen will."

Donna shook her head. "There won't be any men there. The foreman closed everything down when your father had his stroke. Rosemary's the only one there, taking calls."

"Okay; if she doesn't know, then I'll get all the men's numbers, call them." He glanced at his dad's motionless form, and then at Linda. "You have your gun?"

Donna's eyebrows raised, and she looked at Linda.

"It's in my purse."

"Don't leave the room for any reason until I'm back. And if anyone comes in here, even a doctor or a nurse, I want you to watch everything they do."

Linda nodded. "I will."

"What?" Donna said, totally confused.

Rosemary was a chunky, middle-age blonde with a serious look about her. She had a habit of removing her glasses when she spoke, replacing them when she finished. She knew nothing about any business trip his father had made to Jackson. In fact, until she had viewed the television news story about the *Cassandra*'s being found aground, and Robert's body on it, she had assumed her boss and Donna had been enjoying the weekend on the boat.

The foreman was outside in the yard, checking inventory in the shed behind the office, but he didn't know anything about the trip, either.

Clay walked back into the office. Rosemary handed him a list of names and phone numbers.

She removed her glasses. "That's a list of the only six people in Jackson who have ever done business with us," she said. "Most of our customers are out of Louisiana, New Orleans. I thought that if you wanted to, we might call these names; see if any of them had business with your father over the weekend." She replaced her glasses.

Clay looked at the sheet of paper. She was the one who ought to be doing the detective work, he thought. But then she was fresh, her mind working clearly, and his was so fogged from the past week's events that he wasn't sure he was capable of a rational thought. He nodded. "You use one phone and I'll use the other. I'll call the first three names."

It only took fifteen minutes. None of the Jackson customers had done business with his father over the weekend. Only one of them had even spoken with his father in the last month.

Clay leaned back in his chair and thought.

Rosemary removed her glasses. "I'm surprised I didn't know anything about his going to Jackson," she said. "If he was going to make a proposal on any kind of repair work, he would've needed some up-to-date material figures. One or more of them change nearly every week. He relies on me to keep him posted on that."

Driving back to the hospital, Clay worried about both Linda and his father. He had thought about them the entire time it had taken him to stop by the *Cassandra,* shower, shave and put on fresh clothes. He didn't want to leave his father alone with only Donna; there needed to be more than one person there. Neither did he want to go off and leave Linda in Biloxi with Lionel still around. But he was going to go to Jackson. The concern about who his father went to see might just be idle curiosity turned into more only because of his fear of mistaken identity—unfounded, he hoped. Nevertheless, he had to go. It was like the detective told him in Indianapolis—his father's trip to Jackson had given Clay pause for thought. Now he was going to check it out. It might be crazy, but he had to.

When Clay walked into his father's room, he was startled to see two men in their early thirties talking to Donna and Linda.

Linda walked toward him. "I called Rosemary. She said you all couldn't come up with why your father went to Jackson. I knew what that meant: you'd be going there. I wanted to go with you." She turned back toward the two men. "This is Cleve Bullard."

The one she indicated, dressed in slacks and a sport coat, was short, only a couple of inches taller than she was. He looked bookish, sporting thick spectacles and closely cropped brown hair.

"His mother and dad have been my neighbors ever since I was a little girl. He used to torment me to death. Now he's an air policeman stationed at Keesler." She turned toward the other man.

He was nearly six feet, and the more stockily built of the two. He was dressed in coaching shoes, a pair of red shorts that came nearly to his knees and a blue sweatshirt lettered with the word DEFENSE on the front and TEAM on the back.

"This is Paul McGinnis, the winningest football coach around here, and a second degree black belt."

"Third," McGinnis corrected.

Linda turned back to Clay and smiled. "They've promised to stay here until we get back."

CHAPTER

40

It took exactly two hours and fifty-two minutes for Clay to drive up from the coast to Jackson and the hotel where his father had stayed the Saturday night before. He parked his car in the guest garage connected to the hotel, and he and Linda took the elevator down to the lobby. When he presented his credentials to the desk clerk, the bespectacled little man immediately grew wide-eyed.

"Yes, sir. How can I help you?"

Linda handed Clay the photograph taken from an end table next to the couch in his dad's house. He showed it to the clerk.

"This is a Mr. Rodgers," Clay said. "I think he stayed here last Saturday night. Do you remember seeing him?"

The clerk shook his head.

"Is your manager in?"

"Yes, sir. Just a minute."

The clerk disappeared through a doorway at the back of the counter area.

In only a few seconds the middle-aged manager, neat in sharply pressed white slacks and a yellow blazer nearly the color of his thinning hair, came through the doorway and up to the counter. A name tag identified him as Bert. He was much more casual than the clerk had been. He spoke in a soft voice. "Yes, sir?"

Clay showed the photograph. "This is a Mr. Robert Rodgers. I'm interested in knowing if you remember seeing him? I think he was a guest here last Saturday night."

The manager shook his head. "No, sir. I don't recall the gentleman."

"Do you mind going through your records to see if you can find a copy of his bill? He would have checked out sometime Sunday morning." Donna had been unable to find a copy of the bill in the suit his father had worn that day, but she was almost certain where he would've stayed, the same hotel he always frequented when in Jackson.

"Well, I suppose. May I examine your credentials, please?"

Clay reached in his pocket, pulled forth his identification and handed it to the man.

After a few seconds of careful scrutiny, the manager handed the case back across the counter. "Yes, sir, I don't think it'll take but a minute. You said a Mr. Rodgers, is that correct? Related?"

Clay nodded. "My father—Robert Rodgers, Sr."

The manager nodded. "It'll only take a minute." He disappeared through the doorway behind the counter.

A short time later he returned with a sheet of paper. "He did stay here. I took the liberty of copying his bill for you." He handed it across the counter.

Clay studied it. There were no local telephone charges. So his dad hadn't telephoned anyone when he arrived. Maybe he had a meeting already set up some place, a restaurant, or even at someone's house. He glanced back at the bill. There was a restaurant charge listed—room service. Fifty-seven dollars plus tip, too much for one person. His dad had met someone in his room.

Clay raised his face to the manager's. "I need to see a copy of this room service charge—what was ordered."

"Yes, sir. I think we can accommodate you. With the entire bill being paid by credit card, the restaurant should have a copy of the charge on file. Let me call them."

In a few minutes a slim black woman dressed in a waitress's uniform and appearing to be in her middle thirties brought the bill to the front desk and handed it to the manager. He thanked her and handed it to Clay.

The ticket listed prime ribs for two and the trimmings, plus appetizers and a bottle of wine.

"I need to speak to the waiter who delivered this."

"He's off today," the woman said. "I can call his home, see if he's there. In any case he'll be back here. His girlfriend's working tonight. He'll be by to pick her up when she gets off, about eleven."

Clay glanced at his watch. It was a little after six. He'd caught himself nearly falling asleep twice on the trip up from Biloxi. He smiled politely at the woman. "Ma'am, there's no need to call him if you're sure he'll be back. We're going to stay over. If you'll let us know when he arrives we'd appreciate it."

The woman smiled and nodded. "As soon as he stops by I'll send him to the desk."

The manager looked at Clay. "I'll call your room immediately."

Clay reached to a hip pocket of his slacks and pulled out his billfold, produced his credit card.

The manager smiled politely and took the card. "Twin beds or king?" he asked.

After Clay finished checking in, he turned to Linda. "I could use a drink before we go up," he said. "What about you?"

"I've quit," she said.

A small smile came to Clay's face. "What's led to this astounding development?"

"See," she said, nodding her head knowingly. "You think I drink too much, too. You've just been too polite to say anything. I've been thinking about it—if we're getting married that means kids."

"Hey, wait a minute."

The manager smiled.

"You know it does," Linda said. "And if I'm going to set the right example, then I need to slow down some. I started counting my drinks up in my mind; I've been hitting it pretty hard. I'm not going to teetotal, but I'm going to lay off for a month or so. If that bothers me, then I'm going to lay off until it doesn't bother me anymore."

On the way up in the elevator, Clay leaned back against the wall.

Linda stepped to his side and raised her hand to massage the back of his neck. "You're worn out, aren't you?" she asked.

Once inside the room, Clay walked to the telephone on the table between the beds as Linda went into the bathroom and closed the door behind her. He called long distance.

"Hello, Paul McGinnis, here."

"McGinnis, this is Clay. How's Dad?"

"He's doing fine, Mr. Rodgers. Me and Cleve and Mrs. Rodgers are all sitting right in here keeping an eye on him."

"Okay, I'm going to be staying overnight here at the hotel. If anything at all comes up please let me know."

"We'll do that."

After finishing the conversation with McGinnis, Clay rang long distance information, obtained a number and punched it in.

"Hello."

"Jennifer."

"Clay?"

"Yeah, I need to talk to you about something we were discussing earlier."

Her sigh was audible over the line. "Clay, every time you call me I'm on pins and needles waiting to hear whether the call is concerning your father. From now on when you phone, please inform me right off the bat when the call isn't concerning him. Okay? Do you mind?"

"Dad's doing fine. What I wanted to ask you about—earlier when I was talking to you and asked if Dad had any problems with anybody, you jumped off into talking about what difference did it make whether the killer was coming after Dad or Robert, that the important thing was catching the guy."

"Oh, Clay, you're going to drive yourself crazy if you don't quit worrying about every little—"

"I have a reason to be worried, Jennifer. If the killer was coming after Dad and he killed Robert by mistake, he might come back after Dad again."

There was complete silence on the other end of the line.

"Jennifer?"

"Yes . . . I was thinking. What you said hit me like a ton of bricks."

"That's why I wanted to know if you could think of any reason for anybody to be mad at him. Not only somebody mad, even irritated, any trouble of any kind that you might think of that he's had."

"There isn't anything, Clay."

"You can't think of a single problem he's discussed with you?"

"Other than business, no, and nothing about that made anybody mad—just cash flow problems, like I told you earlier."

"Jennifer, everybody has problems with people; I have trouble with my superiors; you have irritated clients. I mean I want you to tell me anything, no matter how little or insignificant it sounds to you. It doesn't make any difference if you think there's nothing to it; it might make something click in my mind."

There was a long silence on the line.

"You can't think of anything at all?" he asked.

"I don't . . . No, Clay, no. Not anybody."

There had been something in her tone, and Clay felt his muscles tighten. Linda came out of the bathroom and walked to the television.

"Jennifer—anything."

"Oh, Clay, this isn't right."

"What?"

"It's nothing Clay, take my word for it."

"What, dammit!" Clay closed his eyes. "I'm sorry."

Linda looked back across her shoulder at him. It was several seconds before Jennifer spoke. "That's all right, Clay, I understand. Your father came in here a couple of months ago saying his relationship with Donna wasn't like it used to be."

Clay, his eyes narrowing, glanced at Linda as Jennifer continued.

"Clay, your father was getting another one of those wild hairs. Remember, I told you how he was. I don't for a minute believe that there was anything at all wrong with the relationship other than he was getting his old itchy feeling back." She paused.

"God, Clay, I wish you would have waited until your father was better and let him tell you about this. I wouldn't have, but —but you put me on such a spot."

"Jennifer, what did Dad mean things weren't like they used to be between him and Donna?"

Linda's brow wrinkled.

"He didn't get into specifics," Jennifer said. "I wouldn't let him. I told you, and I'm positive of what I'm saying—he was just getting itchy feet again."

Clay wished Linda wasn't in the room to hear his next question. "Jennifer, what would come to Donna if Dad was dead? What would she receive—inheritance, insurance, everything?"

Jennifer didn't answer for several seconds. When she finally did, her voice had a note of coldness in it that he had never heard before.

"Clay, if you're assuming on the one hand that your father would have divorced Donna and left her with nothing, it's quite evident she'd end up with a good deal more if he was dead—the house, half ownership in the boatyard, the hundred thousand dollar CD you've posted as a reward. And I think half of the two hundred thousand dollar life insurance policy he's insured himself for goes to her; the other half is listed with you and Robert as beneficiaries." She paused. "Clay, what you're suggesting is preposterous."

After replacing the receiver Clay sat back on the bed and shook his head. Linda continued to stare at him.

He looked at her. "Linda, I need you to do me a favor. If I personally knew those men you have staying in the room, I'd do it myself. But, I don't know them that well."

"Okay, what?"

"I want you to call and tell them that I want one of them to stay in the room with Dad at all times. I don't want them to ever leave Donna alone in the room by herself with him."

Linda shook her head slowly back and forth. "Oh, baby. You don't really believe there's any possibility . . ."

He didn't. Yet how could he just totally ignore the thought. God, was he going crazy?

Linda walked to the telephone, lifted the receiver and punched in the hospital's number.

Clay swung his legs up on the bed and propped his shoulders up against the headboard. He shook his head in disgust with himself.

After Linda finished with the call she turned toward him and nodded. "I talked to Paul. He understands what you're worried about. Everything will be okay."

He nodded. "Thank you."

Linda walked to the foot of the other bed, sat and leaned forward to turn on the television. After flipping through several channels she decided on a movie already in progress.

Clay thought of the old man at the farmhouse—twisting around on the brick stoop, trying to kick the fire away, then dead. Clay shook his head slightly. Here he was thinking of the death of his brother's killer and doing so with a tinge of regret. Was he crazy? Or was the tinge of regret really that he had decided not to say anything about the old man's death? Clay opened his eyes, stared for a moment at Linda sitting at the end of the other bed. He was doing the right thing.

Several minutes later, bored with what she was watching, Linda began going through the channels again, this time stopping on a news program.

She glanced back to the bed. "I'm a little hungry. Would you like to have some sandwiches sent up?"

Clay didn't answer. His eyes were closed. She smiled.

After Lionel had followed Clay's car to the hotel garage, he drove a block farther and parked his car. He watched through the big plate glass windows at the hotel's front until Clay and Linda stepped onto the elevator. Then he hurried inside to see which floor they stopped on. He turned and went to the fire escape door and started up the stairs.

On the proper floor, he opened the heavy fire door and peered for a few seconds into the hallway. After closing the door, he leaned back against the concrete wall.

He raised his hand to the gauze patch covering his left eye, gently touched the tender skin around it, then pulled the patch loose. He wadded the gauze and angrily threw it to the floor.

His jaw tightened, his fists clinched, and he nodded slowly. "You're a dead mother," he said. Then he thought about Linda. He knew Clay had to be still wondering what all had been done to her the first time. He wouldn't have to wonder this time. He was going to get to watch.

CHAPTER

41

Linda, sitting on the end of the bed as she watched television, its volume low, was still hungry. She glanced at Clay, then to her purse sitting on the small table between the beds. She stood and walked quietly between the beds to the table.

After unsnapping her purse, she felt in its bottom and, trying to make as little noise as possible, gathered a handful of change. She walked toward the door, stopping on the way to pick up the room key off the dresser.

Stepping outside the room, she quietly closed the door behind her. She glanced up and down the hall. There wasn't a refreshment center to be seen. She could get by on some snacks and a Coke if she could find some vending machines. She walked toward the exit sign pointing to the fire steps.

There was a musky smell to the fire escape when she opened the door, and the passageway was noticeably hotter than the hall. A small, square gauze bandage lay on the landing next to the door. She started down the steps.

She found the machines on the next floor down.

She selected two packages of cheese-filled crackers and a Diet Coke.

Nibbling a cracker as she walked, she made her way back toward the fire escape.

She pushed the heavy door back and stepped into the passageway.

As the door swung shut behind her, a hand suddenly came over her shoulder and clamped across her mouth; an arm came around her body. The crackers and her drink fell to the floor, the Coke can bouncing and beginning to thump its way down the next flight of stairs.

Struggling, trying to scream through the hand, she was slammed painfully into the concrete wall. A knife flashed at the side of her face.

"Shut up!"

The knife moved to her throat, the sharp point of the blade pressing into her skin. She smelled the cologne. Tears of fear welled in her eyes.

The hand moved slowly away from her mouth, and she gasped for air.

She still had the room key in her hand and Lionel twisted it from her.

"Up the stairs!"

On the next landing, Lionel made her lean back against the wall next to the door. He moved the edge of the blade to her throat as he reached for the door handle, pulled the door open and glanced out into the hall.

He grabbed her by the shoulder and yanked her around, pushed her through the doorway and quickly down the hall.

She had to do something. She glanced back at the knife.

At the door to her room Lionel suddenly slipped a hand back over her mouth and flashed the knife in front of her face.

"You and him both die," Lionel whispered in her ear, "if you make a sound."

She shut her eyes. When she opened them, the knife had moved from her face and Lionel was inserting the key into the door. It opened.

A hard push on her back sent her stumbling forward sprawling to the floor.

Clay sat up in his bed. Lionel pointed a silencer-equipped automatic at him.

Linda scrambled to her feet and backed away from the grinning blond man. She glanced at Clay.

"Lie down," Lionel said to him. "On your face."

Clay did as he was told.

Lionel faced Linda. "Get on the other bed."

She climbed across the end of the bed and onto it, burying her face against the covers.

Lionel stepped to the bedside table and lifted Clay's service automatic from next to the telephone.

After stuffing the weapon in his waistband, he pressed the barrel of his own pistol against the back of Clay's head, then leaned over him and searched him carefully. Satisfied Clay had no other weapons, Lionel reached into his own hip pocket and pulled out a pair of handcuffs.

"Put your left hand behind you," he said.

He quickly snapped a cuff around Clay's wrist, then backed a step away from the bed. "Now," he said, "close the other cuff around the far post."

Clay looked at the square metal bar connecting the far side of the headboard to the bed.

"Now," Lionel said.

The cuff closed with an audible click, and Clay was secured to the bed.

"Now, Mr. Clay Rodgers, you're where we both feel comfortable," Lionel said. "Are you ready for the show?" He looked over at Linda staring wide-eyed at him.

"Over on your back," he said.

Clay glanced at Linda, and back to the gun Lionel held.

Linda rolled over to stare at the ceiling.

Lionel leaned down and reached to the front of her blouse,

gathered a fistful of the material into his hand. Her lip trembled.

A smile across his face, Lionel looked back at Clay, then, still not looking at Linda, he yanked hard on her blouse, ripping it open down the front. She moaned in fear.

Clay's jaw tightened. He glanced back to his handcuffed wrist.

Lionel's smile broadened. "You figured it out now? You're where you can't get at me, yet close enough to enjoy every detail." Without looking back at Linda he groped for the front of her brassiere.

She groaned and slid toward the far side of the bed. He quickly looked down at her, shook his head as he stared coldly into her eyes.

She whimpered.

He smiled back at Clay. "I'm not gonna have hard rocks when I leave this time. Did I tell you I did last time? She's got some tight little body, doesn't she?" Without looking back at Linda he reached and found the front of her brassiere, let his fingers play down the side of her breast.

Clay looked away.

"No, no, no, Mr. Rodgers. You have to watch."

When Clay didn't respond Lionel spoke again, his voice suddenly low and cold. "You watch or I'll cut her."

Clay turned his face back toward Lionel, then dropped his gaze to Linda.

Her wide eyes caught his, and she glanced toward her purse.

Lionel, all the while continuing to look at Clay, reached back toward Linda, gathered a brassiere strap in his hand and slipped it off her shoulder.

"I'm so scared!" Linda suddenly wailed. "I'll do anything if you won't hurt me. Please."

Lionel looked at her and smiled.

"I will," she said. "Please." She clasped his forearm with both of her hands, staring wide-eyed, pleading. "Anything, just don't hurt me. Please." Her head beginning to move in short, jerky nods, she rolled up on her left side and reached behind her to unsnap her skirt. "I will," she said again.

She tugged to pull the skirt past her hips, slid the garment on down her tanned legs.

Clay's free hand slipped inside the purse. Lionel caught the movement out of the corner of his eyes and jerked his head around. Clay gripped the handle and lifted the revolver, purse and all, toward Lionel's face and pulled the trigger.

The firing of the thirty-eight was deafening in the room. Lionel was blown backward head first across the end of Linda's bed. Convulsing once, he rolled limply off the bed and thudded to thc floor.

CHAPTER

42

"Yes, sir, I remember him," the waiter said. "He was with a knockout woman."

Clay took the photograph of his father back from the waiter. He glanced at Linda.

The Jackson police detective stepped to their side.

"Well, Mr. Rodgers. I guess we have everything we need for right now. Before you leave town in the morning, remember to stop by the station and sign your statements."

Clay nodded and turned back to the waiter as the detective walked across the lobby toward the hotel's exit.

"I don't guess there's anything you noticed about them that would tell you what they were doing? Did you see any drawings spread out—like blueprints for a boat, any kind of plans? Or were they just visiting?"

The waiter, obviously uncomfortable, glanced at Linda.

"Excuse me," Linda said, turned, and walked away.

The waiter, a small, slim man of about forty, with short brown hair and dressed in the tapered blue slacks and white short-sleeve dress shirt he had come after his girlfriend in, looked back at Clay. "The man seemed like a real gentleman, Mr. Rodgers. Of course I don't mean the woman wasn't a lady, but I'd pushed the food cart inside, and was standing there getting the check signed when she stepped out of the bathroom without a stitch on. When the man hollered at her that I was in the room, she just stood there for a second, even smiled at me, then sorta took her time as she went back into the bathroom."

"Can you describe her?"

"She had a helluva body. You couldn't help but catch that. Was probably in her middle thirties. Was a redhead." He glanced across his shoulder at Linda several feet away. "A *real* redhead—top and bottom. Caught that right off." He suddenly snapped his fingers. "Angie—that's what the man called her when he told her to get back in the bathroom."

"Angela!" Linda exclaimed.

"No," the waiter said looking toward her. "Angie—I'm certain."

"Red-haired," Linda countered. "The body. The age—Angela looks younger than she really is."

Clay turned toward the manager who had been attentively listening. "You have a fax machine here?"

"Of course."

When Jennifer answered the telephone, she didn't sound like she had been asleep, despite it being only a few minutes until midnight.

"This is Clay."

"Your father—"

"No. He's fine. I'm sorry to bother you, but I didn't know who else to call who I could really trust. I need you to do something for me."

"Okay."

"Down at the Beachfront Bar & Inn, there's a picture hanging on the wall. It's of Brouchard and Angela and another couple. I need you to go down there and get it and then fax it to me in Jackson."

"In Jackson? What are you—"

"Please."

"Okay. Give me about thirty or forty minutes."

"That's her," the waiter said before the replica of the photograph finished coming off the hotel's fax machine.

"That's why she came to Jennifer," Clay said. "I bet that's it."

"What?" Linda asked.

"Jennifer said Angela had been to talk to her about divorcing Brouchard. Angela said it was because of you—his mistress."

The hotel manager smiled.

"Yeah," Linda said, "me and your dad."

The manager's eyes narrowed.

Clay nodded. "And Dad's why she went to Jennifer. He would have told Angela she could trust her."

Back in the new room the hotel had provided them, Clay and Linda faced each other across the table next to the big picture window.

They had discussed everything, thought of every possibility they could bring to mind. They kept coming back to one likely probability.

Clay summed it all up:

"Angela and Dad were seeing each other and Brouchard found out about it. He was extremely jealous, like Carson told you. Brouchard hired Jeffcoat to kill Dad—maybe Angela, too. The night before it was set up to happen, Brouchard went to Miami. When he left, Angela called Dad and told him she was free for the rest of the weekend. Dad cancelled the outing with Donna. Angela got a girlfriend in New Orleans to cover for her then met Dad here.

"Jeffcoat had been told Dad and Donna would probably be taking the boat out to the islands Saturday night. They did nearly every weekend; Brouchard would've known that. So Jeffcoat hid on the boat and waited for them to arrive. What better place to kill somebody than out in the Gulf—miles away from any possible witness.

"Meanwhile, with the *Cassandra* then available because of Dad rushing off up here, Robert agreed to make the pickup of the jettisoned canisters. He needed somebody to help him, so Brouchard's stepdaughter went along. She'd probably helped him before.

"When Robert anchored out by the Chandeleurs, Jeffcoat came out of hiding and, mistaking Robert for Dad, shot him. Then he had to kill the girl, too. But he didn't kill her right away. If he had, then her body would've been left to be found with Robert's. She had to have lived long enough for Jeffcoat to find out who she was. Maybe she threatened him with who her father was."

Linda, a painful expression crossing her face, shook her head. "I don't like thinking about her being kept alive after Robert was killed—what reason Jeffcoat might have had for keeping her alive for a while. Let's hope it was over quick for both her and Robert, and Jeffcoat discovered who she was through finding some identification in her purse—something like that."

Clay nodded. "Maybe he did find some ID. In any case, when he found out who she was, he recognized the name. That's when he knew he had to hide her body hoping nobody would know she'd been with Robert."

Linda nodded. "But Antonio knew."

"Yeah. When she disappeared the same night Robert was killed, Brouchard had to know there was at least a possibility she'd been with him. That has to be the reason he came to the *Cassandra* that night and prayed. He was praying that she hadn't been. When after a couple days she hadn't shown up, he would've then been pretty certain that she'd been on the boat. That's when he went after the killer. Whether he went after him out of revenge, or guilt over what he had set in motion himself or simply because he didn't want to leave anybody around who could tie him back to the murders, I don't know—maybe a combination of all three."

"Clay, the only thing, why did Antonio take so long in finding Jeffcoat if he knew who he was from the start?"

"I'm not so sure he did know right at first. When he first decided on having Dad killed, Brouchard could have gone to someone who he knew would arrange a contract and never had anything to do with the actual hiring itself. Setting it up like that would make sense from Brouchard's point of view. That way if something went wrong and Jeffcoat was caught, then there would be less chance it could lead back to Brouchard. If that was the case, then all he had to do when he got ready to find the killer was start with whoever he originally used to put the contract out and follow the trail back up the line to Jeffcoat."

Linda nodded. "But what do you do now? Whether there was a go-between or not, Jeffcoat's probably the only person we'll ever know who might've been able to connect Brouchard back to the killing—unless maybe Lionel could have. With them both dead how are you ever going to prove it?"

Clay shook his head. "I don't know if it can be proved, not in a court of law. But he's going to pay for it."

Linda's eyes narrowed and she shook her head. "Clay, please, don't get yourself in a mess."

CHAPTER

43

It was shortly after eleven o'clock the next night. Clay sat at the steering wheel of his car parked against the curb a little over a block and a half from Brouchard's gothic-style stone mansion. He had been waiting there for better than three hours and had leaned back in his seat. Now he suddenly sat up and stared down the narrow, tree-lined pavement. Brouchard's dark Lincoln was pulling out of the big circular drive.

After the Lincoln drove past, Clay opened his car door and stepped outside. He started down the sidewalk toward the mansion.

Brouchard, dressed in a white suit, his tie missing and his shirt unbuttoned at the collar, entered his home a few minutes after three in the morning.

Angela, sitting on a couch in the brightly lit living room, stared at him as he walked in from the foyer. She was still dressed in the same dark skirt and light blouse she had been wearing when he had left the house at eleven. She was sitting erect, not leaning back against the couch.

"What you doing up?" he asked.

"Why didn't you tell me you knew Karen had been killed?"

Brouchard, already halfway across the living room toward her, stopped, the casual expression he had carried with him into the room now gone.

Angela continued to stare. "All those nights I was praying she would come back, you already knew she was dead."

"What are you talking about?"

"You never would have told me. You would have let me go on thinking forever that she had run away."

Brouchard glanced around the room. When he looked back at Angela she held an envelope out to him.

His eyes narrowing, he walked to the couch and took it from her hand.

"It was left taped to the door," she said.

He slipped the single sheet of paper from the envelope and unfolded it.

"It says that you knew Karen was still dating Robert," Angela said, "and so you knew from the first that she'd been killed, too."

He raised his eyes from the sheet of paper. "I didn't know she was with him. There was the possibility. I didn't want to worry you."

"That's a lie!" she shouted, no longer able to keep her voice level. "You never would have told me. You'd have let me go on forever thinking that she'd run away. You were afraid that if I knew she had been murdered, then some day when I was wondering why in God's name somebody would kill a couple of kids who hadn't done anything to anybody, it might pop into my mind that somebody had done something to somebody, that Robert's father and I had done something—to you."

Brouchard's eyes narrowed, and his jaw tightened, but he didn't say anything, and Angela spoke again.

"Then would I have thought back to all those times you

threatened to kill me if you ever caught me with a man again? And the man, what about him? You made a mistake with Ben, you said, lost control of yourself and went after him personally, in your own club. You said you wouldn't be that stupid again. How many times, Antonio, how many times did you threaten me like that? Would I think about that and think about how you had suddenly come up with a reason to go to Florida the night before Robert's father and Donna were going out on the boat together? Would I ever think about how much Robert and his father looked alike?" She paused a moment, her cold stare never wavering.

"I called Jake in Miami, Antonio. He said you and a couple of others sat up most of the night playing cards. After the others left, you told him there was no need for him to make the drive home as drunk as he was; so he stayed there. He slept in the bed right next to yours all the time until you woke up and went back to the airport—your alibi. You never did do any business on the trip. There wasn't a business meeting, was there? There was only the card game. And you arranged that to make sure a lot of people could prove you were in Miami all night."

Brouchard shook his head. "You're crazy!"

"Yeah," she said, "crazy for continuing to live with an animal like you—the animal that caused my daughter's death."

Brouchard crushed the sheet of paper angrily between his hands. "That bastard—Clay. He's the one brought this."

"I'm going to the police, Antonio."

"Go ahead, bitch. What are you going to say? They'll think you're crazy."

"No," she said shaking her head. "You're the one that's crazy, an insane cold-blooded killer: your stepfather, Robert and Karen, the old man at the farmhouse."

Brouchard's eyes narrowed, and he glanced down to the paper wadded in his hands. It hadn't contained anything about the old man.

He raised his face back to Angela's. "Clay didn't slip this under no door. He brought it to you. He talked to you."

Brouchard glanced around the room, looked through the entrance into the dining room and into the kitchen.

Returning his eyes to his wife, he suddenly flung the balled-up paper into her face.

She flinched but didn't drop her stare. "If you knew what a pitiful excuse you were for a man compared to Robert's father." A sarcastic smile crossed her face. "The first time I had sex with him was better than all the times with you put together. Everytime I had it with him, it was better."

Brouchard stepped forward and backhanded her hard across the face, knocking her sideways on the couch.

"I ought to kill you, bitch!"

"Pitiful sick," she said, as she moved her hand to her stinging cheek. "All you knew about sex was to just lie there, wasn't it? Is that how you did with your mother? Is that why you killed your stepfather—you weren't the man he was?"

"Why, you sick bitch. I never touched . . ." He lunged toward her. She kicked at him. He knocked her legs aside and grabbed for her throat.

Clay, his service automatic in his hand, stepped quickly from the dining room. "That's enough!"

Brouchard released his grip, and slowly straightened from over his wife. A smile came to his face. "I figured you were here someplace," he said.

Angela, her hand at her throat, struggled to an upright position on the couch. She looked at Clay and shook her head. "He hadn't said enough!" she wailed. "He hadn't said enough. Why didn't you wait?"

Brouchard chuckled. "So what you got now that you didn't have before, Clay?"

Clay stepped to the telephone on the table next to the dining room entrance. "I still have you killing the old man at the farmhouse."

Brouchard shook his head. "You've got assault."

Clay punched in the telephone number of the Biloxi Police station and lifted the receiver to his ear.

"And you've also got my oath," Brouchard added in a cold voice.

The sudden loud shot caused Clay to flinch.

Brouchard's eyes rolled back in his head, his knees buckled and he sat backwards hard on the floor, tottered a moment, then collapsed over onto his side. Blood ran from the back of his head to stain the white carpet.

Angela, an automatic in her hand, stood next to the open drawer of the couch's ornate end table.

CHAPTER

44

The Amtrak train rolled through Alabama on its way from Meridian, Mississippi, to Washington, D.C. Clay and Linda sat on opposite sides of the folding table attached to the window of their sleeping compartment.

The porter placed their desserts and coffee before them, nodded his thanks at Clay's tip and stepped out of the compartment, shutting the door behind him.

Clay looked out the window at the rolling countryside, then glanced above the treetops. The sky was clear again, the sun shining brightly, not a cloud to be seen anywhere.

"I feel sorry for Angela," Linda said.

He turned back from the window, nodding his agreement. "There's no way she's not going to be convicted; she'll serve some time, too."

"It just doesn't seem right," Linda said, shaking her head. "Brouchard hired the killer—I know he did."

Clay nodded. "Murdered the guy at the farmhouse for sure. I'd thought maybe when Angela confronted him that he would lose control—say something. But when I heard him slap her and heard his tone of voice, I started worrying about what he might do if I let it go any farther. She'd already put herself on the line just because of what I'd told her."

"Clay, she put herself on the line because she knew what kind of man he was. I told you Ben Carson said Antonio had abused her for years. When you hate somebody like she did him, it's easy to think the worst of them."

Clay nodded. "I suppose that was part of it. But the biggest thing was his not telling her from the very start that he thought Karen might have been with Robert that night, and hadn't just run away. Had he told her, I don't believe Angela would have believed a word I said. It was his holding that back from her that made her believe he had to have something else to hide."

"Clay, talking about believing, do you think Langston really believes what you told him about your not reporting Brouchard's killing the old man at the farmhouse?"

Clay brought a small smile to his face. "How was I going to get Brouchard to give away that he'd put out the contract if he was locked up for the old man's murder? Only thing bothered Langston was that I hadn't trusted him enough to let him in on what I was doing. I told him that I was sorry, that I should've told him."

"He thinks you'd suspected Brouchard for several days?"

"Told him that I had ever since Jennifer told me about Dad and Angela's relationship."

"What if someday he asks Jennifer about that?"

"She's aware of what I told him. She's a longtime family friend."

"How do you think your father and Donna are going to be?"

"Well, for right now she's just thrilled he's back home again. Whatever she might think in the future, that isn't Dad's main problem. His realizing that if he hadn't been slipping around with Angela that Robert wouldn't have been killed—that's going to be Dad's real punishment." Clay stared at the tabletop for a moment then shook his head. "Jesus, let's get our minds on something a little lighter."

"Okay," Linda said. "When we get to Washington, instead of going to your apartment I want to spend the first night in the same motel we did before."

He smiled.

"Really," she said. "I've dreamed of being back in that motel again, and then this time when we leave you don't say 'no more.' "

He smiled again and nodded. "You've got a deal," he said. "For the whole week if you want—for as long as you want."